Watch As They Fall

M. Nevills

This novel is entirely a work of fiction. The names, characters and incidents portrayed in it are the work of the author's imagination. Any resemblance to actual persons, living or dead, events or localities is entirely coincidental.

Copyright © by Marissa Nevills 2024.

All rights reserved. No part of this publication may be reproduced, stored or transmitted in any form or by any means, electronic, mechanical, photocopying, recording, scanning, or otherwise without written permission from the publisher. It is illegal to copy this book, post it to a website, or distribute it by any other means without permission.

ISBN 979-8-9909530-0-0

WATCH AS THEY FALL

Military Structure Within Azera & Hira*

General - Oversees the entire military
Lieutenant General - Second to General
Colonel - Commands brigade, oversees mission coordination
Lieutenant Colonel - Commands battalion
Captain - Commands company
First Lieutenant - Commands platoon
Sergeant - A junior officer
Soldier

*This is entirely fictional and not meant to be an accurate portrayal of nonfictional rankings

GESTIGE LAND

DAOLAND

♦ CAPITAL

AZURA

NOSAN
SUDWAL
DUWAN

MILITARY BASE

NORA
LAKE EERY

HIRA

THE SOUTHERN ISLES

CHAPTER ONE

Surviving is quite lonely.

*W*as my short-term happiness worth the pain you left me with? Raye could ask that question to almost anyone in her life, past, present, or future. She could ask it repeatedly with no answer that would bring her peace. No family, no friends, no allies left in the world to undo the pain of her life. Was there anyone else to blame but herself, though? She had her hand in every plan. Her sticky fingers maintained the suffering, heartlessness caused the chaos, while her loneliness brought the terror.

What was the undoing of others' worth to her? Anything, it seemed.

Picking the skin around her broken nails, stuck waiting in anticipation, her body and mind grew restless. Sitting straight back and rigid alongside the strangers of the nearby towns as they waited to test; to spar. This would be a turning point in their young lives, for better or worse.

As more groups were called into the room behind the door, Raye caught herself chewing the hangnails off her thumbs. Tucking her hands under her legs, she examined her competition. As far as they knew, they would be sparring against another random attendee while the proctors watched to determine their skill level. If the proctors determined they were skilled enough combined with their written exam scores, the proctors might offer them a spot inside the country's most outstanding military schools.

More groups were called in, but still Raye's name remained uncalled. While not typically anxious about her abilities, the waiting drove her mad. School could be the chance to change her life and rid her of the Kyrfs, her adoptive family's home.

Each time more students were called from the waiting area, the angrier she eyed them, jealous. She nervously rubbed her fingers together while she watched, careful not to pick at them again. The other hopefuls all wore such lovely fitting clothes, handcrafted for the art of fighting. Soft materials flowed with their bodies, snug at the waist before flaring softly down their legs in brightly dyed colors.

Raye's adoptive parents were far from supportive of her future endeavors. She had only managed an oversized shirt and pants from her younger adoptive brother, Finn. The large plain black clothes had her practically swimming in them. She had tied the belt tight enough so the pants would not fall and folded up the sleeves so her hands would stick out.

"Rayana Tyrson," an escort finally called out, shaking her out of her contemplation. She had used her birth name, not 'Kryf' like they had forced her to. They would no longer strip her identity away any longer. She was not the woman who would fit into their mold or take their name. She was born to be a warrior, not a housewife with no autonomy outside a husband.

Women's rights were further stripped away in those days. Even the emperor's daughter had lost her birthright to the throne, as he deemed it unwomanly in that day and age, passing the lineage to his younger son. Not even royalty could overcome the curse of not being a man.

After a glance around, she found she was the only one remaining. Raye was taken back alone, with no other names left to call. She did not enter through the door the others went through. The man led her through a small doorway down dimly lit halls that twisted and turned in all directions. Raye recognized there was no finding her own way out of this maze.

They stopped at the end of a hall in front of an open door before the escort spoke to her again. "Your written test was one of the highest-scored exams. You have been chosen to be seen personally by the masters. You will spar with a current student at the school. If your basic combat is up to par, your acceptance is guaranteed. If you impress any one of the masters, they are permitted to select a certain number of apprentices each year." He gestured toward the young man waiting just inside the room. "That is an apprentice of one of the masters—currently, one of the best. He is your opponent. You don't need to beat him for your acceptance; it is simply to get an understanding and gauge your skill level. Questions?"

Raye let her mind soak up the information given to her while her heart thumped in her ears. She was not expecting to spar with someone already trained by the school. Taking a deep breath, she forced her anxieties down. She could do this.

She could beat him, and she would. It was the only option in her mind. Gaining a master as a personal teacher was beyond what she could have hoped. Such a teacher could hone her skills, shaping her into the fighter she needed to be.

Entering the room, Raye jumped inside her skin as the door closed with a bang behind her. The four masters' attention immediately went to her as she entered. Even sitting blank-faced, they radiated a powerful aura from how they held themselves. She bowed deeply to them at the hips and then stood upright to face where her opponent stood.

He appeared more bored than anything, as if sparring with her were beneath him. She knew the look he wore; he did not expect much from her skills-wise. Of course, he wouldn't; her body melted inside the clothes draped over her, making her appear even smaller than she was. Her blonde hair did not help and made her appear younger, as children's hair tended to grow darker as they aged. He stifled a yawn before cracking his knuckles as if the battle was already won. He glared at her like an animal ready for its meal. Raye looked forward to wiping the cocky look off his face.

The two circled each other for a moment, sizing each other up. Big, arrogant men always thought they could easily win within the first strike of a smaller opponent. She would wait for him to begin the spar. Surprising him was the best option. A similar tactic she used previously in her win against her elder adoptive brother. In an attempt to end things quickly, he aimed at her abdomen with his foot, making no attempt to soften the blow. Bouncing lightly on her feet, Raye twisted out of the way, causing him to stumble before preparing himself for another attempt. He was fast for a large fighter, but Raye was faster.

Allowing no chance to prepare for another attack, Raye launched forward and kicked the back of his knee. He hardly noticed until it was too late, causing his leg to crumple beneath him instantly. His knee slammed into the ground, and his punch fell short.

Raye gave him a chance to get up while she caught her breath. She allowed him to get on his feet before she hit the side of his torso with a kick. A loud grunt of pain forced its way out of his throat, and she could see the shocked look in his eyes. Out of reflex, his hand gripped his pained side. Eyes narrowing, he realized he needed to rethink his strategy. Raye could laugh, but it was far too late for that. She was in control of the fight, steps ahead of him. She had already won—he just had not realized it yet.

Fallen to his knees, Raye gripped his hair between her fingers, gaining control of his head. She yanked him, so his face looked up at her. The surprise in his eyes while he attempted unsuccessfully to claw her hand off him.

A sight she must have been to him. Her slight frame stood over him, tendrils of golden hair escaped from her braid, though she had not broken a sweat while taking him down. The fight appeared to have ended as quickly as it started by a malicious little girl.

Raye kneed his jaw. He fought through the pain and grabbed Raye's clothing, making her fall with him forcefully. She stumbled over next to him on her knees. He impulsively punched and hit the side of her face with a hard impact. Her face flung in the direction of his punch, and her vision went blurry as she fell to her hands and knees. She shook off her daze and rolled away, out of his reach. Blinking her eyes back into normalcy, she sensed the wetness of her blood trickling down her face where he hit her. He was not pulling punches. The drip fell down the curvature of her cheek and around her lips until she felt the warm metallic liquid against her tongue. Nasty and bitter, she spat the blood out the side of her mouth.

She let him watch her pale, blood-covered face while she remained completely unphased. She forced herself to appear like she felt no pain from his blow. The wound he left started to bleed heavier, the side of her face damp. She needed to end this quickly. Her eyes showed no hint of pain, only focused on him like there was no one else in the room. She had learned long ago not to let others read her so easily. She forced herself to become stone in the face of enemies. No pain, fear, or worry was found in her eyes—only a blood thirst within them.

Raye found her footing with a sway while she pulled air deep into her lungs to regain herself. Her chest rose and fell with each heavy inhale and exhale. Her cheek stung, and her body grew hot. She grew out of breath from the match already, but it did not matter. She made her choice and would continue.

He hopped up onto his feet. He, too, did not give up easily, proving himself a worthy opponent. He rushed the distance and went in for a punch, but she was gone. Raye dropped and weaved her way under his arm, so he stood before her. Time seemed to slow down, like she could see the future of every move he might make and counter it. They were always so predictable. She let out a quiet little dry laugh at her thought. He tried to whip around to face her when Raye made her final move.

With a sure quick right hook, Raye struck him in the back of the neck before he could turn around. His body smashed onto the ground. Without waiting to see if he stood again, she turned to the four masters and bowed deeply once again. When her opponent awoke, with a shake of his head, he crawled his way over to lean against the wall and attempted to catch his breath.

Her body felt ecstatic. Victory was better than any drug she could imagine. Her capabilities were beyond even her own awareness. She pushed her joy back down to keep her calm in front of the masters. Their faces expressed a surprised excitement—all but one.

The man sat furthest to the left leaned on the table with his head held up with his palm. Her teeth ground against each other while she tried to take her eyes off him. He was not even looking at her; he merely played with the desk beneath his fingers. Raye's heavy breathing started to slow down as she left the room.

Sat waiting for what came next, she picked the battle apart in her mind. She needed to find a better way to gain strength and not rely on a surprise attack from behind. They would catch on too quickly. She decided she would no longer attempt it. Her fingers picked at her busted-open knuckles while she remained in thought. She needed to acquire a proper outfit and leave her adoptive brother's handed-down stuff alone. She would have bought some years ago if the Kryfs were not as nosy as they are. But gods forbid they catch her with anything they disapprove of.

The unbothered master stood in front of her. She practically jumped from the silent surprise.

"Deciding everything you could've done differently, I assume? I always did the same." He clicked his tongue. His voice was rugged and low but maintained a nonchalantness about it. He was tall and appeared skinnier than the others in his baggy clothes. He did not wear any professional attire to be noticed as a master. A plain outfit similar to hers, with no fancy ornaments. His dark hair mixed with grey hairs throughout. The sun let in through the window lit his light brown eyes.

"I'm Master Sai. Will you accept my offer to attend the Military University of Duwan as my apprentice?" Raye stood up and met his eyes. He stood well over her with a decent posture, and his hands remained in his pants pockets. Her head tilted slightly as she looked him up and down, considering. His character was much different from the others, a casual arrogance. Master Sai gave her a fake smile.

"How about now?" he asked her. *What the fuck is this guy?* She was uncertain of him but did not seem to have other offers. His fake smile dropped to an arrogant one that peeled up at the corners of his lips. She nodded in agreement

"I accept your offer, Master Sai."

"I'll send a ride to the Kryf House for the morning. See you at the university." Sai waved his hand at her in a general goodbye gesture and walked right back out of the room. Raye went over to peek around the corner of the door to watch him return to the exam room, but instead, he left the building entirely.

That night, she would be comfortable in her house. Tomorrow, she would inflict damage.

CHAPTER TWO

How dare you bleed the throats of those who give you everything?

If the country of Daoland did not want the world for themselves, Raye would still be back across the ocean growing up in the land alongside her people, the Gestige. Daoland feared the power of those said to have been touched by gods—Celestials—who carried the elemental powers granted to them by deities to keep justice upon the earth. Celestials had been wiped out decades before they could attack the Gestiges. The two protected each other with their lives—Celestials being living proof of the Gestige's gods. With their missing protectors, the Gestige's abilities were only left to their own—which was not much against a growing army.

The Daos took north of their land to claim the Gestige people and their ways as uncivilized animals—as they did with anyone living differently than themselves—pillaging their villages. Even as strong and feared as they were, Daoland held no care, swarming their villages in the dead of night. Daoland churches worshiped the one single god they believed to be the only one. They disapproved of the Gestige's elemental worship and polytheism ideologies. However, the Gestige was only the start of their plans to conquer the world—religiously, territorially, and imperially. One god, one emperor, one race. The unspoken truth of Daoland. They will *save* everyone; or kill them in the process. *How strange what she could remember from such a young age.*

The weight of mourning the loss of ancestors and culture beat her mind daily since childhood. Earth that belonged to the Gestige people that she might never touch again. All reasons for the resentment brewing inside of her since youth.

◆ ◆ ◆

Raye worried about the reaction her adoptive parents would have. While she didn't care what they thought, part of her felt she should not make them angry after everything they had given her. Thinking about her past, she realized she showed people her kindness and time without expecting anything in return. She enjoyed the selfless act of helping people who deserved it. That was the thought in her mind—until she pushed the guilt out of her chest. They deserved nothing from her. They needed to learn not to throw money at every issue in their lives without remorse.

The house was quiet last year while her elder adoptive brothers were off at secondary military school. The home felt much more joyous with just her and her younger adoptive brother, Finn. He seemed to love Raye no matter what she enjoyed in life. As selfless as Raye had thought she was, Finn was always the one who would do anything for anyone—even if they did not deserve it. The two would often wander the grounds or head to nearby towns to remain unbothered by their parents. The atmosphere would change entirely when their elder brothers would return.

Their wooden swords made contact with each other a few times as Finn defended himself. Raye managed to hit the right spots for Finn to lose control of his sword, which caused it to fly out of his hands. His shoulders shrugged in another defeat. Raye tossed her sword to the side onto the ground with a laugh.

"Aren't you just a master yourself, Rayana." Filip, the eldest of her adoptive brothers, started clapping mockingly. Finn rolled his eyes at his brother. "You should be so proud; you're better than our baby brother, who can barely hold a sword," he laughed at the two.

"Fuck off, dickhead," Raye told him. She stared into his eyes blankly. His lack of effect on her made him furious. Raye caught a glimpse of worry in Finn's eyes. She believed he truly feared his older brother.

"Have you ever even fought anyone else before?" he spat at her.

Raye tilted her head in fake thought and shrugged her shoulders. "Nope," she lied. She would often find fight clubs in town that she participated in to gain skills. The best way to learn to beat a man was to fight them. Finn hated when she did it, but he would always go with her to keep her out of extra trouble.

Rage flickered behind Filip's eyes, but Raye knew he could no longer maintain it when his veins started popping out from under the skin around his face and neck. He clenched his fists, knuckles turning white from squeezing so hard—she knew he hated it when she spoke so casually to him. Filip felt that, as the eldest, he deserved the same respect as his father. The other brothers treated him as such. Raye could not have cared less. Birthright meant nothing to her if he refused to respect her. She could not understand the rage that would come out of him over the tiniest of things.

She would not get too cocky, as she knew Filip took pride in his martial arts abilities. "You want to spar with me; that's what you're trying to get out of me, right?" she asked. A wicked grin across his face. He would not dare ask her outright; he wanted her to ask him, so he had an excuse to hurt her without repercussions.

"I mean, why go through all the trouble of training yourself, Miss High and Mighty? Are you just going to spar with some skin and bones forever?"

How could he be so cruel to his flesh and blood? She did not understand. She could think of excuses for herself; they were not blood-related, and she was not Azeran. Finn had never done wrong to him. He should want to protect Finn like Raye did, not harm him unprovoked.

She kept her face bored at him and wiped the remaining sweat from her forehead with the back of her hand. She readied herself, legs apart, feet flat on the ground solidly, and her arms bent slightly at her sides raising her fists to her cheeks. Her raised brow claimed, *Fight me then*. The corner of her eye saw Finn's, but he knew better than to try to stop her from doing something. He backed up out of the way and remained silent.

Filip got into a similar readying position across from her. She took a deep breath, filling her lungs and releasing it slowly. Her heart rate slowed as she kept her composure. Her eyes flicked through every inch of his body and tracked his movements. The way he stood; one foot held more pressure than the other, ready to pounce forward. She viewed each movement he made so quickly, it felt like time slowed down. Raye had microseconds to thoroughly review his body, anticipate his next move, and how she should counter.

As she expected, he jumped off the back foot and started toward her to close the distance. His mistake was assuming he could take her out in the first hit and not planning past that. Filip was always so short-sighted. As his feet moved, his shoulder rotated in slight preparation to strike her. His movements hid no secrecy. His arm swung forward quickly with much force, aimed directly at her face. Her nostrils flared in excited anticipation. She moved fast. Filip did not realize she was gone until it was too late. She dodged his strike, ducking down under his arm with precision and speed, now fully behind him.

Filip, not landing the blow he thought he would, stumbled forward a couple of steps before regaining his balance.

"*Fuck you,*" he mumbled under his breath.

He pivoted around to face her—the anger burning off his body like fire. Raye knew he would kill her if he could; his blind rage was always his worst fault. Her face remained still. He could still surprise her, so she refused to show him any celebration. She knew better than to give him even a second to become aware.

Raye launched herself at him. Planting her left foot, she swung her near leg upward, slicing through the air swiftly. A dangerous move toward a man she did not know the reaction time of. That was a vulnerable position to leave her leg open for a grab. She had to be quicker than him. She was.

Her foot came into contact with the side of his face like a brick being thrown at him. His skin busted apart from the impact, and blood flung out of the wound, leaving a cut on his face. A slight static shocked the both of them upon impact.

Her kick pushed him to the ground and knocked him out of consciousness. His limp body hit the ground hard and lay there untouched. Raye could only stare at him. She wanted to do so much worse, but still enjoyed the pathetic sight of him.

However, Finn, bright and bug-eyed, let out a laugh that sounded like he had been holding it his entire life. Raye swore he stopped breathing momentarily, but it was only his silent joy. Raye could not bring herself to find too much amusement, not knowing what Filip would do once he awoke.

When he did come to, he groaned as he rubbed his eyes and bloody temple. She could tell he was furious, though he did not explode as she expected. He only stood up carefully with the help of the middle brother, Lukas, and said, "You are fucking insane, Rayana."

He stormed back into the house, surely to tattle to Mommy and Daddy. Finn's look of amusement was gone, replaced with pity directed towards Raye. She did not expect zero repercussions from their parents; the fact was, she no longer cared. She tended to ignore her parents' punishments anymore. If Raye were to do anything, it would always be whatever she wanted.

The staff's energy had been a stressful aura and whispered shouts and chaotic running about. The house staff scurried around, cleaning the home to their maximum capabilities. Raye's adoptive mother would not let her mind go unspoken if they dared have a speck of dirt out of place during her celebration of her son's visit.

Raye glided down the large stairway to the main entrance of the home. The light shone through the big front windows, lighting up the room from the sun. It bounced off the metal decor and brightened the chalky color of the walls. Her stomach growled from her morning hunger. When she entered the dining room for breakfast, her family was already sitting.

"I don't understand why you hate us?" Her adoptive mother cried out to her the second she walked in. Her voice rang with sadness, but her eyes had a tint of anger. Raye was too tired to deal with her nonsense so early in the day. Her temper grew shorter as the sleepless nights grew longer. She took a large breath into her chest and let it out dramatically.

Before Raye could speak, her adoptive father placed a hand on his wife's, signifying her not to speak. Raye clenched her teeth to hide her grudge against her adoptive father's rude authority over his wife. Jex's rage did not tend to be drawn upon Raye. He saved that for his sons. That was his rage now, though.

"What do you plan to achieve, child?" he asked. *Violence, strategy, war.* All things he did not want to hear. She could not answer truthfully when asked why she wanted to learn them. Things they thought a woman was an ill fit. It was not only in her blood, though; she was destined and born for revolution, she knew it.

"To join the military, become an officer, and fight for my country's rights. You can't possibly think that's a bad thing. It's what you've raised the boys to do since birth." Her tone remained firm with her adoptive father; she dared not show weakness when fighting for things out of her reach.

His anger would not shake her. This was bigger than her; it was about humanity within the world. Raye had the ancestral anger of the wronged and undone, a rage much more potent than a rich man could imagine. Yet she forced it inside her mind and knew if it slipped out too much, it would simply be taken as the emotional fool of a woman.

Her adoptive father let out a dry laugh, but his face did not represent it. "I know that you know that will not happen to my daughter. You know your place, and you will be ever so lucky with our status to find a well-off husband—"

"I will not marry some random man," Raye spat out. "I am intelligent, skilled in combat by my own teachings, strong, and willing. What is so fucking bad about that to you?" A slip through the crack she accidentally opened. Arguing like children in front of the entire house.

"Do not interrupt me when I am speaking." His tone was low and frightening. He had always been kind to Raye. She stood there all the same, regaining her composure, and looked at him blankly again. "You will not be violent. Women are not violent." But she was violent, much more than he could ever imagine. Much more than she even knew.

"There will be no learning the world of war, as this is man's job. I wish I could say my daughter had her head up in the clouds, but that would be a mistake. She seems to have her dreams down in the pits of hell." He rubbed his temple with his fingers and unclenched his jaw. "There is nothing more I will say on this. Let it be your only warning, Rayana. Your poor mother is beyond upset and heartbroken by the lack of traditional values you wish to take on."

"Of course, Father." Her response had no emotion. There was no hint of a lie or a doubt that she would disobey them—though she would. That was the future she chose. What else was there to do?

CHAPTER THREE

I must leave the graveyard of my past selves.

A restless night deep in the ideals of her future. The wind was rough, whistling through the trees and roof, pounding on her window. Influential power was the next step in winning the war. She had options the military themselves did not, which were unsafe without help backing her. The propaganda and fears the Daos had put into countries had ruined the face of her heritage and other intimate cultures in the world.

She could only lay still in bed, overpowered by the sorrow felt through generations. Laid flat on her back, hair fanned out around her; she looked for the constellations in the ceiling. Did the gods sleep at night? Maybe that was the blame for her sleepless nights. Though, was there even a night and day where they were from? If not for her living on this plane of existence, would she feel fully rested for once?

Early in the morning, Raye went through the items in her room, deciding what would be worth taking. Nothing in the room felt like hers, like she would borrow it until her next life. She settled on a lightweight grey dress she found comfortable and shoved it into a bag. The bag's strap hung from her shoulder and crossed to her other side. She slipped on simple shoes and was ready to declare war against her family.

Finn sat at the dining table, studying. He was getting ready for his upcoming exams for secondary school next year, the same as she had done. His leg bounced repeatedly, as it always did when his body was restless. If Raye had any respect for their relationship, she needed to let him know before she abandoned them. He was far too kind a brother for her to leave him without explanation. The guilty part wanted her to run away and pretend he never existed. She would not have to face him and the consequences of her choices. Never would she have expected to befriend any of her family members.

Not daring to look at his young, hopeful eyes as she finally betrayed him. Lied to for years, about to be separated by miles, and probably to never see her again, he looked up at her once realizing she had entered the room. Selfishness was carving into her like a sharp knife, spelling out its words across her chest. She wanted only to have him as a true friend and confide in him so many times. But she could not put him in a position of her versus his parents. They were his actual blood relatives and had done no wrong to him.

Finn gave her a grateful smile for interrupting his boredom. "Gods, I was feeling like I hadn't seen you in ages. You done avoiding everyone?" She was sure she had hurt him in the avoidance. Raye pulled out the chair next to him and sat. She set her interlocked fingers on the table, staring at them as her thumbs rubbed each other in nervousness. She could not help but fidget.

"Finn, I am so sorry," she started quietly. She was sure he could see her eyes across from him, full of regret. "I have shame, but I could not change a thing." Her eyes twitched away from him, back at her own hands. She knew the boy was fully capable of protecting himself, but the elder sister in her wanted to fight the world for him, even if it wasn't attacking.

"I passed the secondary exam for Duwan. I leave now," she blurted out. The words hung in the chill morning air until Finn gathered what he had heard. If he was angry with her, he did not look it.

"I assumed so," he started. Raye should have known he knew her better than she thought. He could not have believed she was training with him for fun. "I understand why you thought you could not tell me, so I never asked. There is no malice in me. I am so happy for you, Raye." His face lit up with a genuine smile. Raye's guilt lifted, leaving her shoulders lighter than she thought possible.

When the sound of horses traveled to the dining room, she fought the idea of tears. She embraced him tightly and headed for the door.

"Try not to make too many enemies, Raye," Finn smiled. "Though I am worried for them, not you," he laughed. A small chuckle escaped her lips as she quickly made her way to the exit. Her parents stood outside.

Raye's adoptive mother might have loved her like a daughter if she was only a mirror. Raye was no copy of Lila, though. Her love was always conditional. Raye could never give that much thought to caring about others. Any kind human being was deserving of her love and protection. Both women wished they could save each other for the opposite reasons. However, their fates had been sealed the moment they were born. There was never another option. There would never be a moment of saving.

"I hate you," Lila said to her adoptive daughter. She screamed and cried out in her extravagant ways. Raye had never assumed otherwise from her statement, and she only continued toward the wagon. "You always want to run off to do all these 'amazing' things. You want to run away after all we have ever done for you? I suppose I will always be here as a pile of nothing to you, then." Her anger came out in the way of whiny tears.

"I may not have given birth to you, Rayana, but we are much more alike than you will ever know. I was young once, too." She stared at her pityingly with a grin. "It will pass. As does all craving for adventure in girls." A pleading beg to listen to her husband's wishes. She shook her head at her like the disapproving mother she was. She was always assuming Raye's naivety and recklessness. Raye had lived more life than she ever would. She grasped more understanding of facts than she ever could. No future involved any of the Kryfs with Raye alive beside them. Lila's understanding of womanhood was of her father's and her husband's. Attempting to force Raye to adhere to them had nothing to do with being young or naïve, but with control. May the holy gods forbid she ever become more than Lila did.

Raye was in a far too emotional state that morning to listen to the utter shit spewing out of Lila's mouth. Lila could never love Raye the way she needed a mother to. She almost wished she could cry. She wished she cared enough about her play pretend mother to feel like she wanted to.

"Please, Rayana. Just stay." Her tone indicated this was no longer a plea but a demand. Her adoptive father remained standing next to his wife, unbothered. He had written her off already. That meant less arguing for Raye.

Fuck them, was all she had thought about them. Once she left the property, her brutality held no bounds in the rest of the world. Her cruelty could be unleashed on those deserving; no wicked was safe. The damage of innocence could be repaid. Even her bones could sense the battles ahead.

A lonely trip to Duwan had Raye bored out of her mind. She could only enjoy the view of forests around the city so much. She was missing the thought of home and wanted to be there tremendously. If she did have a home, she did not know where it was. Her mind craved it nonetheless.

Once past the furthest she had been in the country, the scenery outside her hometown was of mass difference. Large vast areas of hills and mountains in the distance, huge meadows full of flowers of all colors she had never seen before. Creeks and rivers flowed through the valleys, small villages, and farmlands housing livestock. Azeran beauty she could only read about until then. These were places she could only see in her dreams. Dreams of her childhood self running through the tall grass and flowers with her birth mother and father. The sky was so blue it could be the ocean, without a cloud in the sky.

The gorgeous landscape of the countryside reminded Raye of the importance of worshiping the earth as her culture within the Gestige always had. The natural beauty it gave to the living should only be protected to grow to its entire intent. Living inside the city walls had made her forget how lovely the world could be. No painting her parents could buy could ever capture the essence of life on the earth.

The days of traveling had finally ended, as she had made her way to the country's eastern side. Some of the highest-ranking academic successors filled Duwan's walls. It held the future of the military, leading the most significant school for military education, placing past students directly into officer positions, and having the most mastered educators who have served themselves. Entering the city was like entering what Raye would imagine a military compound might look like. The roads and buildings were built of stone, giving it a uniform and modern look. While some cities had incorporated stonework into elements, Duwan was the first to use it within the city as an aesthetic rather than just for military buildings that needed extra protection.

Even so, the city was still bright with its added landscape. As Raye traveled through the city, she watched the streets and buildings full of people. There were many shops, restaurants, and places to see within the city. Duwan was the second largest city besides the capital, but Raye could not imagine a city bigger than Duwan. Once entirely in the city, she could no longer see the outer edge, which made it appear like it had gone on forever. The crowds were much more diverse than most of the smaller areas she had been to. People from their neighboring country, Hira, lived within the city, and people with different complexions and features she had not seen in person before.

Raye had reached the eastern edge of the city limits where the school sat with enough land and trees to cover its location until they got close. She hopped out of the wagon and stretched her achy limbs. Students wandered about the school, keeping a busy presence. Many people her age were pursuing the same goal. Raye did not know if she felt comforted or opposed by them.

No one gave any mind to Raye as she entered the building in search of the main hall. They did not need to look in her direction; she was just another student. Knowing herself well, she wondered how long that would last.

Students, both nervous and excited, filled the hall, scattered amongst the pews. Mostly, men filled the room. Raye wandered mindlessly into a random row and sat beside a tall, skinny, dark bronzed-skinned woman. Her skin was a warm tan with a blush color that radiated from within her. Her cheeks were perfectly rosy, her lips large, and her dark features, like her eyebrows and eyelashes, made her appear a flawlessly dolled-up woman. The large black ringlets fell to her chin and covered her forehead in a little round bob surrounding her face. Raye could only be jealous of her natural beauty.

The woman made eye contact as Raye sat and gave her a wide smile. Her long, dark lashes fell over her golden brown eyes. Stunned by her silky, smooth appearance, Raye examined her, entranced. She appeared to look like what Raye might assume a sun goddess would.

"Hi, I'm Raye." She smiled back at her.

"Anala. Nice to meet you," her voice was smooth and intimate. Something about the two felt entirely familiar. Neither knew what it was, but their souls tugged them into that moment to find each other. They were two old souls searching for one other in their new lives. They had found each other. The familiar aura of one another. They were both exactly where they needed to be.

"Are you from the city?" Anala asked. Her hands sat in her lap, one on top of the other.

"No, I grew up mostly in Sudwal with my adoptive family. You?" Raye replied.

"South, in a town called Daran."

An older gentleman made his way onto the raised stage, and the

room's volume dropped in preparation.
"That's the headmaster," Anala whispered near Raye.
The headmaster clasped his hands before him as he stood tall and powerful. He had an almost full head of grey that fell past his shoulders and a well-wrinkled face of a life lived.
"I congratulate you all. It is no easy feat to excel in the country's most prestigious academy. It will be the easiest thing you do here, though." The tension among the already uneasy students thickened from the extra anxiety handed to them. Raye did not fear a school or its teachings.
"I am Headmaster Lorcan," he announced. "I graduated from this school many decades ago, and after serving in the Azeran military, I find myself back here to help with the teachings of the future soldiers. The opportunities you can earn here are truly life-changing," he boasted. "The main office will give you your class schedule, uniform, and dormitory. Classes will start in two days at the start of the week, while the remainder of students arrive. Please use your time wisely to get situated with the campus." The headmaster bowed his head.

"Rayana Tyrson," she answered when the clerk asked. The woman handed her a schedule, key, room number, and a folded pile of black clothes. Raye bowed her head as a thank you and walked out of the office into the hall to wait for Anala.
Raye peered at the paintings on the walls. The beautiful scenery similar to her views on her way there hung in gorgeous golden frames. She stepped closer for a better look at the sizable hand-painted map of the entire country hung across from her. It was a stylized version one would assume to be in a military building. The map covered the entirety of Azera and the border of Hira. The edges painted in gold ink, and the swirls of colors added onto drawings to represent different towns or land occupations drew her eye in further. It looked more like a work of art than anything, but still maintained the correct basis of the country.
To help retreat from their anxieties about first-day classes, Anala and Raye made their way around the halls, preparing to find their classrooms and dorm rooms. More art filled each hall they walked through.
Anala's passion for artwork shone through as she listed facts about most paintings they stumbled onto. One vast landscape caught Raye's eye—a sense of familiarity enveloped her. It depicted a mountainous range with a large, flat land between them all. A large meadow touched

each of the start of the mountains. Brightly colored flowers in shades of orange and yellow filled the meadow. Dark purples and blues saturate the mountains while the sun shone brightly on the flowers. Raye tried to see precisely what Anala was looking so deeply at.

M. NEVILLS

CHAPTER FOUR

The beginning of the end.

Master Sai sat in a regular wooden desk chair, like he had drug it out from an office, reading a book underneath the only tree in the back center of the private courtyard. Built with stone walls and flooring, the courtyard mirrored the outside of the building. The outer edges had built-up spots full of flowers and bushes.

Without lifting an eye off the book, he sensed her walk in. He did not raise his head or stop reading. There was no one else in the courtyard with them. Raye stared at the man, expecting him to speak eventually, but he only kept reading and flipping his pages.

"Don't you have other students to teach besides me?" Raye asked, the biggest question coming to her as he sat and did nothing.

"You're my apprentice," he stated, flipping another page in his book. Raye gave him a sideways look of confusion, though he did not see it.

"Right . . . But what about the others?" Raye was starting to get angry with his lack of focus on her—a great master to teach her who would not give her a single look this morning.

"Others?" he asked. "You're my only apprentice," he shrugged his shoulders. Raye stepped closer to him.

"I was told all the masters took on a few students, so my confusion was valid." Raye snatched the book out of his hand to get his attention. He looked up at her for the first time. He gave her a pout like a child. She could only respond with a dirty, annoyed look.

Master Sai sighed and leaned back in his chair, setting his folded hands on his lap.

"The others do. I don't." Another casual shoulder shrug. "You're the first one I've had in a few years. Hm." He looked upwards, tapping his finger on his lips, pretending to think about it. "I didn't like anyone else until you came along. Not many people have the talent or mental skills to catch my attention. They all learn the basics from their little tutors and think they're the best—" he rambled.

"So why the fuck did you decide I was your choice, then? You didn't even let me leave the building before asking me. And why do you not have to have students every year, but others do? Who even are you, exactly?" Raye interrupts.

"Celestials, you're fucking loud this early. If you wanted some compliments, you could have just asked." He rubbed in between his eyes in annoyance. "I can do whatever I want because I'm the best at what I do. Not everyone can be the best, but everyone wants the best. I create the best soldiers and officers. It's a talent; few others can develop students near my skill level. They can go on and on about themselves and the great masters they are, but anyone can personally train a handful of students, and they will be better than those without a personal teacher. I'm better at it." His nonchalantness acted like he was not giving himself the highest of praises. It was only facts to him.

"First lesson of today: control your anger and allow patience. I was almost done with my chapter." He stuck his hand out for her to return his book. Raye placed it back into his hand. "You want to get places, but no superior will enjoy your presence if you treat them like that. You are quite disrespectful to your master." He wagged his finger back and forth in a mocking shame, then pointed at her. "I chose you because you're fucking crazy, but you managed to teach yourself better than most do with a tutor. You have some impressive drive. But you are still crazy, so handle that."

"You know I'm self-taught?" she asked, ignoring his name-calling.

"Yes. You stand, move, and kick, all differently than those taught the same. Most teachers are too afraid to continue with a self-taught student, assuming they don't know the basics and will never understand them. But when done correctly, you make yourself stand out in a fight by being unpredictable. Everyone is taught the same thing and has a formula they follow while you do whatever is necessary. Your discipline is much better; the ability to force yourself to learn hard things is not something everyone is born with. I can tell you know your strengths, and you see other's weaknesses."

Raye eyed him up and down, still confused about the man before her. He seemed to see exactly who she was. "So, what are we doing today then?"

Raye was still determining their relationship and how they would get along. He seemed borderline insufferable. As long as he helped hone her skills, she could not complain. Though she probably would anyway if he continued being annoying.

"Alright, get into the fighting stance you would normally before starting a spar." Once Raye bent her knees, spread her feet, and had her arms on her sides at the ready, Sai went closer to tweak her body. He kicked her feet apart wider, repositioned her hands, and straightened her posture. Her body seemed to fall into place better, and she naturally found her center of gravity quickly.

"Now stay exactly like this, and do not move a single hair until I say so." Master Sai opened his book to the page he was on previously and sat comfortably back in his seat to continue reading. This request utterly confused Raye.

"You're joking."

"No. You have your discipline, but it can always improve, and the best way to replace this correct positioning in your mind is to continue doing it. The body remembers. Discipline over your mind and body; use it and remain still until I say." He was no longer looking at her and was back to being entrapped by his book. She was choosing to trust him and would force herself to stay. However, after some time, both her thighs and core were feeling weary, and this would be much harder than she had hoped.

Raye stood still all morning, attempting to keep her mind at peace from her screeching body. She wanted an influential teacher to force the best version of her body and mind out. Even one day of doing this could build muscles up exactly where she needed them. Beads of sweat pooled up on her face and body, dripping from the day's heat.

The sun rose fully to the height of the day. It beat down on her with full force. Where she stood had become fully exposed as the sun's victim. The vigorous pain and heat her body felt as time went on only continued to be felt stronger and stronger, as her mind could only force down so much pain away.

Her entire forehead glistened with her soaking sweat, all while her new master sat unbothered by her presence, finishing off his book. Every noise felt a million times louder the longer she stood. Each sound of the page flipping dramatically made her left eye twitch. He was not her enemy; she tried to remind herself. She instead decided to focus her energy on her breathing: long deep inhales followed by long deep exhales to try to take control of her body once again. Eyes closed, body still, she now faced the sun head-on in the sky, soaking up its rays instead of fighting them. She could not move her position, and neither would the sun. The head would remain. Instead of battling it, she drank it up the best she could. Though her legs wanted to shake and collapse, she sank lower into her knees, forcing herself to lean into the pain instead of ignoring or running away. Pain could make her stronger if she let it.

Sai shut his book, causing Raye to jump inside her body. Her head jerked to him as if he had awoken her from a deep slumber.

"I have finished my book," he announced. He stretched his arms out, clasping his hands above his head and moving side to side. He let out a loud yawn. Raye stared at him, unamused.

"Don't you want to ask me how it was?" Offended, she had not already asked.

"No."

"It was quite awful, actually. Horrible ending." Raye grimaced at him without meaning to.

"Am I done then, or would you like to begin another book?" Raye asked sarcastically. Sai leaned forward in his chair, leaning his body weight onto his arm propped on to the arm of the chair. His fingers tapped his face one at a time, the pointer to pinky rotating repeatedly. Raye inhaled a deep breath of patience and pushed it down to her stomach.

"Yes, you may be done," he paused. "I honestly forgot you were still listening to my order. I stopped paying attention a while ago. Great job, though. You're improving at a much quicker rate than expected." He gave her a big grin and a thumbs up.

Raye's eyes bulged at his words and the pain in her body as it shook until she stumbled to the ground when trying to break free of her stance. If she had any feeling in her body, she might have wanted to kick him. Instead, she let her body lie flat on the warm pavement. Sai stood up, grabbed the chair by the back, and dragged it on the ground on the back to legs. They made a loud and awful sound, scraping the wooden legs across the hard stone floor. Sai drug it towards the exit door before stopping right above Raye. "See you tomorrow!" He smiled and waved a hand at her before continuing on his way, dragging like nails on a chalkboard.

Raye's body jumped and cringed at the awful dragging noise. She remained on the ground for a few more moments until her mind regained entrance inside of her body. A pathetic sight she was sure she was.

A sore Raye wandered down to get dinner; finally feeling as though she could topple over at the slightest breeze. Her stomach gurgled, and her throat was dry, in need of water. After getting a meal, she found Anala sitting in the dining hall alone. Anala looked up at her and smiled until her face dropped into concern.

"Celestials, are you alright?" Anala asked, shocked. Raye started grabbing at her face, assuming she was bleeding or something worse. "Your face is bright red," she giggled at Raye before being able to rein it back in. Raye's cheeks and forehead burned hot and stung once she touched them.

"Shit, I was in the sun all day, I got burnt," Raye said. Tomorrow would be a day of pain from head to toe. Thank gods her uniform covered her arms and legs entirely.

"Bad first day?" Anala asked in a sorry voice.

"Just intense, I suppose," Raye said, though she could only bring herself to laugh at the day she had, causing a worrying look from Anala. It was unconventional learning, but her body felt the work.

Raye asked Anala about her first day and tried her best to listen, but her mind melted like her body. She grasped the basics of Anala enjoying herself and all her medical studies, but she was not interested in being a fighter, more of a healer. She said they will start learning about the entire human body before learning anything medical. Raye could not understand most things she said on an average day, let alone with her fragile mind today. She did not know much about technical things within the body, nor was she very interested in it.

"We were told today that we will have tests on the material every week. It is a very study-based course, that's for sure. But after passing so many tests in the first half, we will get to join and help out at the actual infirmary in our second year!" Anala explained.

"So, what you're saying is, don't get too hurt, or I'll have a bunch of students trying to sew me back up?" Raye joked. Anala laughed then immediately went back into her stressful situation.

"How am I supposed to do all of this? It's only the first day, and I'm overwhelmed by the workload just being explained. They need medics for the military, but they make it so hard."

"I'm sure it's overwhelming now, but it's spaced out through the next two years. Don't freak yourself out too much yet; I'm sure you'll be alright. You already seem much smarter than me talking about the stuff you'll learn," Raye told her kindly.

"You're right, thanks."

"It's alright. If you just wanted me to compliment you," Raye winked at her, "you can just ask next time."

Anala laughed at her and lightheartedly hit her on the arm across the table. It hurt Raye's sore body more than she would admit, but she enjoyed having a friend in her new place.

She tossed and turned for most of the night as her aching body found no rest—neither could her mind. If her mind managed to drift away for a second, it would only wander into the darkest parts she hated the most. Dark and familiar, the forceful images of past, present, and future burst into her mind. Her least favorite loved to come back the most; the more she pushed it away, the harder it pushed back—her final image of her birth mother.

At that point, no matter how often she had seen the memory play in her mind, she could no longer remember her mother's face. A blurry recreation of a blank-faced woman she knew to be her mother lay lifeless and limp in her mind. She would rather forget at this point than continue to mourn. Mourning did nothing but torture her mind. She could not remember any complete memories of either of her parents, their faces now both a blur. The two blurry beings haunted her mind, claiming to be her once parents.

That night, it felt like her mother fought back harder than ever. Her body lay on the ground, blood pouring out of her, paler than usual, drained of any blushing life force. Dead for who knows how long at that point. She began at the same moment in the memory where she always did. The soldier in a stained, blue uniform, had decided young Raye was next. The Dao man looked at her with a menacing face—drenched in sweat and blood. A nasty smile plastered across his face below his villainous eyes. He was done with her mother, and she would be next.

Her mind clung to that memory—the final memory. For even when all faces faded, she would still remember. Raye could only pray to the gods to give her another memory she knew she once had of her robust, powerful mother to replace the torturous, distraught, and lifeless one she had. Not even the gods could control what the mind stored, though.

Raye's tossing and turning felt like it lasted the rest of the night. She was sure she would never sleep again. Eyes open, mind awake, she stared out the window next to her bed into the night clouds where the moon peaked.

Her body would not allow her to leave bed if she wished, so she did not try. She traced the lines in the sky with her eyes for hours, asking herself the most mundane questions. Questions of the future instead of the past. *If she could not sleep through tonight, how could she ever? For it was only day one.*

For that was only the beginning of her life.

M. NEVILLS

CHAPTER FIVE

Escape the faith.

"War has no victors," the history professor stated. He enjoyed the dramatics, though most of his students bore the repeated history lessons. The dull faces of young students he had been teaching for weeks made him feel like he was preaching to chickens. The older man tapped his fingers on the desk he stood over, waiting for someone to ask the question he knew they would.

"Someone has to win the war for it to end, though." A boy in the second row finally spoke up.

"Yes, but there are no true victors. Unless you count the wealthy men making all the calls, but they were already winning. As an entire country, we lose. Lives, food, funds, water, health, land, morale. Is that a victory for most of the country's working class?" he asked the room.

The original student nodded his head in a slow understanding of his point. "I see. The emperor will always eat, sleep, bathe, and have protection. While the majority of the people who fought the war are left to suffer," he stated.

"Of course, the emperor will get that treatment; he is a valuable head of state to our country," another student told him nastily.

"Why?" The professor intervened.

"He is the head of state . . ." the student started.

"No, why does he deserve that over others?"

"He makes hard decisions for the—"

"Could anyone, in theory, not make decisions? Should the person making all decisions for a country not face the repercussions of those decisions the mass majority does?" He paced back and forth slowly in the front of the class.

"Do you think the emperor of Daoland, for example, had decided for the betterment of the country to slaughter and convert the entire world as they please? What does that do for the regular citizen besides force their sons into war? Do you believe he is doing this out of the kindness of his heart, so the world is not eternally damned by the single god they believe in?

"Or is this not a convenient way for him to gain the most prominent, fastest-growing army and power over other countries? It's always about more power; it's addicting. An emperor bore into wealth without care and does not always understand or care about the average experience of their citizens. They believe their god—or gods—chose them to lead, and their royal bloodline is sacred. The closest a person could be to a god. Of course, the world's people think they deserve an extraordinary life.

"I do not say to let go of your beliefs in religion or our empire; I ask you to question things further than the majority. Everything can be used as a facade to convince the masses of something. You were smart enough in the country to make it into this school. Do not maintain a naïve mind forever. Everything you had been taught up until this point could be considered a tool to keep your mind exactly where it should be to put trust in our emperor. The exact ways used in Daoland to give them the best perspective of their actions."

Raye sat at her desk, fidgeting with her pencil in her fingers. *A facade used as a tool*, the only note she wrote in her notebook by the end of the class. Everything she knew could be true; she was only surprised he was saying them. She doubted anyone else in the room would understand that what he said was relevant to their empire. The wealthy students of the world who could use the most change were the ones brainwashed on the world's perfection, as it benefited them the most—the same ones who would never claim a form of brainwashing.

"Are you a philosopher or a history teacher? Sounds more like your opinions to shit," a boy from the back shouted, causing most people in the class to giggle. Raye's lips pressed together and rolled her eyes at them.

"Claim these as opinions if you must; I simply ask you to keep an open mind when you view the country around you. These tactics can be translated into strategy if you are smart enough to see that. Either way, emperors are not inherently evil nor inherently virtuous. To assume either would be incorrect. Most things are not the absolutes we were taught to believe." His voice was neither malicious nor kind; it was coated in a warning layer.

He then sat down at his desk and motioned that the class was over. The students jumped out of their seats and went to the hall. Raye was in no rush to be pushed around by the sea of students and stayed in her seat. Her palm held her chin up from the elbow resting on the desk as she watched the student shuffle through the single door. Her finger moved on the skin of her face, feeling her soft cheek in a dazed-like habitual movement.

When her eyes peered over to the left side of the classroom where the other students once sat, she noticed a boy sitting a few rows over from her near the center of the classroom. His head lay in his arms on his desk; he appeared to be sleeping. Raye's eyebrow raised as she turned her head to view him. She eyed him up and down. Though she could only see the top of his dark-skinned head, his hair cut short all around. She made the decision to wake the poor boy up.

Raye gently nudged the young man's shoulder until he started moving. He came to, slowly sitting up, squinting and rubbing his eyes as if trying to regain focus looking in Raye's direction. Raye stared at him blankly while checking to see if he was alright. His eyes were low and tired, with dark circles underneath. His irises were so dark she could not tell the difference between them and his pupil. The man's skin was darker than she had ever seen in person, a deep brown color that lay smooth over his chiseled face.

"You alright?" Raye asked him. His eyes focused on her face in a squint, trying to make out who she was. Raye lent her butt on the desk next to his. Her eyebrows popped up, and she shook her head at him, waiting for an answer he had not provided. The entire classroom, including the professor, had emptied out of the room, so it was relatively silent.

He blinked away his confusion. "Yeah, sorry." He looked around the room quickly in realization. "Fuck, did the class end?" he asked disappointedly. Raye only nodded her head yes. "Shit. I stayed up too late writing a paper for another class last night. Celestials above . . ." He rubbed his face with one of his hands while the other still held the pencil he should have used for notes prior.

"I don't really care, sorry," Raye replied before he had the chance to continue. She stood up, about to leave, when her eyes dropped to his notebook, which had nothing written. She let out a quick, dry laugh to herself.

He gave her a nasty, confused look at her remark, "Gods, sorry, you're the one who came to me first." He gathered his supplies, spread across his desk, and shoved them into his arms as Raye made her way down the first few steps to exit the room.

Out of Raye's peripheral view, she noticed he was suddenly right next to her. Her head snapped to the left to verify he had caught up to her, now on the lecture room's ground floor near the exit. Her eyes looked up at his head, at least a foot taller than her, then scanned his whole body to the ground.

A tall, borderline skinny man. He had some muscle but was at a smaller level than some of the other stronger students. He had a good potential build to become a large man and strong fighter if he worked at it better.

He flashed her a bright smile, showing off his light teeth, "I'm Zeki." Raye stopped moving and stood before him, eyeing him in confusion.

"Sorry, am I annoying you? I honestly don't have any friends at school yet, and you don't talk to anyone in the class, so I got hopeful when you approached me," his voice was a natural, robust, and low sound, but he drug it through his awkwardness, removing what could have been power. Raye's mouth cracked into a smile at his goofiness. The awkward, anxious man reminded her of her younger brother, Finn.

"Maybe you should plan your course load better, and you won't be sleeping through classes," Raye claimed rudely. She continued her approach to the exit with an attempt to leave him be.

"It's hard. Master Yarrow is teaching me as their apprentice, and their daily training is beyond exhausting for my body. I feel like all I do is get beaten repeatedly by the other apprentices during our spars," Zeki complained, walking alongside her.

"You're an apprentice?" Raye asked, ignoring the remainder. She stopped in her tracks. His brow furrowed in confusion.

"Yes, I just said that. To Master Yarrow," he replied obviously.

"Interesting. Me too. I haven't had a chance to meet anyone else here who was." Raye shifted her weight to one leg, getting comfortable in her conversation.

"Who are you apprenticing with?"

"Master Sai, though I might regret it, he's quite annoying." Raye grimaced at the thought of returning to his presence for two years.

"Oh wow, you're his only apprentice in a few years. Guess you must be pretty good then!" Zeki claimed excitedly.

"I guess, or maybe no one wanted to work with him," she shrugged and smiled. "My name's Raye," she said.

Finn often enjoyed the educational part of life most, which differed from their elder brothers. That was the exact reason the two got along so well. Finn would gladly help her catch up on her studies and teach her the basic things about their country. If not for Finn, she probably would have never fallen in love with history. She loved listening to him explain the laws, the hierarchy of the empire, and the military history and layout. He only had her craving for more knowledge. It became an obsession with history and understanding the country's past wars and military.

Raye was unaware of the countries neighboring Azera before living with the Kryfs. Finn showed her the world map, and she could only look at it and point out where she lived once he showed her. Hira was their eastern neighboring country, attached by land. Finn explained Hira was their ally. Unlike Daoland, the only other country in the world she knew of. Finn was very passionate about the economic understanding of the country. He knew all the items the country sold for their exports and where they got their imports, and the county's trade routes fascinated him. Upon learning Raye was from one of their biggest ports, he was amused to ask her any questions about what she knew, which was nothing. Until, of course, she explained it had been destroyed by Daos in the same operation, creating her homelessness once again and leaving the young boy very disappointed.

"The emperor makes most of his money by selling all our farm grains. I'm sure he'll have it rebuilt as quickly as possible to get it back up and running, but we still have the southern port as well," he explained.

Raye truly wanted to know the reason for the Dao's attack on the ports. The trending gossip seemed that they sent it as a message, whether because they helped Gestige refugees or simply to let them know they were next. Daoland was known for sending fear into its victims in many ways. Their army had grown so prominent and influential in the world that they had no reason to fear a thing. Everything was a fun game for them.

The library was Raye's favorite room. It's filled with so many books stacked from floor to ceiling that you had to use the ladder for some. She was most excited to learn about anything she could. The Kryfs paid for her private education alongside her brothers. Everything Raye had ever craved as a child; they would give to her. She and Finn spent many days inside searching for the perfect novels in nonfiction and fiction to occupy their time.

Often, when Finn should have practiced drills for his tutor to help with his future combat classes, he would hide away inside the library reading. Raye would only help encourage his behavior, as she understood his cravings for knowledge rather than the violent acts of war expected to be learned. Raye's understanding only made Finn adore her further, as he finally had an older sibling who understood his true desires of the world.

How could their family expect such a sweet young boy who had a passion for academics and not for the sword to join the military? They had two elder sons willing to attend school to fight for their country. Even Raye's young self, not even double digits in age yet, knew she too would join them. That was her purpose, as Finn's was education. Many jobs within the cities involved educated scholars, if only the Kryfs allowed them to. As the Kryfs had their traditional views on women in their family, they also had their views on the men. Other sons could be accountants if they chose, but no son of Jex Kryf's would do anything other than rank in the army, as he did in his youth.

While Finn would run and hide in his younger years, he eventually grew to learn what his family thought was his place. He knew his fate and came to accept it. Raye was never thoroughly convinced—though he never honestly told her otherwise. Raye did force him to reteach her what he had learned so she could spar with him. Finn was not a great sparring partner; he was great at understanding and reteaching his learnings to her. He could not execute them as well as her.

Raye's most significant disadvantage was always her size. She had become fully grown but still quite petite compared to the other women she had met. Not by much, but every bit mattered to her when calculating a win. Doctors had assumed the malnutrition of her youth stopped her from growing as tall as average. Minor setbacks would not destroy her determination. She would have different advantages against men larger than her if she became as strong as possible.

Addicted to the breaths of winning, learning to fight physically became a challenge. With her constant gain in strength, she could physically lift large amounts and fight against her brother well. Her greatest strength of all was how rapid she was. Her contained statue made it easy to control at all times, whereas the larger Finn grew, the slower he did. Even if she could do nothing else, she could avoid and evade like it was nothing.

Her entire body could become like a flash of light.

CHAPTER SIX

Death is a comforting promise.

Zeki and Raye sat across from each other for lunch. Zeki sat hunched over, leaning over his meal, and resting his head on his hand. His fidgety elbow rested on the table, the other hand tapping repeatedly next to his plate. His eyes stared off in the distance at nothing far past Raye's head as he spoke. She learned he was not from a noble family, unlike most students in attendance. He was an immigrant from one of the southern island countries below Azera, which Raye had not heard of before. When Zeki would stop tapping his fingers, he would rub them together in his hand, similar to Raye's habits.

"It was easy for them to take over each small island. There's nowhere to run or hide, and any military they had could only be as large as the island itself," he said. All his knowledge was secondhand from his parents' experience. Raye being accidentally hidden when she was younger was the only reason she's alive. If the Dao were determined to collect the entire island, any hiders would not have lasted a search. Her stomach churned at the thoughts of living through her horrors with nowhere to turn. To be left alone in the dark with yourself, hoping no one would discover you, only to be punished further for fleeing felt unimaginable.

"My family was lucky," a slight sadness in his voice, "they started with other islands and managed to get word. They couldn't take everyone off the island though, so they prioritized families with children. Strange to think I'm alive because I was allowed to be."

"Do you remember any of it for yourself?" Raye asked without

37

thinking. Her memories haunted her like no other; how dare she assume he would even want to speak of his childhood memories?

Zeki sat still, no more fidgeting. Raye had thought she had made a mistake and triggered something she should not have. The bitter taste of guilt spread throughout her mouth, and her eyes bulged open as she was about to take back what she had said. Zeki stopped glancing in the distance and looked at the hand before him as he picked at the dirt underneath his fingernails.

"Some, I think." He paused, collecting his thoughts on how to word the emotions and feelings inside his mind. Raye knew the wordless things she felt herself and understood his struggle. "Sometimes it's hard to remember what was real versus what has only become nightmares I may or may not have lived out. If that makes any sense . . ." he trailed off, unsure if his words had any meanings.

"I think I get it. However, if it did or did not happen to you at the time, it does not take away the real feelings and nightmares you might have now. Who's to say what's real or not real, anyway?" Raye replied.

Even though he claimed no noble lineage, Raye could tell he was far too educated not to have had some form of formal education. He did not portray the cadence of uneducated civilians like those Raye had spent time with as a child. He spoke like he could fit in with any other man of wealth, but with more charisma.

Zeki had a likable charm about himself that was incapable of being taught to others. Once she got through the layer of awkward anxieties he held at the forefront of his mind, his authentic charm came out with ease. If only he could gain the confidence to rid his mind of his apprehension. Raye saw the potential he had to be the type of leader who would follow without question. A strength of his covered by the weakness to which Raye could see both of.

"Did you have a formal education, then? How could you have ended up here?" Raye questioned.

"Both of my parents worked to provide an education for me. They felt I was smart enough to have a good future, making it worth it for them." He stared at his fingers, dazed. "I'm just glad they no longer need to overwork themselves for me." His eyes stared ahead wide open. The sense of guilt showed all so clearly to Raye. "My only goal is to make enough to send back to them, so all their time was worth it."

"You don't believe they already think it was worth it?" Raye asked as she played with her fork in her hands. The two's conversation of strangers had been long gone. Zeki's eye met Raye's at the thought of her question. He did not answer. Raye assumed as much.

Zeki's eyes snapped out of his thoughts. "What about you, Miss Gestige? How did you end up here?" he asked.

"My adopted family, the Kryfs, formally educated me on the basics. My three brothers all received the same, plus a combat tutor to help with military schooling. Unfortunately, they do not believe a woman's place will ever be in war. So, I left without asking. If they knew any history of the women warriors of the Gestige, they should not be too surprised by my decision," Raye replied. Her lips could not help but twist into a coy little smile. "So, fuck them, I guess," she shrugged her shoulders like it was nothing more than mundane, lousy news.

Zeki's laugh at Raye's arrogance was a sound of natural amusement. Like he was born to be a happy man, that was what the earth expected of his future. Raye's face popped into a smile from the warmth of her new friend. She felt the polar opposite of him, though. Like she was born to have a life of loneliness and sorrow; maybe that would change.

The bombs went off at the boat harbor. The town of Norsan was under attack. Daoland soldiers had sailed across the ocean unknowingly to Azera. As the planted bombs had gone off, the soldiers poured in from the southern lands of the town.

Rayana was only eight. She was sitting on the ground of her orphanage reading when the building shook like a beast. The children then trembled with fear and cried. Raye peaked out the window to see the sight of Dao soldiers charging into the town, slaughtering all in the streets. The roads were splattered with blood, and dead bodies slumped to the ground. She recognized their dark blue uniforms and deadly stares from when she was young enough not to remember much else.

Ms. Bruner, the orphanage keeper, was shouting at Raye from across the room. Raye did not bother listening to what she said.

"Get away from the window, Rayana!" Ms. Bruner yanked Raye away by her arm, dragging her back onto the floor with the other children. Ms. Bruner always assumed she had a lousy sense of danger or would not listen to the rules—a troublesome child. Raye could not bring herself away from watching the chaos. She sometimes thought she could observe from afar and determine the threat, the enemy's movements. She

39

might have just craved the violence she had always had in her life—a strange comfort.

Ms. Bruner, clearly in a panicked state, was telling everyone to stay calm.

"Stay away from the windows; the Azeran military will be here to help us," she stated, as if she was not on the edge of tears in fear. Raye watched with a strangely calm demeanor as Ms. Bruner tried to convince the children and herself to remain calm.

Raye could tell from Ms. Bruner's energy, Raye's lack of terror was creating more worry for her. She probably thought Raye was stupid and did not understand what was happening. Raye had heard the whispers of the assumption of the Gestige education. Or she thought she was maybe a psychopath. Idiotic, blood-hungry warriors. Raye was unsure of her mind.

Whether it be the desensitization from previous encounters with brutal violence or that she knew the world had a way of getting exactly what it wanted. Her death had caught up with her after surviving her original attack, and the world must be put back in order. Or could it have been that the violence she secretly craved . . . craved her back? There was not one without the other.

Raye, off in the world of her mind, only heard the mumblings of Ms. Bruner in the background until she snapped out of her thoughts as they shuffled her off with the others. Ms. Bruner had shoved them all in the nearest closet to protect them as long as she could while the Daos made their way further and further into the city. Raye saw the strength it took for Ms. Bruner to try to protect the children to the best of her abilities. She knew it would not end well for her. One of the most selfless and kind adults Raye had known in Azera. A young woman with no family or husband who gave up everything to care for many unloved and lonely children. Shattering to Raye's young heart that this was all the life she would live.

Raye peaked through the crack of the closet door and listened closely. "Please, it's just children in here." The soldiers had entered the building. "Just leave them be, please," she pleaded to them with all her being. Raye could hear it in her voice. The begging of life to those who have no right to take it ate at Raye's chest like poison. Raye snapped out of her acceptance of death. One of the first times she decided to live. It was too late.

The men's cackling filled the building. Raye watched between the small crack as a soldier's sword slammed into Ms. Bruner's head, and she fell to the ground. Her head hit the floor with a hard thud from the force. He did not strike hard enough to kill her. Her heart still beat, and her lungs still took in breath—though mangled. The soldier yanked his blade out and slammed it down again. Again, and again, and again. Her blood splattered onto the men's uniforms. Her body was limp on the ground while her blood pooled through the floor far enough that even the soldiers were standing in it. It soaked through the floor, the wood planks probably stained from the remainder of the woman.

If she had awoken out of her selfish stupor, she could have prevented her death. Instead, she hid in the shadows of the closet, waiting for them to come and kill her, too. Raye was furious at herself. Angry at the men. How could she let that happen? Ms. Bruner was innocent, just like Raye's own family. If she had gotten over her depressed sulking, she could have helped her. She could not let these innocent children die. How could she let her own family history get away from her? Their entire life was spent protecting the innocent lives of the world. Her grief had distracted her from reality. From her heritage.

Raye shoved the door open and faced the soldiers. The children remaining in the closet gasped and screamed at her actions. She stared at the men with anger as they laughed in her face. Their humor did not bother her; she could imagine how silly she looked from their perspective. She strengthened her legs and feet into a fighting stance and tightened her core.

Her breath steadied as the electric strings flew and snapped around and off her body. Her flyaway hairs stood up from the power, and the bits of bolts surrounded her face, cracking and popping in the air. Raye forced down a swallow of anxiety as she stuck out her right arm at them. She enjoyed the look of fear she suddenly struck into them. They were too scared to run away from the monster they were viewing, not that they would have been faster than lightning.

Raye forced the electric feeling from her chest down her arm to her fingertips. Her eyes shut from the pain as the lightning wrapped itself around her arm downward until it bounced off her fingertips. It ran through and around her arm like her own veins. She had done nothing on this large of a scale and knew the risks of hurting herself, but at that moment, protecting the others was more important. The electricity sprung from her, exiting her fingertips. It was too late when the soldiers seemed to understand exactly what she was. Within mere seconds, they had laughed at her like the child she was to meeting their painful death.

She had far too much control for an escape, a gift she had also granted, along with her abilities. The fiery rage was released onto them. Her bolts traveled up their swords in a beautiful display of a blue-tinted light.

She did not need to move for one man at a time; she knew she had the power to kill them all at once. Lightning was a powerful weapon, unharnessed by the mundane man. The bolts continued moving down her arm in excruciating pain; she could only grit her teeth to prevent a scream. Her victims screamed in agony as they fell to the floor. Their bodies were struck by lightning to a degree no man had ever faced in the past. To a degree, no man would ever live through. Their flesh charred and burnt in the markings of her fire bolts. The marks flowed up their body like a river, up each of their necks—now covered in the same marks one would see on a stormy day in the sky—onto their faces, scarring them entirely before consuming their bodies.

Raye could not hear their cries over loud and sharp, cracking light in her ears. She was heading toward a lack of stability. As much control as she had naturally, harnessing the amount of power she had was difficult as a child. Electrocuted to death simultaneously, all three soldiers now lay in front of her. She stopped her stream of light as the pain in her arm became too much. A euphoric feeling of power remained which died down quickly, only to be replaced by the stinging of her open wounds.

Blood swirled around her right arm trailing downwards. It dripped onto the ground, splatting and mixing with the pools of blood of her former caretaker and soldiers. Raye could see the markings of some of her crackling wounds wrapped around her arm, down to her inner palm and fingertips. The exact formation of sparks one would notice in the sky that she had created left permanent lesions. A once beautiful light now burned into her skin, the mark of an untrained girl.

Her mind, still in survivor mode, would not let her tears fall down her face. Instead, she knew they needed to leave before more soldiers came. The children behind her appeared more scared than before. Raye could not blame them for that. She knew if they did not leave with her, they would undoubtedly die. She took slow steps toward the others, which caused some to step back away from her.

"I will not hurt you, only them." She gestured to the dead men. "If you do not leave the town with me, you will die. More soldiers will come."

"But the military will come and save us," a child said. The others did not seem convinced that was true, but they wanted to know Raye's response, as if she had learned more than them. She did not, but she knew she had to say or do something because if no one else took charge, they would all die.

"The chances of them making it in time are not good," Raye claimed. "I feel like running is better than staying if they come." She saw understanding in some faces. She gathered those that would follow her to the back door. Opening it a crack, she peeked out around the corner for nearby danger—she mainly saw chaos. The whole town appeared on fire from her view, civilians and soldiers from both sides running around after each other, blood, slaughtering, and screaming all around—a massacre of mankind. By morning, the town would level down from the spreading fires alone. Raye imagined this was what the Daos had done to her home and her people.

The surrounding area was clear enough to dash for it—the men too distracted with their violence to notice them yet. The four children who decided to follow her looked at her with wide, worried eyes. One child held their baby sibling in their arms tightly, hoping to save them both.

"Grab a hand so we can stay together. If you can't keep up, we can't go back for you," she said sternly, with a sense of sadness behind it. Some of these children had never known life or death situations; she wanted to paint the picture as accurately as possible. She grabbed the hand of the boy next to her and gave them all a sad excuse for a smile. 'It's going to be okay,' was what she was trying to convey, but she knew it would not be okay in her body. She had a feeling in her chest that someone would not make it. Attempting to ignore the feeling, she readied them and flung the door open. She took to a sprint toward the woods. She knew the general direction of the next town over, Sudwal, but she had never left the village of Norsan before. Don't look back, don't look back, don't look back. Just keep running; she told herself, *it's not your fault if someone didn't make it.*

She ran as quickly as possible, the other children trying to keep up the best possible. They ran into the start of the wooded area when Raye whipped her head around to make sure they were not being followed. The only person she noticed was the girl at the end of the line, and the baby she carried had fallen to the ground as soon as they took off running. She lay on the ground face down; Raye could not make out her sibling, only blood on the ground smashed beneath her. Whipping her head back forward, she kept running, now covered by the trees. Refusing to stop until they could not bear to continue. So focused on their escape that tunnel vision had made her ignore the boy behind her, begging her to stop until she finally snapped out of it.

The kids plopped onto the ground like dead weights. With her adrenaline and fear calming down, the guilt in her throat for not stopping sooner. The twinges of pain from her blood-soaked arm had come back at full force as well. Her arm was exposed entirely due to her short-sleeved dress—and she had nothing to clean herself off with or to cover the wound. The entire right side of her dress was now a darkened, wet, red color from her shoulder blade down. Twisting her head to try to see the start of her bloody mess, she assumed the burn marks had started near the middle of her back. From the back of her chest to her fingertips, where she released her energy. If she had lived somewhere more private, she would have been able to try to gain better control and not harm herself, but she had only been able to practice small amounts in secret. She would have done it again to protect the others, though, only sooner to protect Ms. Bruner—a regret she would have to live with forever.

In the far distance, coming through the eastern woods, Raye heard the faint sounds of horses running. They must have been near the path connecting Norsan to the next town over. She could almost feel it in the ground. Raye dropped her head, ear placed up against the ground, listening. She heard them even better now, meaning there was enough to make an impact. A skill children of Gestige were taught young, a hunter's mastery was needed to provide. All were hunters and gatherers to them.

"It has to be the military; it's coming from the direction of the other town, not Norsan," she exclaimed. The most petite girl popped her head up in hope.

"You think so?" she asked. "Will they help us, you think?" Her hopeful eyes stared into Raye's soul. She could not give them false hope.

"I'll go check it out to make sure it's them and if it's safe," Raye said.

CHAPTER SEVEN

Are we worth saving?

The Daos flattened another home. All that remained were death and vile crimes that would loom in the air for eternity. Though Raye had only lived in the town briefly, with no friends or family, she still mourned the loss of others' homes and lives. She mourned the place that taught her the language—the hours she had spent reading, speaking, and learning to fit in with the other children.

Sitting at the military infirmary, the doctors and nurses eyed her lighting-stricken arm. Not one asked her questions about it, though. Raye was far too exhausted to care. She eyed around the room she was in, trying to ignore the pang in her chest. On the table, she sat feet off the ground and swung her feet back and forth while she examined the tools scattered around the room, guessing their use. Her arm was washed, covered in a paste, and then wrapped in a cloth. They wrapped it around her arm and palm; then, her two most affected fingers—her pointer and middle, stuck together and wrapped up completely.

"These look like a scorched knife has cut you," a doctor told her. He did not ask whether this was true; he seemed only to assume the worst. The poor man thought she had gone through a horrible tragedy when she only harmed herself. "With both the slices and the burns, I don't think there's any chance of you not scarring. I'm sorry." She assumed this would be the outcome, though she was still disappointed it was not more positive.

Whispered voices coming from the outside of the door caught Raye's attention. She tilted her body to the left so her head could peek out from behind the doctor. The deep voices traveled quickly to her ears, though she could not make out their words. A knock on the door caused the doctor to whip his gaze behind him. A richly dressed man walked through the door.

His face stayed polite, but his eyes read a slight gross disgust for the child. Her wild, ratty waves framed her blood and dirt-covered face. Her blood-soaked rags of clothing hung over her, multiple sizes too large. The tightly bandaged cloth went up her entire small arm. An interesting sight for him. He did not dare step too close to her.

He attempted a smile to cover his disgust from her current condition. "My name is Jex Kryf. Yours?" He nodded her way, his dark eyes staring at her, waiting for her answer.

Uneasiness sat in her stomach as she looked him in the eyes. She knew best to trust her gut about people; she was too bright not to follow her instinct.

She was a child, and children, by nature, are naïve. How could a young, lonely child see the red flags through the fine silks and embroidered clothes laid on the man before her? A clean, well-kept man who wore rings worth more than she could imagine and had shoes on his feet that looked like they had never touched the ground. Idolization left the girl with insufficient air to breathe at the want of a life like that.

"Raye," she spoke up, daring to maintain still his dark, grim gazes hidden under the smile of a kind man.

He let out a small chuckle, showing off his white teeth. "Your full name," he told her.

"Rayana Tyrson . . . sir," she stumbled. She did not know how to speak to adults properly, which she assumed should be to the man.

"Rayana, lovely name. Kind to meet you." He placed his hands into his front pants pockets, appearing more casual. "The government has notified me about you. That is what they wish of me, to give you a proper home. I live right here in Sudwal." His eyebrows raised gently, waiting for a response. After further thought, he realized the girl—who had seen all she had at a young age—knew better than to wander off with a strange man. "I have three sons, two older than you, and my wife, Lila. She is very excited at the thought of a daughter."

✦ ✦ ✦

Two familiar faces now occupied the once-lonely halls of Duwan's university, both of whom helped determine her future. As the cold winter passed, they often found themselves stuck inside with each other. As the weeks of repetitive training and teachings passed by quickly, her only source of comfort was the time she spent with her friends. With the movement in time, the level of difficulties crept higher and higher with each of her sessions with Master Sai. He was practically beating her body to the bone, only to rebuild it when he decided.

"I'm going to be honest; sometimes I might think you're lying about the drills Master Sai gives you." Anala laughed and flipped another page in the book she was reading. "Like, how are you even doing some of this shit? If I were you, I'd have been dead simply listening to his instructions." She looked across the floor to Raye's exhausted eyes. Raye did not find the same amusement in the pain Anala seemed to. She glared back at her friend, allowing a hint of amusement to break through. Raye pulled up her long black pant legs to expose her pale, sickly, bruised legs. The shades of blue, purple, and even older green popped up all over the white canvas of her legs.

"Fucking heavens; put those pasty things away. Gods, Raye," Zeki, finally looking up from his homework, yelled at her. "I need a warning next time for something that bright, alright?" He tried to maintain his serious demeanor but could not help but chuckle at his jokes.

Raye took off a shoe and threw it at him without warning. He ducked his head behind his arms, the shoe hitting them.

"Fuck off, you're not funny," she claimed through her laughter.

"What did you do to bruise your legs so badly?" Anala's face, unlike Zeki's, showed genuine concern.

"The other day, I had to do an entire routine with only my legs," Raye sighed, letting her face fall into her hand.

"Was your opponent a rock?" Zeki asked.

"No, a solid wooden staff he likes to use as a target. This target hits back, though." Raye mimicked Master Sai, using his staff to slam into her ankles repeatedly, mockingly.

Raye's mood lowered even further once seeing the time. Master Sai awaited her once again.

While she may have poked fun at him around her peers, she truly did enjoy his presence to some degree. She felt at ease around him, as unorthodox as his teaching might be. She did not need to pretend to be anyone other than herself for a second. Any little bits and pieces she could gather from his life made them seem to have some things in common.

She felt powerful before attending school; she honestly had not thought she could gain this much skill. Thinking she was much closer to the end goal before, she would not allow her confidence to get out of line again. Every cold morning it snowed, and she was forced to shovel it away to create her own working space before her next torturous activity.

Sai was creating a perfect soldier's body, mind, and skills. On the downhill of her first year, her mind became her most significant obstacle to Sai. His newest enjoyment was attempting to distract her with his quizzes, to surprise and knock her off her feet. Then, he would only tell her to pay better attention. While he was probably right, that she should be able to focus on her surroundings while speaking or listening, she did not enjoy the constant fall onto the freezing hard ground.

"If you can't listen and focus, you might as well just be another front-line soldier," he claimed. He would shrug his shoulders like most front-line soldiers aren't just sent off to their imminent deaths.

"Thinking does not require you to move, Rayana." The joy he found in using her full name like a punishing parent. He thought he was the pinnacle of comedy. She should have maintained her center of gravity and strong position so she would not be knocked over too quickly, just as without the questions. But sometimes, he would ask or say the most confusing things to trip her up, which worked to distract her.

CHAPTER EIGHT

How my times have changed.

The two girls lay on the floor of Raye's dorm room—a small room with a tiny window, bed, and desk with barely enough floor space. Anala was taking a break from her constant studying, which Raye assumed was all she did. Raye sat up and leaned her back against her bed for support. Anala looked up at her movement with her big brown eyes. Raye had convinced Anala to grow her hair out like she had wanted. Raye would not follow the rules for the men, and there was no harm in having their hair long if they pulled back in battle. Over the months, her big bouncy curls had grown slightly past her shoulders.

Raye could see how smooth and silky Anala's skin was, even in the dimly lit room. The yellow light from the small lamp on her desk was the only faint illumination source.

The closer Raye got to Anala, the more jealousy grew—her marred skin a stark contrast. Raye had never thought herself ugly, but her skin was far from made of silk. Even from childhood, she had always had minor marks and scars. Reminders that she was still alive. Anala would shine in every room whether she meant to or not. Raye did not shine, though—this she knew. She did not burn; she was a shocking presence. Her presence seemed much more jarring and less attractive compared to her friend. While Raye could convince herself of her contentedness, a part would always wish she was more lovable. Oh, what it could feel like to have a handsome man look at her like the only star in the sky.

The silence of the room was a comfort. The perfect friend was one Raye could sit with without saying a word if she wished to. Raye could no longer remember the times she once feared—never to find a friend who would allow her comfort. Raye watched calmly as Anala raised her hand, checking her fingernails. Her long, slender fingers ended with perfectly cut nails that hung slightly off the free edge. How could she maintain the maintenance and not break a nail in school? Raye could not understand. She did enjoy the more feminine things in life compared to Raye. However, even if Raye did want them, her lifestyle did not. Her hands were scarred and ragged. Bloody and beaten knuckles, calloused palms, and short, broken nails.

"Do you know of a Sebastian?" Anala questioned while still eying her nails. Raye tried to think of the few names she knew in the school.

"Hm, not sure." Her mind came up blank Anala looked up from her nails, leaned back on her hand, and stretched her long legs across the floor, crossing one over the other.

"He's in your and Zeki's history class. He's an asshole," she stated.

Raye might have remembered Zeki mentioning Sebastian. Raye tended to try to zone out when the obnoxious boys tended to attempt to speak up.

"I think I know who you're talking about now."

Anala's head turned to Raye with a nasty look twisted on her face. "He's in one of my classes with me, too." Anala paused, and a sadness flashed on her face when her eyes fell off Raye's face. "He's started being a real dick to me. I haven't done anything, but I'm now his amusement for the class period with his buddies."

Horror struck Raye's heart. Her stomach felt in her toes with how quickly it dropped. "What the fuck do you mean? What is he saying about you?" Her voice instantly slicked in low, angered hatred.

"Typical pasty, rich boy shit," Anala alluded.

"Yeah, it's just so fucking annoying. I'm just here to do my fucking classes and graduate. I wish he'd leave me alone," Anala said, defeated. Raye used to pick fights with the little boys who would misbehave toward the innocent girls back in Sudwal. It seemed like she would need to once again to protect her best friend.

An aggressive, loud knocking interrupted them before Raye could express her anger further. Their heads both whipped to the door. Raye got herself off the ground and opened the door to Zeki, ultimately pushing past her before she could open it more than a crack. Raye twitched around to scold him for his rudeness, but he silenced her before she got the opportunity. Her eyebrows raised, and her eyes bulged at the confusion in Zeki's attitude. He guided the door closed fully with Raye's hand, still holding the doorknob in shock.

When Raye examined Zeki's face under the faint light, she could see his widened, goofy smile and exhilarated eyes. Her face dropped from shock to her usual face of annoyance. Zeki pulled a bottle out from underneath the jacket he was wearing. Raye read the label to see it was a honey wine. Her lips flattened into a line of anger.

"Are you trying to get expelled by smuggling fucking alcohol into the school?" Raye asked him in a quiet, angered voice. "Where did you even get this?"

"I already got it here, so I'm not expelled. I thought you'd be so excited and proud of me, Raye." He gave her a fake, sad pout, quickly turning into a laugh at himself. Raye shook her face at him in a reminder of the unanswered question. "I made friends with Master Yarrow's other apprentices. One of them got it for me. Do not act like you've ever followed a rule in your life."

"I never claimed to, only that you typically do," Raye retorted.

Anala hopped off the ground to take the bottle from Zeki's hands and read it. "Seems like Raye is a terrible influence on you, Ze. Aren't you scared you'll get in trouble?" Anala laughed.

"Very much so," he replied.

Her eyes flushed out any sadness, only excitement with their new plans remained. "Looks like we're drinking tonight," she squealed. "Know any fun Gestige drinking games, Raye?"

Zeki giggled at her. "An, she'd had to have learned them before the age of, like, five." Anala's face turned a shade of red out of silly embarrassment, but she laughed it off. Zeki took the lid off the bottle and handed it to Raye first.

"For the influencer first," he said as he handed it, smiling at her. Raye grabbed the bottle and smelt it. A mix of the sweet honey smell and a pungent scent that felt like it singed her nose hairs. She took a quick swig of the bottle, and her face instantly shrunk up into her nose. The pungent smell was a fiery liquid down her throat—a bitter like no other she had before. Once the fire made its way fully down, the burning sensation crept up into her ears. A strange sensation that took too long to leave.

Her mouth smacked in disgust as she passed the bottle to Zeki, who threw the liquid to the back of his throat.

The alcohol had taken its effects on them.

"You owe me a bottle after being negative," Zeki claimed, his eyelids hung heavy. Raye laughed at him.

"Fine, alright. You're such a needy person, Ze." She smiled at him. Anala's flushed face giggled at her friends. Raye leaned her head onto the side of her wall.

"You know when I was watching your last spar," Raye started. Zeki rolled his eyes.

"Here we go. Even drunk Raye can't help but go on a tangent." Zeki laughed. She pouted at him before continuing. He smiled one of his cocky smiles that made her stomach turn as she stared at his face.

"No, it's not that." She smiled back at him. "I was gonna say that you're the best fighter out of," she paused, "well, probably everyone." He raised an eyebrow.

"Nah," he started. She did not let him continue.

"I'm so serious, Ze. You're fucking massive. I mean, like—You could beat any of them in your sleep with your power and skill, for sure. If you just went full confidence with your attacks, you'd wipe the fucking floor with them. You're stronger than all of them. For sure."

"For sure," he mocked humorously.

Raye lay in the grass near the sunshine. The days of occasional warmer weather had finally come upon the school, and most students spent more time outside on the grounds enjoying it before exams would quickly start, marking the end of the year. It felt to her it had ended as quickly as it began.

Anala ran her fingers through Raye's long waves, brushing them further into a poof of frizz. "I wish my hair was easier to maintain, but still pretty, like yours. I love your hair; I'm so jealous. I love my curls when they're long, though; I feel like a boy with them when they are so short." There was sadness in her voice over losing her length; she was now jealous of Raye's extreme length. Her refusal to adhere to dress code standards had yet to get her into trouble, and she only continued allowing her hair to grow, now almost to her waist, undone.

The midday sunlight had most students outside who were not in class. The grass was an extra bright green, and the flowers around the school started blooming within days. A group of boys were playing some game off to the side. It was not something Raye had seen or heard of before, but it involved a ball, and she had yet to understand the rules while watching.

There were few actual activities around the school. Raye sat up, holding her knees to her chest and her bare feet planted in the grass. Anala split Raye's hair down the middle to braid it into two braids starting at the top of her head. She held the strands of hair in her fingers, weaving them over and under each other and then adding more hair.

"It's only manageable because I toss it up in a braid and don't typically wear it down," Raye responded.

"That's true. I'm just glad you convinced me to let it grow; I hate feeling all boyish. I'd rather pull it back when necessary than look like a little boy," she laughed. The air around her seemed to drop the happiness. "I almost hate that I enjoy more feminine things because my father wishes his firstborn was a boy. Or any born, actually. I bet he'd adore you as his eldest, though," she said humorously. "You're much more interested and good at what he wants from his children. You'd be the perfect child."

The perfect child was quite ironic to Raye. If only they had been switched in childhood, they could have had the life they wanted.

"I'm sorry, An. You're completely perfect how you are, though. Your father's worries are not your own." Raye attempted to be helpful, but she knew it was easier said than done. She could easily not care about her adopted parents' opinions, but the parents who bore her were different. Who was to know how she would have felt if her birth parents had turned out that way?

"He's just a big crybaby over being cursed with all daughters," Anala laughed, though Raye did not believe there was humor in her statement. A silent moment passed, both unknowing of what else to say. "Hey, Zeki's out there playing that game with those guys. Maybe he could explain the rules to us." Anala laughed, pointing out Zeki in the mess of men.

As Raye understood, Celestials had become a modern-day myth to Azerans, thanks to the Daos.

"Celestials, as I'm sure you all know, are those believed to be touched by the gods of elemental earth. The original gods and those who created the world we live in. In some cultures, they are the only godly existence believed in. In more modern society, however, we now believe in a vast majority of gods for more intricate ideas." Raye's interest finally peaked in her history class.

"These Celestials are humans with the same god-like power to control elements of the earth. Elements can be anything from fire or water to potentially more intricate things we might not know. These humans were to be chosen by their god to keep the peace of the world and undo the injustice of the innocent. Some today believe them to be a myth entirely, as there have not been any sightings in decades and only spoken of. Though that would be the work of the fear-ridden Daoland." A student's hand shot up in the front.

"So, you're saying Celestials are real and not some myth the Daos created in an excuse to commit genocide?" The student scoffed at the idea. "It seems like a mythological story we pass down."

"Yes, many people do not believe in the existence of Celestials due to never seeing the power of one in reality. I do believe, however, that the Daos did not lie; they truly feared their power and had spent decades picking them off in casual genocide. The Gestige were the largest group of modern believers before their massacre. They had become the biggest protectors of their gods' will. They were said to have spent their last life protecting Celestials. The Daos feared their skills, and if any Celestials hid there, they removed them. The Gestige saw Celestials as proof of their gods, so they were meant to protect those touched by them."

"Guess that didn't work out too well for any of them then. Gestige died protecting mythological magic people that didn't even save them," a boy let out with a laugh.

Giggles erupted throughout the room, while others only turned in shock to Raye. Raye did not enjoy the attention brought on. They all knew the blonde-haired student was a remaining Gestige, which was precisely why he said what he did.

"Sebastian, watch your disrespect before I send you to the headmaster," the professor scowled at him.

Raye did not honestly care what the boy said. He wanted her to rage out at him, to prove the exact violent Gestige he assumed she was. While her blood wanted to boil over, she would not allow herself any control from that boy. Raye would not allow her reputation to be the crazy woman any more than it might already be. Any survivor of the Dao was not someone they typically wanted to poke fun at; even if she was a small child when it happened, they did not understand that.

Raye looked at the culprit to find Sebastian staring directly at her, trying to enjoy the misery she did not even have. She had never interacted with the boy before that very moment. His bright blue eyes stared like daggers at her. He seemed to enjoy picking at people until they broke, no matter who they might be. His targets had a pattern of being people he assumed were less than him. Like poor Anala, people he believed would do nothing about his remarks.

Unfortunately for Sebastian, Raye had never been one to leave things be. She did not brush things off or let petty boys attempt to walk on her. He knew nothing of her, which was only a mistake for him. She would make him believe in Celestials when he prayed for one to save him from her wraith.

Raye sat stone-faced and unbothered as ever, unaware the boy had spoken. She did not feel angry, no. Her body was on fire from the vengeance she knew she would bring upon him when the time was right. He started a game he did not know how to play with an opponent far superior to himself.

Though as normal as ever outside, her rage boiled inside of her. She could have smashed his skull in with her bare hands right there if she had let herself. A geyser of her hot blood that tried to pop over the top only remained inside her body with the tightening of her fists. The whitened knuckles and red hands she hid under her desk were the only say to her barely controllable rage. She only looked Sebastian in the eyes from across the room and gave a slight emotionless, closed-mouth smile that hid her clenched teeth. He did not realize the anger that seeped through her cracks, because he only grew annoyed at her arrogance. He could see she was trying to prove his lack of power.

Holding in her anger in front of him made time feel like an infinite amount in the seconds that passed. The professor finally took hold of his class after clearing his throat and continued.

"The centuries of sacrifice the Gestige had given for the hope of a better, more humane life, years before you were ever even thought of existence, are acts of selfishness you could never even wrap your mind around. A sense of community and acts of pure compassion for the sacredness of life brought these groups together. Any acts of violence were only for the correct recipients. They were among the first historical groups to accept all humans as equals."

Sebastian rolled his eyes at the entire situation, causing the professor to notice and think to himself for a moment.

"I hope you learn some selfishness while you enjoy your time cleaning up the school alongside the janitorial team as punishment, young Sebastian. Do not speak up in my class again unless you have something of substance to say."

The class broke out into laughter directed at Sebastian. His veil of calm utterly ripped from him. His face was pale from embarrassment and shock as he was expected to help the janitorial team, about whom Raye could only expect the rich boy's opinion. Raye turned to a laughing Zeki, who appeared proud of her for holding her tongue. If only he knew holding her tongue would result in a much greater punishment for Sebastian.

The only way to get a cocky man to shut up is to do the worst thing imaginable in their minds. Same as she did her elder brother. She would punish him for thinking he was above all else when they all stood on the same ground in the same place.

CHAPTER NINE

You can never go back.
You can never go back.
You can never go back.

Silence filled the campus as final exams came around. Failing them could mean no longer being allowed back into their final year. The school was never willing to allow students to slack in their abilities. If you could not make yourself the best every second, you did not belong here, as only the best did. The eerie air felt the stress. Almost all students attempted to gather as much information into their brains as possible. Even the country's best and highest testing students were still worried about maintaining their status to remain at school.

Graduating from Duwan meant higher positions, pay, opportunities, and bragging rights for their parents. The more significant opportunities within the military meant the lesser chance for the average student to be forced into actual battle time. Raye wanted a position of power but would not fear backing behind the lines, while others fought head-on with fewer fighting skills than she did. She could only hope to have more chances to kill Dao soldiers.

Sai had no exam for Raye; he only asked her to study in her other classes and not fail out of the academy, so he wouldn't have to try to find someone else who would put up with him as much as she did. She did not think she put up with him too kindly, but that may be enough for him. She wanted next year to come quicker than ever so she could enjoy the sparring of the second year against her fellow students. Raye needed to attempt her newly honed skills on other great fighters and would not allow Sai to try to get another apprentice as long as she was there. She needed his full attention to fight other students, and he could tell her exactly what details to fix.

Raye walked down the highly decorated halls toward the library, right past the same paintings she had wandered by during her first days with Anala. Around the corner, she heard the sloshing of a mop being taken out of a bucket. She had not thought much more of it until she had turned the corner, and all too late, she realized who it was mopping.

Sebastian's eyes flipped up at her as quickly as she turned the corner, realizing who she was. Raye stopped in her tracks and let out a sigh of irritation at the sight of him. His nostrils flared with his fury toward her. He chucked his mop down at the ground, splattering water all along the wall upon impact.

"It is your fucking fault I'm mopping the fucking floors, you bitch!" he yelled. His veins popped out in his angry rant, and his face turned red with fury. Raye let out a laugh at his idiocy.

"I've never even spoken to you," she laughed again. "Did I get amnesia and forget holding a knife to your throat to spout bullshit about myself or something?" Her coy half-grin and humorous eyes looked right at him. "I guess I didn't realize how scared you were of me; I do apologize for your fear of me." She mockingly fluttered her eyes down at him. She got a sick taste of joy from poking the bear. She could only imagine that was what he felt, though targets were only innocent bystanders.

Raye couldn't stop herself from continuing the same pettiness Sebastian gave others. She knew better than to let herself get out of control, but the sweet taste it gave her was more than addicting. "Bet you never thought you'd end up doing housework, huh? Thought you'd graduate in some high military position as the best in our class or something? Reality tastes like shit it seems." Pure joy radiated from her face; that should have been the end.

Sebastian was far past his breaking point. She saw it. Knew it. And continued. It was a mistake an arrogant idiot might make, not Raye. She prided herself on her control, but when faced with real demons, it was too easy to give in. She took a few steps closer and lowered herself to a condescending whisper.

"Hope you enjoy taking orders from a woman 'cause no matter how good you think you are, I'm better. No matter who you think your family is, I'll have a better recommendation. You will never outrank me while life breathes inside you," she claimed, wickedly. *Stop. Stop. Stop. Stop. You're getting far too ahead of yourself without knowing the future. This could easily bite you in the ass.*

"Though . . . I'm sure you already knew all of this, right? Since you hate me for no reason, it must be jealousy, correct?" Wicked but calm. Raging yet collected. Her voice was fluid and calm in her insults. Her natural state. She was taking her sharp blade and stabbing him repeatedly. In and out, in and out, the knife went smooth and buttery. Whether she should have stopped, she did not. She maintained as much grace as her out-of-control mind would allow herself to give Sebastian.

She swore his blue eyes had turned darker with anger. His fists wound up so tightly within themselves, she thought his blood vessels might burst. He was going to try to strike her; she saw his hand move, reading his power. He was about to launch, but Raye had already anticipated his movement. She prepared herself to dodge but would not dare give herself away as he did—maintaining eye contact as her peripheral view watched his body. She knew better than to strike him in retaliation; there was too much to lose at this school and could not break the rules and get away with it the same way he could.

Sebastian's fist flung forward, directed at her face. Quickly, it went flying toward her. The power behind it could have broken bones in her face if she let him hit her. It whipped through the wind with all its strength and speed; Raye was faster. His whole body followed through with his arm, wanting Raye's blood on his hands. She jumped back, shuffling her feet a few steps backward out of his reach, and watched the rest of her show.

Sebastian, full force, expecting to hit Raye directly, fell entirely through the air instead. Far too cocky in his abilities against an opponent he had never seen. He landed on the ground fast and hard, knocking over the bucket of water on the way down. Soaked in his mop puddle, Raye squatted down to him, laughing directly in his face. She could not have planned it out better in her mind. He lay on the ground, defeated.

"Don't fuck with me. You wouldn't be the first man I've killed," she told him sinisterly. The power she had over him felt electrifying in her veins. Her familiar, violent joy filled her body until her mind tried to ignore it. A game she had become the master of. The mental one Sebastian did not know they were playing until it was too late, and he lay in a puddle of his mess.

Raye now knew some of his pieces. He was a powerful fighter, much quicker than most larger men, but he provoked easily and was careless.

He was instantly too arrogant without knowing his enemy's value.

Raye stood up and started to walk away before gesturing to the water spill with her chin. "You might want to clean that up." The water spread as Sebastian slowly crawled his way off the floor. When Raye continued down the hallway, leaving him far behind her, her heartbeat with the joys of his singular downfall. She could not get ahead of herself and let her outbursts get the best of her. But it felt good. She did not even have to be violent to win.

Was the taste left in her mouth a sweet or bitter sensation? She could not tell which she felt more, angry at her childish outburst in the middle of school, which would probably lead to more issues with Sebastian, or at her satisfaction from giving in to violence.

Two things could always be true at once.

Raye's friends already sat together at a table in the corner. The filled library was found with only hushed whispers to others at their tables. Anala's energy was not of her calm and kind usual self. She read and wrote from her textbooks with an uneasy stress Raye could feel the second she sat down. Raye laughed at her, causing Anala to look up at her angrily.

"What is so fucking funny?" she asked. Raye practically jumped at the question, not expecting hostility from Anala. Raye's eyes quickly flashed to Zeki's, where he was full of silent warnings. Swallowing down her thoughts, Raye tried to be gentle to her friend.

"I just thought you looked a little frantic, and it was silly to me, is all. I know you know the material well; no need to put yourself into a panic," she said as sweetly as she could manage. Raye's high had been quickly brought down to the level of Anala.

"There *is* a need for panic; my exams are difficult, and I can not be kicked out of this school. Are you even here to study Raye or to poke your 'fun' at me?" Anala scolded her. "Just because you're some master's apprentice doesn't make you immune if you fail your other classes. Are you even doing well, or do you just fuck off in class, too?"

Anala's anger did not need to be directed at her. Raye let out a scoff and rolled her eyes. If Anala wanted to be bitter and argue, she'd win no battle against an angry Raye. Anala had no clue about the vengefulness Raye constantly kept bottled up inside of herself, and having her best friend pick fights over nothing was not something to do with someone who was about to boil over.

"I'm doing perfectly fine—for your information. All I'm saying is you don't need to be so fucking stressed and moody over some dumb exams you know you'll pass. No need to be a bitch to me for attempting to calm you down. I only meant it out of kindness, but if you're too stressed to see that, then maybe don't ask for my fucking help." Raye was attempting her best to bite her tongue. She did not need to lose one of her only friends.

Anala took heavy breaths through her angrily flared nostrils. She set her pencil down and stretched her fingers while she stared at Raye with annoyance. "Do not call me a bitch. I was just—"

Raye did not want to hear her stupid reasoning for being rude to her only friend. "Here I was in a perfect mood, here to bring you both joyous news, and you're taking all your bullshit out on me. Fuck off with the attitude, An."

Zeki's eyes shot back and forth through their conversation, astonished by their attitudes and hostility toward each other. He finally lost his calm and slammed his fist on the table, causing the entire room to turn and look at the loud noise that echoed throughout the room. Both Raye and Anala jumped, shocked by his hostility and lack of care at the entire library now looking at him.

"Both of you shut the fuck up. For the love of Celestials, you're the worst possible people to study with," he announced with a slightly lowered voice, considering the attention he had already gotten. Raye was now just as annoyed at Zeki for being unreasonable. She had done nothing wrong; the two of them were both annoyed with her, and he caused a scene in the silent library.

All three were escorted out for breaking the one rule during silent study hours. They all sat outside in silent annoyance with one another.

The last few weeks of classes had meant the edge of summer. The sun shone exceptionally bright, lighting the property in its harsh rays. Raye's fair skin burned warm and tingly; the heat powerful from mere minutes outside. The countless days of sitting inside classrooms for exams, her recent outdoor activity had been in the courtyard with Sai. Exam-less and Sai-less, today could have been an enjoyable warm day.

Instead, the warm outside air was consumed by a cold environment as the three sat outside together, but separately. None seemed too bothered by their argument or lack of library time, as they secretly did not want to study. Raye sat in the dirt off to the side of the bench Anala sat on while Zeki stood to the other side of Raye, pulling matches out of his pocket. His other hand revealed tobacco rolled in its brown leaves, leading Raye to let a grimaced look slip out.

"You smoke that shit now? Not even gonna ask us ladies if we mind before you light it?" She scolded him and threw an appalled facade at him, but Zeki's mouth corners twitched into a cocky grin before he stuck the stick in between his lips. He struck the match to catch fire.

He sucked in a deep breath of smoke and held it in while plucking the cigarette out of his mouth and sank into the dirt alongside Raye. Zeki leaned his arms over his knees, resting them casually.

"You two just drove me to it," he claimed sarcastically after he let out his breath of smoke. Raye dramatically waved the smoke away from the air surrounding her. She rolled her eyes and laughed at his accusation. Anala sat on the bench in silence, staring off into the distance.

"What put you in your good mood today, Raye?" Zeki asked her. He offered her an inhale of his cigarette with a gesture in his hand and raised eyebrows. She yanked it from his hand and inhaled the smoke, pushing it down her throat into her lungs. Zeki laughed at her unexpectedly. It burned and tickled far worse than her attempt at alcohol, both as it went down and came back up. Her chest and throat felt thick as she let it out with her exhale. She choked it out with coughs. When she coughed off to the side, she saw a disgusted Anala look like Raye had just killed her cat.

Raye faced Zeki again, as she was no longer in any mood for the drama. "Just excited for these exams is all." She flashed him a smile identical to one of his little smirks.

"Guess so." He inhaled again.

Now was no longer the time to explain the fool she had made Sebastian out to be. Since she had settled down from her pivotal moment, she knew Zeki would be frustrated with her for not leaving it alone. Even though it did happen to fall into her lap while walking down the hallway and only tried to move out of the way of his physical attack, she knew Zeki would not see it that way. Raye felt it would have been disrespectful to the gods themselves for putting her into this position and not to take advantage. He would undoubtedly find out once Sebastian attempted retaliation—a problem for later.

"You two just try to brush everything bad off like it never even happened, don't you?" Anala finally spoke up. "You were rude, Raye; you can't just pretend we weren't arguing a few minutes ago."

"I'm not pretending; I'm moving on. It was stupid, and I'm over it," Raye explained without looking at her. Anala let out a huff.

"Maybe I'm not over it," she mumbled back.

"Well, you should be; you were rude first, anyway." Raye turned to face her.

Anala sighed. "You can just be so assuming about my schoolwork. I'm not like you guys; I don't have the entire fucking school memorized. I have to try at shit. If I want to panic over exams, I will."

"An, this is a stupid fucking argument. I'm only saying you're smart, and that's the end. You're smart. Why do you even compare yourself to us?" Raye responded.

"You compare yourself to everyone at the fucking school. How could I not? I'm sure you compare us in your mind."

"Yeah, and I'm not perfect by any means. When I compare us, it's out of jealousy," Raye quietly admitted to her friend. She only ever craved Anala's highest opinions.

"Oh," she said, shrinking into herself.

"You're more than enough already, alright?"

Would Raye miss the moments she could never return to? The moments in her friendship where they could never return to that innocence? When the biggest fight could be over a rude comment? The thoughts tended to take her out of reality, as if she knew what would come. Instead of enjoying her life with her friends, she could only focus on the impending doom that lurked that might change her relationships forever. Most of her impending doom was a simple result of her deep anxieties. Other times, it was accurate to the future. She had never been one with such a positive outlook on the world. But there were still questions she did not know the answer to. Anxieties crept up inside her darkness.

It was the silent war they were not yet fighting. Did friendship exist in war?

A distraction came soon enough for her. Decorations filled the schools and streets of the city in celebration of Unity Day—their longtime shared day of celebrations with Hira for their allyship. It brought back memories of the uneventful days she would spend alone while her family celebrated with friends. Each year seemed to grow in the despair it caused her.

An emptiness filled her lungs with each step she took up the stairs. She was unable to stop the darkened shadows of her mind from fully taking over when they chose to. She could be the most powerful person in the world, and they remained catastrophic within her. She only wanted to rest by herself, as she always did.

Raye made it about halfway up the stairs before her mother's voice jumped her back outside her body, aware of herself now.

"You're not celebrating with us, Rayana?" Lila slurred her dramatically sad words; she had been celebrating early with some drinking. That was the only time her mother acted like a happy, carefree woman. Raye stopped feeling bad for her through the years since the exact life expectations were being forced onto her. Raye would think she would want to protect her daughter from the same fate.

"No need to be upset; I know no one cares if I'm not that," she replied.

"That is not even tr—" her mother half-argued.

"I'm not feeling well, anyway. I'm going to head off to bed early if that's alright."

Her mother swayed on her feet momentarily in her drunken thoughts, then waved Raye off with her hand. Raye was not one to enjoy being politically fake to a room of people who did not care about her.

She continued climbing the stairs and drifted into her bedroom. Raye stripped her dress off and wandered to her bathroom. She dipped her legs into the bath until she sank in entirely, each body part tingled from the burn of the hot water. She lay in her bath with only her face and knees outside.

The water framed a circle around her face, and her long waves of hair melted around her underneath the water. Her breath raised her body higher in the bath and sank with each release. Her head finally sank under, and she let her face completely submerge until her head bumped into the bottom of the tub.

When she was underneath the water, every sound rang further away in her ears, out of reach from her person. The party outside rang with the noise of instruments and laughter far away, like she was listening to the world outside her body, a place between reality and not. She remained submerged, listening to the world outside, the world she did not seem to live in fully.

She ran her fingers through her hair at the front of her scalp until it got trapped between the knots. She remained for as long as she could until her lungs might collapse. *Maybe they would,* she thought.

She yanked herself upwards toward the air her lungs needed to breathe. Coughing and gasping for air, she flicked the water out of her eyes. Drowning would be painful inside her body. If she were indeed outside her body, it would be easy to watch herself drown from a distance, holding her own body down while she tried to gasp for air.

She still sat in her warm bath. When she opened her eyes, the laughter somehow felt further away than before.

CHAPTER TEN

It was woman.

Anala's excitement in trying to bring Raye a joyous Unity Day permeated off her body.

The musical tunes burst from the performers who played their instruments masterfully. Upbeat, happy tunes played out to the crowds of people within the town streets on the warm summer night of celebrations. Celebrations for nothing except the fact it was summer. A festive night full of vendors brought outside and filled the streets with smells of delicious foods and florals. The sun filled the sky as much as possible as it sat right above the city skyline, slowly sinking behind the buildings.

Raye enjoyed the cheery music. She could feel the strong beats of each instrument pounding through her body, her heart pounded along with each note. The crowds were heavy and hot to squirm through. Anala tracked in front of her, weaving through the sea of people toward the live music, guiding Raye with an interlocked hand so she would not get lost.

Anala's smile lit up her whole face, a natural piece of her face Raye could never find on her own. Maybe Anala felt happiness more naturally than Raye did; she was unsure, but Raye could never have a sense of natural joy on her face. Her grins were typically more forced in nature than those brought on by genuine cheerfulness. Her resting face was one of a much meaner, more powerful demeanor, and while it had most of the effects she had wanted, sometimes it seemed nice to be seen kindly. Occasionally, she wanted to be nothing more than a girl like Anala.

Raye had been examining Anala's face when they stopped near the group of musicians and only realized it once she turned to face her. Anala came closer to her face so she could hear her in the loud streets: "I love music!" Her eyes lit up with a dark golden glow from joy and the setting sun. When she turned away to watch others near them, Raye followed her eyesight. Women and girls danced all around.

"Then let's dance," Raye offered, grabbing Anala's hand, ready to yank her toward the front. Anala's face turned to utter distress.

"No, I don't want to be embarrassed, Raye," she screamed out anxiously. Her once joyous eyes were full of nerves. She was always nervous about doing the 'wrong things' in life. Raye did not feel a sense of embarrassment over the idea of dancing. How could joy be embarrassing? She wanted to find joy with her friend and Anala may be her own worst enemy, holding herself back from life—Raye would not allow it. Raye took hold of her hand tighter and pushed her way through the people around them to dance alongside the other carefree girls.

Raye had never danced before and usually liked to do things only after being adequately trained and perfected. She did not care that night. She only saw Anala in front of her, hands held as she danced and twirled to the music like all the others around them.

The two danced until they could barely breathe. Sweat dripped down their bodies from the heat. They swung each other around in circles and in between their arms. They danced with strangers, all in child-like beings' intimate and chaotic dancing. As if they had not experienced freedom until that moment, grins spread across their faces. Faces sore from the laughter. Anala's dark curls jumped around in her movement, and Raye's light waves swung freely around her. Their dresses portrayed the same feminine movement their bodies did. The peachy tone of Anala's dress only made her skin glow brighter than before. Raye watched as the fabric of her dark grey dress swam around the air.

With each of Anala's twirls, the skirt of her dress spun around her, exposing its layers. The music ran through the air, down and around their bodies, allowing their legs to move faster than their minds to whatever rhythm was playing. Their laughter filled the surrounding air until it was all they could hear. Two women who knew this was their last chance to pretend to be girls again, to not care about those who found it immature or unbecoming to dance freely, to laugh at themselves and their terrible dancing.

Anala brought her lips close to Raye's ear to speak through the music. The heat of Anala's face brushed against Raye's cheek.

"This makes me miss my little sisters so much," she said. "We always have so much fun together. You would love them Raye. I bet we'd all get along so well."

Though the mention of her sisters brought a pang of jealousy during their own fun together, Raye smiled gleefully through her clenched jaw—unwilling to spoil their night.

Out of breath, they gleefully walked through the rest of the festivities. Raye led Anala by the hand, weaving through the crowds like a snake in the grass. They slithered through the waves from edge to edge, looking through the merchant booths—jewelry, baked goods, food, clothes, accessories, and everything imaginable. They were stuffing their faces with sweet goodies as the sun set on the town.

In the sun's setting, the street was now illuminated by the colorful lights of vendors, streetlights, and buildings. The two walked through most of the streets and stepped away from the crowds near a pond where a few others rested. They sat on the edge of the wooden fishing dock, feet hanging inches from the water. Raye's legs swung gently back and forth over the open air. Anala leaned back onto her arms behind her, staring up at the almost dark sky. The sun now only touched the tops of the furthest buildings ever so slightly, creating an array of pink and yellow sky before fading into a vast darkness above them.

Raye listened distantly as her friend spoke, her focus remaining inward as usual, on the thoughts inside her mind. Thinking of the lonesome life she had convinced herself she would live, to her remaining days being spent with people who seemed to understand her. About having a relationship with another woman who understood her like no other . . . one to relate to. No matter what Anala was, the two ended up in the same selective school and, simultaneously, both for a bigger purpose than their own life. Anala could understand the parts of Raye's life like no one else. They both fought the odds of being women and secured themselves a spot in the best military school in the country.

If neither wanted it, it did not matter. Their bigger purpose had them here: to join the Azeran military to fight a common enemy and protect the civilians of their home. She wholeheartedly supported Raye's decisions, more so than Zeki even. Zeki understood Raye wanted change, but Anala knew that to change the unjust, Raye had to fight for it. A bad idea for Zeki might be the only option for her. The two girls were opposites in many ways but did not rival each other like many women felt they needed to.

Raye stared downward into the pond reflecting the sky above. Her reflection stared back at her.

"If I fall in, will you jump in to get me?" Raye giggled at her question and turned to Anala.

"Of course, I will; we're in this together," she laughed.

Would Anala follow her to the darkest parts of her mind when reality came? Raye wished for Anala to remain the pure and kind woman she was. She feared even sharing the whole truth of her past with her. Anala had never imagined situations like those she had lived through.

Raye could have the possibility of never seeing her again after graduation. She hoped not, but the war they would fight was real, and their placements could be anywhere in the country.

"Yes," she whispered. "But reality would be the opposite, I'd imagine." Raye turned her gaze into her eyes; the pink and yellow sky reflected off them, and she forced a small smile toward her friend.

If a god gave us anything, it was woman. The only thing they seemed to have was each other in the world.

They clung onto each other on their exhausted walk back to the school. They made their way, stumbling through the twists of the school and up the stairs. The quiet giggles and shushing of each other bounced off the hall's walls. The lack of ability to maintain silence did not help their laughter. They plopped down onto the bed of the closest room they could reach. They lay on the pillow facing each other, only inches away from each other's noses.

"We need to sleep now," Anala said, utterly exhausted. Raye agreed and rolled over to face the opposite direction. Only a moment passed before Anala spoke up again.

"You know how I despise rodents?" she asked, causing Raye to laugh at the randomness and choke a *yes* out.

"I was just thinking about the time I found a mouse in the sparring room during class and thought I was going to die." They broke into shared laughter. "Everyone made fun of me so bad, but no one would help the teacher remove it."

"Alright, I'll actually sleep now," Raye said once the giggling slowed. Her mind would not relax, though. She flipped back over to face Anala, who was already facing her; her eyes popped open.

"You know," she started, eager to continue. Anala stared deeply into her eyes, waiting for the remainder. "I think Zeki has a crush on you," Raye whispered as if others could hear. Anala's face scrunched up, and she giggled; her smile spread across her face, causing her cheeks to become even more pronounced.

"You think so?" she asked genuinely, surprising Raye. How could she even ask questions like that? Her beauty radiated inside a room the second she entered, and her kindness was always undisputed.

"Um, yeah."

"How can you tell?" Anala prompted. She adjusted her head on the pillow to focus on Raye better.

"I don't know; I feel like I can just tell. He acts differently when you're around than when it's just us," she explained. "He looks at you differently. He doesn't look at me like that, you know? Like, I'm his friend, nothing more. But he wants more from you," Raye giggled at her comment. "Behind his eyes, it's like you're the prettiest person in the world to him. Like he can't even look at you, or his eyes will explode."

Anala placed her hands on her face out of embarrassment. Raye could tell it was good news to her, though. She seemed to enjoy Zeki's presence more than just in a friendly way. With the time he had spent with Raye in their friendship, he had gained the confidence he needed. Everyone in the school seemed to notice, mainly the women who found his new, natural, bold personality attractive. Everyone had found his charm and physical looks more appealing than ever. The growth in his sturdy, muscular appearance might have aided further, though she was unsure.

NEVILLS

CHAPTER ELEVEN

May they witness my rage.

Sebastian was out for blood.

He had been patiently waiting his turn to spar against Raye. With the progression in her strength and weekly matches, the crowds had grown bigger and bigger to see when her winning streak might end. When her winning streak continued, Sai had forced her into a more challenging position out of nowhere to push far past any limits she might have left. Sebastian would not get his one-on-one spar, which left him frustrated.

Sai had hand-picked her opponent lineup for each fight. Long ago, he decided Sebastian was the least of her worries and forced her into more difficult matches, leaving Sebastian in more personal embarrassment. Every robust and cocky man wanted to have their moment in the ring with Raye, but only Sai would approve of whom he found sufficient. Sebastian, alongside another more petite male fighter, had their chance against Raye. Her first attempt at more than one enemy at a time. Sai expressed his concern about how anyone could fight one soldier, but if she were faced with an actual situation, would she be able to hold her own or die trying?

A safe, monitored practice was a much better idea than Sai finding out she would only die on a battlefield. She would not survive in an officer position as a woman. After the first two months of weekly sparring against other qualified students, he found her winning far too quickly. Things needed to be shaken up for Raye and the rest of the student body. Sai would shove the wrath of Raye down their throats until they saw and respected the warrior she was. She would be the changing tide in the war against the Daos—of this, Sai was sure. Everyone else needed to be sure, too.

Every over-eager man ready to be the one to defeat Raye had fought her at least once. After months of additional training, some attempted again. Raye could not get caught behind.

Zeki was the only opponent she had not sparred against that Sai thought would be worthy enough. Sai had asked her if she was comfortable fighting against her good friend. Raised fighting with the only boy who would let her, Finn, she didn't see an issue. Nothing ever came of it, though, and they never did spar. At least not yet, Raye assumed.

The embarrassment she had left inside Sebastian was his clear fuel in their battle. While sparring with another fighter in the ring, Raye was less than bothered by his presence —only focusing on Sebastian. She knew the fight was personal, making him willing to do anything. The other kid was an unlucky student thrown into the ring full of preexisting hatred.

The fight started. Sebastian had no patience, and Raye dashed forward, ducked under his attempted jab, and ran right past him entirely to the other poor boy behind him. She was boiling to the touch with the fire she maintained, ready for this existing fight. Her senses now heightened like never before. She could smell the stress pouring off the worried boy, and she streamlined for him. The sound of Sebastian's stumble onto the ground with his feet from the missed action hit her ears. He would soon turn around and refocus.

The punch she landed in the poor boy's abdomen contained all the force of her quick dash. Raye could sense Sebastian slowly realizing how quickly she avoided him while her attacked victim let out a painful grunt from the blow he took. The contact she made with him was solid, and she forced him backward until he stumbled onto the ground within the first few seconds of the fight. He would get back up; Raye knew that. She only needed enough time to get Sebastian to fuck off.

Thinking he got the best of her, Sebastian tried to retaliate, coming toward her back for a blow. Raye whipped her body around to face him, her thick braided ponytail slicing through the air, hitting her face once the momentum stopped. She was unflinching to it, more worried about her leap to the side evading Sebastian's contact. When he flung past the side of her, his face was hot red with anger while he breathed heavily. He would be idiotic to waste his energy early on, but his rage might cloud his best judgment. That was the issue with an enormous stature; it took more energy for each heavy movement, and Raye knew that.

Out of the side of her eye, she saw the kid crawling up from the ground slowly, holding his abdomen. Sebastian wasted no time changing direction, pivoting toward her once again. She could not win the fight by dodging the entire time. Her breaths were heavier from each movement she took, and her fists clenched as she rubbed the back of her fingers in her decision-making. Her eyes flashed back and forth between the boys as she calculated her next move. She would not underestimate Sebastian's abilities, knowing how much time had passed, and the personal anger he held toward her.

Raye did not decide fast enough, and now, all three of them circled each other in small movements, determining who would make the first move. Each move she dodged from Sebastian fueled him with more frustration and a desire to strike her hard. His biggest weakness was his painfully obvious lack of control over his anger. But it would also make him desperate and cause him to lose all decorum. Separation would be Raye's best option, as she was an easy, tiny target for the two.

Sebastian was taller than the other boy; she would have had a better chance of knocking him over and throwing off his balance. She had to be fast, or he would see it coming and ready his stance. While her body and eyes faced the other boy in an attempt to confuse them, she quickly dashed directly toward Sebastian, aiming for his torso to knock him over. Her feet pushed off the ground with all the momentum she could. Her arms wrapped around his waist, ramming her body into him with her full force. He let out a loud gasp of air that she forced out of him, his face full of utter shock as his body fell backward onto the ground.

His back hit the ground hard, knocking the wind out of him. Raye, arms still wrapped around his waist from ramming him, crashed half as hard as he did, landing on top of his body. She was able to force herself off him before he grabbed her and gained any control over her. The room felt blurry around the edges of her eyesight as she crawled to her knees, trying to regain control. Sebastian started squirming, trying to roll over onto his side. Raye whipped her head around to view the third person in the ring, who seemed too shocked or scared to come anywhere near the two of them.

Raye painfully forced her body onto her feet as she rocked back and forth, slightly disoriented. With Sebastian now on his side trying to get up, Raye kicked his gut as hard as she could manage. She kicked him again and again, each kick to the stomach causing groans of pain to launch out of his mouth. The final blow had him coughing up blood before the other opponent stopped her.

The boy had made his way over without her noticing and landed a hard fist into her stomach. Her body instinctively curled up within her stomach, and she let out a sound of pain and shock. She allowed herself to become too distracted by Sebastian and mentally shamed herself for it. Raye elbowed the chest of her assaulter, knocking the breath out of his lungs, punching him hard in the temple, then shoulder-checking him to the ground.

She was not done with Sebastian. Her knee rested on his chest once she shoved his back flat to the ground again. Her left fist clenched his shirt with the last year of anger, while her right swung toward his face with mighty blows of agony. She managed two punches to his face, now bloody and swollen, before a painful yank to her ponytail caused her head to jerk back. Raye tried to whip her head free from his hand's grip but failed. The boy wrapped his arm around her neck tight enough that she struggled to get air.

Both her hands gripped the arm torturing her neck, trying to claw her way to air. Her blood-covered hands could not get a good enough grip around him, and he only pulled his arm tighter, choking her further. His heavy breathing pushed into her ear as he struggled to control her flailing body. Raye could feel her face turning redder with each gasp. She tried to control her mind, tried to remain calm for a moment long enough to break out of his hold. Her entire body stopped moving, and she allowed the boy to put all his strength into his choke hold.

Raye kicked the front of his knees as hard as she could, forcing his arms to loosen up due to the pain. With a deep inhale, she kicked the front of his knee a second time with more force. She swore she heard a crack in the second kick, and he released her entirely, falling to the ground, crying out in pain as he held his knee. Her body fell onto all fours out of exhaustion and needing more air inside her lungs. Neither of the boys got up. She did not for a moment either, until after they announced her name as the winner, and the students crowding around the room cheered for the bloody show.

Each swallow hurt her throat, her knuckles had busted open from the hard hits she repeatedly landed on Sebastian, and her vision was dizzy, but she had won. On her two feet, Zeki came up to her for physical support. He looked at her with more worry than anything and helped her walk away from the crowd. While everyone in the room was obsessed with her violent victory, Zeki was the only one with a somber look. Raye felt as fine as she could, though; she felt euphoric. She was the greatest fighter in the school and the most influential student. Zeki's stress would not downplay the greatness she felt in herself.

Zeki helped her into the infirmary to have her checked out. "Are you alright? You're pretty bloody and beaten this time." She did not hear him; she was lost in the euphoria of her mind. "Raye? Gods, did you hit your head? Are you alright?" He tried again. His arm wrapped around her back, holding her up by her torso while the other gripped her arm as he did not think she would stand upright alone.

Raye looked up at him in confusion, "I'm perfectly fine, Ze." she whispered joyfully. He looked at her with further distress. She had yet to see her own bloody and bruised face, as he did. She had not even let her previous cuts fully heal before going and getting more around her face. Scars that primarily outlined the outside of her face, but with each spar came bigger ones caused by the impact of her opponents. Zeki had to keep convincing her to get them adequately stitched up while she still could at school, but she did not mind a few scars on her face. Zeki insisted if not for the aesthetics of a smaller, straighter scar, then at least to try to prevent infection.

She became a completely different person after each more incredible fight she would win. She became lost in her powerful mind, feeling godly compared to the average man, building a reputation as a vicious victor and nothing less. She heard even the new first year's whisper about how frightful she could become.

Anala came rushing to her aid once they entered the infirmary, forcing her to sit on a bed to begin cleaning her up. She obliged, as while she had adrenaline, even she could admit Zeki was the only thing keeping her on her feet. Anala always looked so happy while she cleaned off her copious amounts of blood and sweat and bandaged her up.

Once again, Raye had won, as she always had. That could teach Sebastian and others like him to watch their rotten mouths. While Raye hated to prove their Gestige beliefs true, she was a violent warrior. She had realized over time here that she could never force them to believe a different view of themselves, and there was no reason she should not be exactly who she was—a hunter to kill its prey.

Did they love or fear her? She did not care. No one would prevent her from potential destruction.

Sitting on the bed while Anala tended her wounds, her energy plummeted. Her eyes were heavy, as was her mind. Anala cleaned up her face as she sat in a now stoic posture. Sweat beads dripped off the tip of her nose before Anala wiped them away. Her eyelids drooped lower than before into a comfortable place while she stared off into the space of nothingness. She let her vision go blurred entirely to avoid the true dizziness she was dealing with.

As always, brought to the front of her mind were the visions of her faceless mother. *Could she not even enjoy a victory without her mind taking over?* Forced to remember how much they differ in their age. Gentle and kind were the two things she could remember of her. What would she have been like at a different time? The guilt in her stomach churned as it always did. She could only hope those were not what her late mother craved for her because Raye was far from it. She used to be so kind and giving to the communities around her growing up. Kindness did not get her far enough, though. Raye needed to fight through the mass to get to the root. It would always have the chance of growing back—even if she did not.

The urge for death heavy in her chest made her guilt only grow. She did not know who the urge was for. Her enemies? Sebastian during their fight? Herself? Was all of the above an option? Unsure and uncaring. She let her mind relax for the remainder of her tending. She could see Zeki softly staring at her face while Anala cleaned her up. The softness probably came from the fact she looked awful; she could only assume. Zeki tended to worry far too much about her. If only she were as calm as Anala, she might not cause him to worry over her. She did not want to bother her caring friends.

She was surrounded by her best friends, who took care of her after she had won her most challenging fight to date.

That was victory.

CHAPTER TWELVE

Is it evil if my heart meant good?

Each strike against the practice body with her wooden sword echoed through the courtyard. Sai stood silently, carefully watching every slight move she made. With each mistake, he would force her to start from the beginning. She encouraged his ideas to help push her past her prior limits. Each morning she woke up, her desire to be better was more significant than the last, and she crept her way up in strength and abilities.

Any emotions she had within herself, she was able to take out beating the dummy to 'death' until her knuckles bled. Her raging violence had grown with each step closer to the actual military. Sai had recently forced the sword on her, the most used weapon in war—typically—she anticipated spending future training sessions this way.

Her breaths entered and exited her nose heavily as she had been at this for hours. The further she pushed through any exhaustion, the worse she would trip over her footwork, causing her to restart. "Exhaustion doesn't go away on a battlefield," Sai would say. She knew this, of course, but on the battlefield, perfection was not expected. She would not argue with Sai; she was all for letting out her anger onto the fake man with no arms while she gained skill.

Sai was pushing her as far as he could. Once she beat all the worthy opponents, he started doubling them, like the fight with Sebastian. Once she could easily manage that, he'd force three against her to see how far she could go. What he did not know for sure—that Raye did know—was she could go as far as he would let her. Her abilities outranked any average person.

Raye felt like the second her body stopped moving, it might collapse on itself, so she did not stop. She did not break her continued sword movements as Sai broke his silence.

"I did some research," he stated factually, much more severe than she had ever heard him speak. "Most might not notice the connection between certain things, as most would not know the accurate facts of history, but I have become most intrigued the longer I've known you. I was curious to see if I was correct in my assumptions, as I usually am."

Raye's movements slowed as she listened to what he said, curious about what the man had to say. While most people at the school found Sai annoyingly immature or unsettling, Raye knew better than that. He was a brilliant and attentive man who knew more than anyone could imagine.

"Back in Norsan," he started. Raye grunted with annoyance.

"Three Daos soldiers electrocuted to death, right? Completely covered in the scars of lightning-like burns." He laughed at the thought. So much for their unspoken agreement to mind their own business. Raye did not fully acknowledge his words and continued.

A step forward, then a hop onto her other foot as her hands gripped the wooden sword she swung across the body in front of her. She sliced, much more substantial than she meant to, and the force from the unsharpened blade alone split the thick cotton covering in two, causing the tightly piled straw to burst out of the stuffed body.

Raye ground her teeth out of annoyance at the now broken dummy. She tossed her sword out of her left hand, allowing her right hand to maintain a tight grip, dropping her arm to her side. Her angered grip tightened, her knuckles turning a bright red and white. Her eyelid twitched from her internal stress.

She assumed Sai had paused his words for Raye's full attention. She tapped the sword tip onto the ground a few times to gather herself before turning to face Sai, raising her eyebrows out of the question. The mess on the ground drew Sai's attention.

"That building used to be an orphanage, right?" he finally asked, still staring blankly at the pile of straw before eventually meeting Raye's gaze. She blinked slowly a few times before nodding her head in agreement. He pursed his lips strangely at her while he shook his head. He could be the most infuriating human with his manners.

"The bodies had scars, like your own arm," he said. Raye released a sigh, waiting for him to admit he knew about her. He lets out a round of laughter, causing Raye to look even more confused.

"Here I am, spending my time training you to be some machine soldier, only for you to already possess the power of a lifetime. Assuming you can control it better now." He gestured to her scars.

"What made you put that together?" Raye asked blankly.

"Your progression should have peaked already. Yet your strength is inhuman. Because it is godlike, I realized." He shook his head as he spoke. "No offense, but your strength outweighs your skinny arms."

Raye looked down at her covered arm she knew was to be left with lesions for the rest of her life. She rubbed her fingers together, viewing the scars she could see on her palm and digits. "I was eight then, I think."

His face fell slightly to a sad look at the thought of it. She would have scolded him deeply a year ago at the idea of him digging into her past. It was different now, though. Their relationship had grown to a more profound mentorship than she would have known possible. Ultimately, he always saw through her—just as she saw through him.

"How did you know the details of the soldiers?" Raye felt it was acceptable to ask since he had done his prying.

"I led the city's cleanup with my team after the Daos were gone," Sai replied. A glimpse into his military past for once. He did not elaborate past that statement, and Raye felt there was no more room to ask.

The looming sense of fear hung over the courtyard as her master now knew the secret she had been so desperate to hide. The world was not safe for Celestials anymore, not with the world against her in the possibility of being handed over. Raye knew she could win many fights, but not one by herself against the entire masses. She trusted Sai fully, but this was unfamiliar territory for her. No one knew of her abilities—besides the children she saved many years ago. She knew no one would trust the sights of fear-ridden children from over a decade ago if they ever were to tell the tale of the child who saved them. She hoped they knew better than that, though.

Sai had used the last year to rip her apart mentally and physically to rebuild her exactly how they both knew she needed to be. However, she feared what he might do with his newfound knowledge.

He claimed to have picked her as his student because he always knew what she was meant to do, and how she could change the tide of the war. Perhaps he always assumed her secret. Their conversation had ended, so she would not ask him further questions, because he would not bother answering.

Her fingers grew cold from the chilly afternoon as they clenched the sword tightly. She turned her attention back onto the sliced open dummy and continued her routine, ignoring the gash through the middle. The air only seemed to grow colder as time passed

✦ ✦ ✦

"Years before the massacre of Celestials, some of you may or may not believe occurred; there are many famous stories of powerful and well-known Celestials throughout history." The professor paused for a moment to ensure no one interrupted him. He glanced at Sebastian, who did not utter a word or even look up from his desk, and then continued.

"Lucian, with the ability to form the earth, and Silas, controller of the winds, are the most recent stories shared across Azera. I am sure many of you know the basis of the story in one form or another, since fables, warnings, songs, and bedtime stories have interwoven it into their narratives. It is the story of a man who had gone mad, and his dearest friend was forced to slay him. The capital city, Nora, being torn to shreds from storms is well known historically.

Raye had not been told this story as a child. The orphanage did not tend to tell stories of death to children without families, and the Kryfs did not believe in the realness of any Celestial beings. While some might be fiction, she knew more than any other person alive knew how real Celestials were, so there could be more truth to their story than people might believe. She had not known any stories of past Celestial beings other than the consensus that they kept the world at peace.

"The general story goes as follows." He coughed out of the back of his throat to warm his voice up.

"Our great Lucian is known for the feat he won in the capital. His best friend, Silas, had grown alongside him their entire lives. Both men were born with Celestial powers. After weeks of Lucian having no contact with Silas, he appeared out of nowhere in the capital, using the wind to rip the buildings apart. He ripped trees out of the ground, flung apart brick buildings, and tore wooden wagons and buildings to shreds in seconds.

"He was to destroy the entire city. Lucian was in the capital then and had no choice but to battle his friend after a failed attempt to calm him down. The two fought while the remainder of the city got as hidden away as they could be. Between the two of them, they destroyed the entire center of the capital, resulting in it needing to be rebuilt later. In the end, Lucian had defeated his friend, who would not listen for any reason, and with no other option, he buried Silas in the ground below.

"What stands today in the center of the capital is where they claimed Lucian buried Silas; the statue of Lucian to honor his brave efforts in the saving of the remainder of the city. Rebuilt better than ever, the city now contains beautiful marble elements. I truly recommend viewing his statue if you have not.

"As I said before, this is how the story we know went, and I am sure the truth is less dramatic. Humanity will probably never know the exact truths to the details, as any regular human in the area would have had their body ripped to shreds before living to tell the tale. People love to speculate about what might have caused Silas to suddenly lash out at his own country like this.

"It is interesting to know that was the last big moment of any living Celestials, and their disappearance swept across our nation shortly after. The questions I ask you all to keep you thinking about this after class would be: do we believe this situation had anything to do with the mysterious slaughtering of the Celestials of the world? What might drive a regularly good man like Silas to this point? If Lucian had listened, what differences would our country face? This can cause many speculations and theories.

"I want you to study the details I gave you as to what could have happened and avoid making the same potential mistakes. We can learn from historical fiction, even if that's not what happened. What significant differences would our country face with that one moment in history being different if Lucian had found whatever Silas claimed to be true?"

The Daos had been hunting the Celestial for decades; that happened at the beginning of the disappearances in Azera. What would the odds be of Silas trying to get his friend's attention so desperately, only for his friend and every other known living Celestial to be wiped from the nation?

As the class swam toward the classroom exit in mass amounts, Zeki and Raye sat in their corner seats, waiting for the struggle to die down before they attempted to get up. Zeki leaned back into his seat, tapping his fingers on the desk before him as Raye watched his fingers hit the table one at a time, zoning out.

"I am surprised that some of the shit he implies hasn't gotten him fired yet," he said casually—a slight giggle released from Raye's lips.

Zeki reached a hand into his pants pockets to take out a cigarette, rolled it in between his fingers for a moment, then tucked it behind his ear in preparation for them to head outside after class.

"I think he enjoys the slight implication that our government is worse than we think," Raye responded quietly within earshot of Zeki as they made their way down the steps to the now empty exit. Raye's tongue picked at her teeth, wondering if she should say what her mind was thinking. Zeki tended to agree with her on most things, as their values tended to align.

"I think he's right, too," she confessed. Zeki kept walking without saying a word toward the building's back exit door. Raye kept looking at his face for an answer on whether he wildly disagreed with her. She only meant to test the waters to know his true feelings for Azera.

"You think he's right?" he asked her quietly in return.

The two entered the chilly backside of the university. Raye felt she could only manage her mind if she felt the sun or breathed in the fresh air once a day, training with Sai not counting as relaxing outdoor time. She would get so cooped up inside the building and the classrooms that even the colder weather did not keep her away, and Zeki enjoyed the company alongside his smoking habit.

The leaves around the school had just begun to change into the yellows and oranges of autumn around the campus area. The slight breeze rustled the branches of the trees high above, and the shaking sound of them hitting each other filled their ears. Raye sat on the regular bench. They enjoyed most of their time together outside the door. Zeki sat beside her, lighting the end of his cigarette with the flame.

"I think the Azeran Empire is not as good as they try to convince everyone they are." The lack of response left Raye's words hanging in the air. An eternity could have passed with what it felt inside her mind. Was Zeki secretly a loyal, blinded, patriotic man?

He left her words looming while he remained in his thoughts. His exhale of smoke lingered in the air.

CHAPTER THIRTEEN

There is only sorrow underneath my calluses.

Each day became weeks, merging inside Raye's mind. The subconscious repeated through her mind daily, creating an undead living persona moving from class to class. Hardly needing to use her mind, her other classes were easy conquers compared to the physical progress Sai forced. The sweetness left inside her mouth from each victorious task was almost enough to push her past any remaining boundaries.

"I fear addiction may come for you, Raye." Sai circled her, watching her form as usual. Raye huffed and puffed as she continued punching the air in repeated formations. Her eyes squinted at the statement, confused, but she maintained her repetitions.

"What the fuck are you even talking about right now?" Raye spit out at him. Master Sai continued his slow pace around her, merely looking at her fighting stance up and down, stroking his chin.

"The success," he started. "Each time, I can see it further inside your eyes. Each defeat sends you into a state of exhilaration."

"Fuck are you saying about me?" Raye interrupted; her fuse was extra short today.

"I'm saying you will become fucking bloodthirsty if you do not mind yourself, girl," Sai raised his voice ever so slightly, but more than enough to let Raye know he was serious. He had never spoken to her in a more than casual way. Raye's arms dropped as her head snapped in his direction.

"You think I'm addicted to winning? Won't I only want to win more? Can't be so bad, right?" Raye added some humor to her voice to soften the tension between them.

"Euphoria clouds the mind like drugs; I only warn that you fight for a reason, not for the blood lust to chase your highs." He was back to his usual calm.

Once again, Sai could see precisely what Raye thought. She was enjoying her time in the ring, winning battles against her classmates, but her master did not view it as she did. She blinked back her watery eyes and continued her routine. It felt like everything Sai ever told her was conflicting information. Be the best, but do not enjoy it. Become a killer, but only within reason. How was one girl supposed to know where the line was?

Sai giggled at her frustration. "I'm sorry. I did not mean to upset you. I forget how dramatic you can get." Raye's chest wanted to pop open and explode the boiling bubbles within.

"I just don't understand what exactly you want from me. A big, powerful, world-changing Celestial? Or a well-behaved girl without flaws?" she whispered angrily, just loud enough for him to hear the words escape her lips.

She let out a scoff of irritation at allowing her comment to leave her mouth. Control seemed much more challenging to maintain with each passing day. Every time one hand grasped power stronger than before, her other released her control the same way. Her fingers squeezed even tighter within her fists of frustration as they flung through the chilled air in front of her.

Sai stood still, seemingly dark in the shadows of her out-of-reach vision. The gloomy day's darkness crept further over the courtyard, casting more shadows of darkness than light. Dead plants maintained the mood of the training as Raye grew more sleep-deprived and exhausted, only to take out her pain on her instructor. Silence filled by her hateful remarks made everything else Raye was feeling even more painful. Her bright red ears and nose were cold and runny. Her eyes stung, feeling like they never closed longer than a blink at a time. Her lips cracked and chapped from the winter weather and the obsessive picking of the dead skin on them.

She would not turn to face Sai like she would not face any real problems she was dealing with. Raye convinced her mind she did not care if he was upset with her as of late. She was tired and beaten regularly; she acted rudely occasionally. Sai would physically and mentally push her to the edge of a cliff, only to have her hang off by her fingers and pull herself back up and expect to act grateful. At that moment, she was not appreciative; she was tired. She could not handle the constant back and forth with him. To be the best or not to be? Sai should have answered that question within himself before pushing her this far. Raye had passed the line of reeling herself back in; she could only ever strive for greatness. She would only ever strive to win. Why would she not?

Sai broke the silence of Raye's thoughts. "You're right, Raye. I should not have expected a child to understand," he whispered to her.

It was not hateful, only laced with sadness, because she did not understand. But there was nothing for her to understand. There were no issues with her wanting to win her fight; she craved it so severely that her whole body wanted it. It's what she had wanted since childhood; she would need it badly. Raye knew herself better than Sai thought he did. Raye had only ever had the good of other people in her heart and mind to maintain the peace of the innocent.

Raye wanted so badly to explain that he had nothing to fear. How angelic her heart was to the unjust, kind humans of the world. How she would fight for the equality she craved so profoundly for the citizens of Azera. But the exhausted version of Raye did not have the fuse for her explanation. She only got more upset at his statement. She had not been a child long before her recent adulthood. Her entire youth lost to enemies and war.

"I am not a fucking child, Sai," she growled. "I've done more shit than you ever have, whatever the fuck that is. You've suddenly changed your mind about wanting me to be this all-powerful being to take back the war. You've already pushed me this far. Are you upset that I enjoy winning against the other students? What do you expect? These people are the same people who think my poor child self didn't deserve rights! Who wouldn't revel in every win when you're an undefeated woman against a bunch of rich, cocky assholes who have been and will be handed every single thing in life unless someone changes shit?" With each point she made, her voice rose higher until she was yelling at Sai. She had never snapped so hard at him, even in all his regular annoyance. She did not feel bad, and she did not care; she was angry.

"Take a nap, Raye. The session is over," his voice, a scary stern she had not heard before, shocked her back into her body and the words she spewed at him.

He left her alone in the courtyard, shocked. Shocked by the words she spit at him like scum, or the anger inside him she never knew existed? A secret rage he let slip out from his usual calm and collected self. Unsure of the answer, she gathered herself. Maybe the two were more similar than she initially thought.

✦ ✦ ✦

Sai stood up from his chair and shook the hand of the Lieutenant General across from him. He then walked to the other side of the desk and placed a hand on his friend's back before escorting him out.

"As I said, my current student is unlike any skilled master you could imagine. Their dedication to skills is unlike any I've met before, which only pushes their drive for physical and mental education. I look forward to receiving your letter when you decide." He smiled at the Lieutenant General.

A once close friend he would have died for on the battlefield, now just another person to pull the strings of war, precisely how Raye needed them. Sai had always been quite the manipulator when the guilt did not eat him alive. That was always the difference he found between himself and young Rayana.

His pain and guilt ate at him until he became paralyzed in fear of his position, whereas Raye seemed to let it linger in the background and do what needed to be done. That was assuming she felt any guilt or remorse for anything. A part of Sai assumed she might know what must happen, and that was that. But the more humane part of him knows she was a person, a person with great empathy that she tried to hide in her cold persona.

"Well, if the great Master Sai claims it to be so, I only pray that your student will accept the offer I sent him," he replied, returning the pat on the shoulder. The inside of Sai's mind winced, and he let out a big grin to hide it. "I shall see you later, my friend."

Sai dipped his head and casually waved goodbye. "Looking forward to hearing from you, Zion." The door closed behind him as he left Sai's office. He gave constant empty promises to his friend. His fingers rubbed in between his eyes from stress. He could only pray to the gods that Raye would live up to the potential she had and not fuck this up for the entire country. He could no longer do as much as he wished—if only she let it be this one last thing.

The ethics of his current situation left a nasty taste in his mouth. He sighed in remembrance of his youthful, unethical days. He needn't worry about right from wrong when you get overall progress for the country. Until his conscience would no longer allow it anymore, that was. If only he were a better man, he might maintain true friendships. He would not have been exactly where he was if he were only a better man.

His moral compass believed that was the correct action plan, though. Raye was the proper plan of action. Raye would never enter into a rightful rank without an underhand, not only due to being a woman, but being what the military would assume 'uncivilized,' too. She needed protection and soldiers behind her and required the influence that Sai no longer entirely held within the military. She could end the war if they let her, but she could not do it alone. Without protection, she would get snatched up and offered as a Celestial to Daoland. Lieutenant General Zion was the only friend who knew Sai well enough and trusted him with everything.

She was confident enough to right the wrongs, as he once attempted. Could Sai let himself allow Raye to be so vile?

A great warrior . . . the great warrior he trained, would bring order to the world. The Daos would be stopped in their massacre attempts.

Once she considered something warranted, all hell would rain down. Sai wished he had the strength to help her longer on the path, but he could only keep his faith in her once she entered the never-ending war. Raye enjoyed a meticulous game she knew she could win in one swoop. They barely held off the game approaching her. She had been planning it for a decade and a half now.

If anyone could rip the rug out from under the arguing idiots at the top and take matters into her own hands, it would be Raye. She cared not about the bureaucracies of politics—an unmannerly trait, but one that would excel her whether they liked it or not.

May the world never see her coming.

She was always willing to go far. Would she be willing to see what was *too* far?

Uneasiness filled his stomach as he picked up the loose wood on his desk. She reminded him too much of his younger self and it prevented him from making any other choice. No matter how she acted, he would give her every opportunity. That was that.

May the gods give her their guidance to make the correct choices.

❖ ❖ ❖

"This will be our goodbyes, Raye," Sai said. They stood in the courtyard that they had spent many hours in over the last two years. It looked the same as when she started. The sun shone directly over them into the courtyard, casting shadows from the large tree. The flowers around the edge bloomed in bright colors, and the vines crawled up the side walls.

"That's it?" Raye asked. Unsure how she felt leaving the master whom she trained with for years. "Will I ever see you again, Sai?"

"No," he claimed. A lingering silence fell over them while Raye stood, shocked.

"How do you know that so surely?" she cried out like a small child. He always said things so plainly, like fact. "What if we win the war? What if *I* win the war? You wouldn't even try to see me after? I'm—I'm so sorry for how I acted before. You don't have to leave me forever; I'm sorry, Master Sai. I'm so sorry." Her throat felt thick as she tried to keep her tears inside.

"That's not what I said, Raye." He offered her no comfort. She did not understand why she felt so angered and upset by the situation. How could he be so cold-hearted?

"Realistically, you will not be able to see me again," he remained calm. She felt defeated. There were so many unanswered questions about Sai and his life. There was so much she wanted to know about him. As annoying as she found him, she would miss him.

Her eyes watered, which only increased her frustration. She rushed the distance between them and wrapped her arms around him while burying her face in his chest. Sai jumped from the surprise before letting out a small laugh. He laid his chin on her head and embraced her.

Raye had never felt emotional leaving someone, and she did not understand why she did so with him. He was a stupid old man. He treated her as almost equal since the second they met, though. If he was capable of love, she thought he might love her a little. Raye loved him back for the time he spent teaching her.

She let out cries she had not in a long time. They did not want to stop once the tears started flowing from her eyes and into Sai's shirt. He did not pull away from her before she was ready. How quickly one could go from pushing people away to clawing onto the people who try to leave them. She never found true comfort in any person, not one who knew everything about her. Not one who saw her as she indeed was.

She was not just a warrior, but she was a girl, too. Sai saw that.

CHAPTER FOURTEEN

I am but a ghost who roams around in a body I used to call mine.

Two years of education to be thrown toward a longstanding enemy with no prior knowledge. Sai was long gone, supposedly to be never seen again according to him. Though he was a much greater man than others to send her unknowingly into their army. He claimed he had a once great friend in high places who would treat her the same he did—the lieutenant general of all things. Raye had no idea how he claimed to have these connections to people and opportunities, as he would not share a single ounce of his life before teaching.

Returning to Norsan felt like something Raye would never have done in that lifetime again. There she was, though, shoved into the back of a horse-drawn wagon, trekking the journey with other graduates assigned there. It was uncomfortable and long, and the others smelled due to warmer weather. Not only could her senses not relax on her trip, but her mind could not. Memories flooded her mind the same way they did on her first journey to school, but now with the added memories of abandoned families and lost homes.

Resurfaced at the top were the memories of her short-lived home in Norsan when she first arrived in Azera. To step onto the soil of the town she had not touched since her single digits in age left her queasy. She had no expectations of how it would look. Torn down and scarred from the Daos and built on top to look like an entirely new town? She did not know what would feel worse inside of her.

Norsan was not a place of easily digestible memories she could shove into the pits of her stomach or store in the dark, quiet corners of her brain. No, Norsan was what brought life back into her young self. A purpose of fighting, killing, and winning. Another true sight into what the Daos were capable of. Norsan had become their highest military presence in the country—the most accessible spot on the shoreline to protect their ships and maintain watchful eyes on their enemy's direction.

Raye was the only woman in the wagon of newly trained soldiers from school. Once they arrived, they were to escort her as quickly as possible to meet with the Lieutenant General personally. While confident in herself, she still felt the anxieties creeping up her throat with this sudden toss into the real world. She still did not understand what sort of power or authority Sai held, but she knew that had to be the reason for her visit with the lieutenant general.

The lack of information was about what she expected based on the small amount Sai prepared her expectations. None of them knew anything besides where they were heading, and most of them were going to Norsan, as it was their most significant base. She only overheard things; no one would speak to her directly, as none of the ill-mannered men cared to acknowledge her. Raye did not mind being left unbothered by them, anyway.

She wondered where they sent her friends. A part of her felt like she could not do it without Anala alongside her. Raye had become used to being alone her entire life, but when she had someone supporting her for years, it was hard to go back to being alone.

Anala had probably already made friends with the other medical personnel. She attracted people easily with her bright, kind heart. Jealousy panged around Raye's chest, twisting and turning inside of her. She wanted to be Anala's closest friend. But that was the thing about Anala—everyone wanted to be close to her.

Raye was certain Zeki had made buddies with whoever he was working with. Every woman wanted to be near him, and every man wanted to be friends with him. By the time they reunite, Raye assumed he would no longer need her friendship. His charm frustrated Raye, while it brought everyone else closer to him, craving to be alongside his calm aura. Raye found it all stupid.

The town appeared much different from it once was in her childhood. Twelve years allowed them plenty of time to build the little shacks into a full-fledged city of stone buildings. The salty air and muddy streets were still the same as before.

It had become a more complex shoreline town for trekking items in and out of. Norsan had become a fortress of its own to prevent prior tragedies. The town had become entirely focused on its military presence. At the same time, the civilians lived around it—buildings of offices and storage for the military with the occasional home or shop in between them.

A giant stone fortress stood at the edge where the ocean met the town. It only grew in scale the closer they got to the military base. A long stone wall that almost resembled a boat appeared. The front of the fortress that faced the sea, the part their enemies would see, appeared as a tiny little building with random towers throughout.

The reality was hidden in its wideness and the slight hill off the back to cover. Raye entered the first door through the wall to find a large, grassy courtyard as most of the area in front of her. The large building to the left stood four stories tall and connected the entire structure's exterior, including the insides of the walls and towers.

The courtyard was a busy location full of soldiers in constant movement, heading from location to location. Shuffling weaponry and supplies around in their correct places as more shipments got brought in. Raye followed suit as they shuffled her into the building along with the other new soldiers. The office she got escorted into smelled of warm and sweaty people, as her entire trip did. The overworked soldiers gave Raye her uniform and emblems needed and gave her general directions to the lieutenant general's office upstairs.

The folded clothes in her hand were a dark red cotton base with dyed black leather chest armor and a belt to hold a sheath. The base seemed similar to her school uniform, long pants and a long-sleeved top to protect her from the elements. Raye rubbed the material under her thumb in circles before climbing the stairs to his office.

Raye did not know what to expect of the lieutenant general. Sai had told her they were close friends, and he gladly accepted any position of Sai's student in high regard. A friend of Sai's could be anyone from a lunatic to a rude old man, so her expectations were low. Whoever he was, though, he seemed to have blind faith in Raye, which was precisely what she needed, and Sai knew that. A man that close to the top with that much power blindly trusting her like that . . . she would hope he could do it until she managed what needed to be done.

The stairs took her into a small room with a door on one side and a tiny passage further into the building. The room smelled like cigarette smoke lingering from the soldiers smoking below. That seemed like their only relief from stress. Raye wafted the stink out of her nose and knocked on the officer's door before entering.

The lieutenant sat at his desk in the tiny stone room with no windows. The interior remained unfinished and made of stone, beside the wooden walls of the open-concept bedrooms the masses shared. The man seemed about the same age as Master Sai, so she assumed they served together. Would he have answers about whatever made Sai so powerful in the military school to do whatever he wanted? His eyes had youth in them, a light, fiery brown color, but his face told years of stories with each scar and fold. His forehead had the deepest wrinkles from a worried brow, and the circles under his eyes reminded Raye of her own, dark like ink. He raised a brow at Raye's presence, unsure who stood before him.

"Rayana Tyrson, sir." Raye bowed her head in respect to her superior. His face softened into one of humor, now realizing his past mistake, and laughed at the joke only he understood. Raye returned with a puzzled look.

"I should have known better than to assume anything from Sai." He clicked his tongue, reprimanding himself, then rubbed his temples.

"I'm not sure I understand."

"I was not expecting a woman, is all. Your abilities and strengths Sai spoke of, I assumed otherwise. My deepest apologies for my misunderstanding. I take no issue, but the news of our exciting new Lieutenant Colonel Tyrson being a woman will not please others." He paused. "They typically do not promote women this high as an officer, which I realize is why Sai didn't mention it. Guess you must have been worth it." He motioned for her to take a seat across from him.

"It will be best for me to give you a general rundown on our current situation before I throw you into the waters. You'll have two captains, each with their section of soldiers to worry about. If you go in barking orders about shit you don't know while they've been in for years, they will not react too kindly." He paused once and again shifted awkwardly in his seat before continuing.

"While your direct superior would normally be the one to speak to you and give you your information, I know you're a special case. Sai's ability to know people better than they know themselves is something I've always trusted and found true in him. I truly hope this remains true for you."

Azera's plan up until she came seemed nonexistent. They were only slowly building up their army, and now that shit got serious, they were rushing to be prepared. The Daos had made massive movements in preparation to invade Azera, and that had known for months. The lieutenant general had no hope of surviving this without Raye.

Lieutenant General Zion, the plaque on his desk read. Raye tapped her fingers on the desk as he pointed out where each of their military camps sat throughout the country. The most significant one right where she sat was Norsan, with smaller groups ready for additional reasons. South of Norsan, along the shore, was another base prepared for protection against Daoland. They could easily see a ship near and send for backup up north the hour ride if needed. They set up a miniature base along the border of Hira. They wanted to remain close in case Hiran officials changed their minds and decided to aid Azera. Hira seemed to have no plans to do that, but Zion and the general hoped to convince them.

"If Hira is so clearly uninterested in helping aid us against a Dao invasion, why keep troops camped out there in case?" Raye asked, the question not finding a clear answer in her head. Raye was unsure whether they knew why Hira would not help alongside Azera's military, as they seemed to share no clear reasoning for lack of help.

"Things are different now."

Raye let out a chuckle of air through her nostrils. Nothing was different. Azera was in for a giant shit show against the Daos and alone. The Daos would then move on to Hira; their lack of aiding Azera would not stop their demise if they even postponed it.

"How so?" she asked the lieutenant general.

"You can convince them." To Raye's shock, Zion seemed to trust Sai's word, trusting her far too much for what he was expecting. Hira had denied aid for years; how could she change their minds? She was sure she could try, but an entire country not willing to help fight alongside their allies for decades did not seem like it could be so quickly redirected back onto the course by a young woman.

Zion was grinning like a joyous child with a secret he should not know. Because he *did* have a secret he should not know.

"You will bring faith to their general." He motioned to her scarred arm, which Sai must have told him all about. Instinctively, she covered her entire hand with her sleeve. She no longer felt as safe there as she once did. The knowledge her superior officer had of her was blindsiding. Her eyes bulged open in shock, staring at his audacity to out himself so quickly. Was it a power move? To show he knew exactly what she was and the leverage he now held over her? Fuck. Raye felt utterly fucked. She was also alone. No friends or Sai to protect her here in the wild.

She assumed he had been rambling on with excitement over his newfound weapon, and she zoned out his words, shoved into the interior of her mind in panic. She held up her hand so he could stop talking. "I don't understand."

Then, silence as Zion stared at her in shock. Her cold demeanor confused him, how angry she was at Sai at that moment. How dare he trust some idiot man? A man he had not known for years. If that was his plan, a warning might have been nice.

"Before you start with your team, I'm sending you on our last attempt to rein in Hiran aide. I truly believe that if they see a Celestial in the flesh on our side, they will have more faith in our forces," he explained, confused by her lack of excitement. "There will be no issue; Hira is known for having nonviolent healing Celestials of their own. They cause you no harm, and you will be in no danger like you are here."

"Alright, but how the fuck do you know? And do you even understand how nonchalantly you're talking about this? People could have me hunted and handed over, especially with the Daos on their way over." Raye started to get heated with each word.

"I do apologize, Raye. Sai informed me only for your use and protection. I am no—"

"Use?" she scoffed, disgusted. "You don't get to decide when to use my power; it's not some little thing that I can hide. The destruction is too big; the masses must be ready to accept that before I go around flailing fucking lightning around unnaturally."

"No, no, no, of course. I only worship Celestials and the gods; I mean no harm to you, and I will die before I tell a soul of your existence." He seemed genuine, though anger still simmered in Raye by her presence being known. While it might be nice for someone to know and fully trust her, she would not be told when or how to use her abilities if he thought that was the case.

"I will protect you with my life, blessed Celestial. I swear to that," he claimed. His eyes were full of fear that he had offended her. Raye now realized he was not to be worried about, but he was an idiot blinded by his deep faith, too afraid to offend one of the god's greatest creations.

"That is not necessary," she gritted her teeth. She tried to give him a slight laugh to relax him, though she was not the naturally at-ease type. If only Zeki were here to bring his charm and casually repair her aggression attempts. "I only need you to remain discreet."

Raye had her first mission to worry about. She knew she could handle it well, but convincing her team to put faith and respect in her might be difficult.

Raye's time in Norsan was less than an entire day. Hira was her new target. They could have wasted less time if they were made aware before traveling across the country in the wrong direction. The military did not seem to mind wasting time, just as Sai had warned her. Every second mattered in war; she would force change into these ignorant officers. They underestimate the Daos' power and capabilities and have only been so lucky thus far due to whatever else the Daos have been focusing on. They could have entered the country at any point, even with a warning, and Azera would have no choice but to surrender.

If Raye managed to get the Hiran army on her side during her first days as a lieutenant colonel, the military would be unable to ignore her. She needed to secure a good standing with enough officers to maintain support. Unable to meet her subordinate officers during her short time in Norsan, she only hoped they would forgive her when she returned, hopefully with Hiran's aide, and find themselves accepting of her. If her captains were unwilling to listen to her, she had no chance of anyone in the army listening, let alone the world she needed to change for the better.

Raye finally had the chance to slip into her officer uniform and out of her school uniform. Stripped of the old childish uniform worn during trivial arguments, she slid perfectly into her new, much sturdier, deep red clothes. The representation of the actual battles ahead. She knew she was past the time of fighting stupid boys and ready to be the killer of men she needed to be. Or was she? The tiny voice in the back of her head loved to creep up into her present consciousness.

She fastened the strap around her waist to allow her pants to fit correctly. They ended at her ankles perfectly, and her shirt draped over her body ever so big. The sleeves went slightly past her wrists, which she did not mind as they covered her scars more, keeping her mind at ease. She tucked the end of the shirt into her pants, allowing her waist to be cinched. Raye tossed her dark chest piece over her head and squeezed her arms through before tightening the sides appropriately through the metal ringlets. It sat on top of her body, snuggly but not tight enough for her to be immobile.

Her fingers caressed the soft leather from the top of her breastplate until it ended near her stomach—an animal's soft, smooth skin. Raye stared at the woman in the mirror as her fingers gracefully ran over each new element of her garments, tilting her head to view each new item. She felt the stitching of the patches sewn onto her left sleeve over her bicep. Three long black rectangles stitched down the side, one on top of the other, identifying her rank of lieutenant colonel. Each position up the hierarchy meant another patch slapped on.

    She turned her left shoulder toward the mirror, eying her status symbol. Even with the symbols, her young face made them feel useless.

CHAPTER FIFTEEN

Does the Devil know they're the Devil?

No longer a training exercise or a lesson to be learned. The numbers in her game were now real lives, not metaphorical. Raye had much to think about on her long haul back to the other side of her country. Most of the things were not so positive, but they were the things pushing to the forefront of her mind, as always.

It was a chill morning when she reached the edge of Hira, where their military base stood. The entire country had a different aura than all of Azera. A calm day for them. As if a war would not be approaching so soon. A chilly in between. Between the night and day, before the sun could conquer the weather. Raye felt like shit. From the uncomfortable long ride back to the chilly morning that made her nose run uncontrollably, she was in a shit mood, which was no mood to greet the general of Hira's military.

Raye wiped her nose with her sleeve before letting out a deep, hot breath, creating a small cloud. It was far too early in the year for it to be such a cold day. The two accompanying soldiers hopped out of the wagon and rode in. She wanted to attend alone, but Zion wanted her to have other protection in an emergency. Whatever. She did not think she mumbled a word to them the entire trip.

The atmosphere was like the quiet calm of a library. The opposite experience of the one she had when entering Norsan. Hira's military compound was a simple, large building with a yard so big it filled up with all sizes of artillery. From catapults and archery to bomb mechanics, they were an organized system with nothing thrown around out of perfect order, like Norsan.

The building was more academic-like than a military base. Like her old school, it stood taller than wide—an essential foundation with many windows into offices and meeting rooms. There were no men standing guard anywhere. Raye and her men walked in through the front door. Right inside stood a giant directory for the offices. Easy enough.

Men wandered around the hallways on the third floor with some leisurely job after Raye climbed the stairs. No one paid her any mind, even when she found the general's office door cracked open and slid right in, closing it behind her. He sat, hardly noticing, reading over his paperwork. When he looked up at her and registered his confusion, she interrupted before he could question her.

"I was sent by Lieutenant General Zion, sir," she stated matter-of-factually. "You repeatedly ignore our requests in aid against Daoland, so I have come personally—"

"Personally." He made fun of her. "And who the fuck are you, exactly?" He almost laughed in her face.

Not quite taken aback, Raye continued. "I have private information I have brought to share with you. If you would have let me finish, I'd have gotten to that." She fake smiled at him, already pissed off. Chill out, Raye. "Lieutenant Colonel Raye Tyrson, sir."

She looked further into his face. A man probably the same as her father's, with his inky black hair slicked back into a tight ponytail tied off in the back of his head. His slim eyes were just as jet black as his hair, and his pointy chin and long face gave him sharp features, even for someone aged. He only blinked his slender eyes at her with no emotion behind his face in response. Raye took that as a continuation; whether it was or not, she did not care.

"I'm sure you know the Daos will come for you no matter what. They have an inhuman-like thirst for destruction and blood. So why doom yourself in isolation?" she asked.

"Even without isolation, we are doomed; why waste my manpower failing to defend you?" he replied. Raye said nothing in response, but raised her eyebrows in suspicion. There was an underlying reason he was not speaking.

The general clenched his jaw so hard Raye could see it bursting out the sides as he ground his teeth.

"Wealth, power, greed. That is what your emperor had allowed Azera to become. You think I don't know about the uprisings and rebels inside your country?" he asked. He might have known, but that was the first of it Raye had been aware of. Seeing her confusion, he let out a dry laugh. "Your citizens know the country is letting them die and starve only to make their powerful even richer. We disagree with what the country has become, so we are pulling any aid we might have offered to the empire."

"And who does that harm the most?" Raye was getting heated by his argument. "What rich people are getting harmed in war more than the impoverished and front-line soldiers? Be serious about your thought process, General. Offering the people help against the empire would be better than doing nothing!" Raye claimed in anger. The general's expression was pure shock. Raye was sure no one had ever dared speak to him like that, especially after meeting someone so shortly. Raye claimed no prejudice over who her anger could claim, though.

"If we waste our efforts helping your civilians, once the Daos reach us, what's left??" he retorted.

"So, you sit back and watch as you do nothing?" Raye asked genuinely.

"W-Well . . ." The general grew frustrated by her remarks. His fists balled up onto his desk, hitting it in annoyance. He had no response for the girl. Though he had no honest answer for her, Raye knew. Had he given much thought to his so-called plan at all? She understood putting his country first, but to claim neutrality in the situation was weak.

"Seems as though your true plan is to let us die from the Daos to buy yourself even more time," Raye stated coldly. "You've all had decades to prepare, yet the threat surprises you all."

The silence filled the room from wall to wall. The general, rendered speechless, stared into Raye's intense, hateful, icy eyes. When she felt he had enough of his suffering in silence, she continued.

Raye's composure remained the same chill she entered with. "I've brought a deal with me. You will agree."

Astonishment and anger filled his eyes as his mouth tried to tell her off, only to be cut off by Raye's voice. "Azera is your biggest and strongest ally, and to lose them, and the resources they give would ruin you. I agree, it is taking a chance, but I can guarantee an entirely new empire. But only after you aid me in the defeat of Daoland." Raye offered.

He only laughed at her. "Oh, I'm sure if you guarantee it must happen."

Raye's eyes lit up in bright anger, and the snaps and pops came off her body quicker than his laughter turned to pure fear. The light flicked off and around her, popping into the air. What did she have to lose? It seemed her power was no longer only known to herself. Her irises were a lighter, brighter version of themselves, similar to the lightning flung around the small room. Raye sent a single, small lightning mark toward the general, only to send a slight shock to the tip of his finger at the hand he had reached out to protect his face.

He gasped in his slight pain and shook his hand off as if there was something on it. The springs of tiny sparks stopped immediately, and the room was again silent. She only stared into his eyes, unbothered as the fear and realization set into him. He now had a choice to make Raye an ally or a new enemy. Raye's mouth cracked into a slight grin at the situation, and she could not stop. It only made her appear more insane than she already had, and the man's fear came back across his face.

"Fucking Celestials above, for the love of all the gods..." he whispered curses to himself. "You're a fucking—" he stared her body up and down in further examination. "Celestial," he said, only louder than a whisper. His eyes were wide open, bulging out of his skull, for if he blinked, she might disappear in front of him now.

Raye's right fingers and hand twitched and shook ever so slightly, a side effect from the damaged nerves from her wounds, she assumed. His eyes jetted to her twitchy hand; like he thought she was itching for a kill or something. Everything was in her perfect favor, to be seen as the scary and powerful being she was. She knew he would make the right decision after coming to his senses. She felt powerful at that moment. As she always seemed to when people had a genuine fear of her. Humans feared powerful things.

"I am humbled to allow my nephew to work alongside you during this war. Lieutenant General Jin." Stress coated his throat as each word slipped out. How quickly they change. Their discussion had now pivoted to one of human and deity.

The door behind her whipped open swiftly, and the young man entered. Raye snapped her head around to view him as she sat across from the general.

"Uncle, are you aware of the Azeran soldiers lingering in the hallways?" His eyes went straight to Raye after he said it. The man's features were striking, with his snow-pale skin and inky dark hair like his uncle. His slim eyes seemed even darker than the previous ones she had seen, like looking into an endless void of black. His hair swept perfectly from his part across the sides of his head in a swoop around his ears, a slightly shaggy but boyish haircut much more modern than the general's. He stood tall and robust, the actual build of a skilled fighter, looming over Raye. He stood outfitted in the golden version of Raye's uniform, making her stand out as an Azeran. The man stared at her in exasperated shock. His uncle let out a very dry, awkward chuckle at his nephew, his eyes pleading silence. The general acted as if it was not his office and Raye was holding him hostage. Brutal men were never as tough as they like to appear.

Raye stopped herself from looking at each detail in his pretty face and gave him a smile with only arrogance behind her eyes. She had zero intention of harming any of them, but if that was what he needed to believe to agree with her, who was she to deny? The general cleared his throat loudly and stood up with his hands on the desk.

"Jin, this is Lieutenant Colonel Raye Tyrson." He spoke slowly and clearly. "She has brought information, and I have decided to help aid her against the Dao." Jin stared in disbelief and tightened his fists in anger.

"You decided, did you?" He scoffed at him. "I was under the impression nothing would change your mind." The general's veins popped out of his neck as he tightened his jaw harder.

"Watch yourself," a deepened voice meant to cause fear in his nephew's disrespect. Raye wanted to laugh at the way men tried to intimidate each other. Whose voice would go the lowest? Who could punch an object the loudest? She remained quiet when Jin's face settled and his eyes lowered. Raye felt a pang of guilt for the grown man being belittled in front of her, though she ignored it. It was how things were, how respect worked in the world. She disagreed with the order of most things.

"This situation is much different," he trailed off slightly, begging with his eyes for Jin to leave it at that. Raye was sure this sight confused him, so she did not blame Jin's attitude. A young woman somehow struck fear into the general of an army, convincing him to bring the aid he opposed regularly.

"You will aid Ms. Tyrson personally." Jin hid any emotions he might have had well. His army was hers.

◆ ◆ ◆

The mountainous range between the borders was always the worst of the journey. Once they got past the worst, the trip could continue easily. A squadron traveled slower than just her person with a horse. One chilly morning was no indicator of the remaining weather. The heat felt unbearable, walking at a constant incline, and the journey would take even longer up and through the mountains.

The hundreds of soldiers and supplies made their way through the tallest part of the range and approached the capital city area. Almost three hundred miles of land to cross once again. What would be the situation when Raye returned to Norsan a month after she had last been? Downhill was much easier for the group.

Jin was more than capable as lieutenant general, and he made sure to make Raye aware of that. His uncle made it seem like they would be working together, but that differed from what Jin wanted. She could understand his poor ego being affected, he was of a much higher status, but what power was there in status alone compared to her entity? He was making every call on their trip down to the exact path they would take. She did not care to argue with him, though; it was not as if she knew the eastern part of Azera any better.

Jin did not speak to anyone besides his soldiers in direct rank below him; the youngest one was still not as young as himself. Other than that, he maintained his cold sense of silence. He reminded her of herself, of course. The need to be respected in your authority can be difficult for groups of men who have years on you unless proven otherwise. He did not dare to show any amount of immaturity. She found herself respecting that enough.

He was mostly uninterested in Raye, though. He occasionally flashed a glance at her, but his look never faltered, and his questions never asked. His soldiers whispered their gossip and jokes about herself, though. The whispers of her name would make their way to her ears a few times, whether it be the simple shit-talking of her being put in charge of them or the questioning of how that came to be. She could assume most of what they would be guessing.

If Raye's name made its way to Jin's ears, though, he was not so forgiving. The mixture of respect and fear blended around the air with him and his soldiers. The raging looks he would shoot at them had them shaking where they stood for fear of punishment. They would stop for a few hours until an unknowing party committed again. He craved respect from his supporting officers, but front-line soldiers were always disposable to the military.

When their group made their way to the flatlands of Azera, on the southern side of the capital, hidden by the trees, they laid their camp as the sun set on the day. The Hiran soldiers built their camp quickly, like thorough professionals, as they did every time. They made the fire in what felt like the slowest possible time, though. After becoming accustomed to Anala's mastery, Raye forgot how long it can take. Jin's team had the rest of their jobs down to perfection though, and before Raye could even figure out an attempt to help, they already served the food.

She sat silently alone, eating her food, lost in the thought of her friend she missed dearly. She eyed the others and watched their interactions and comradery. Like how she used to behave in school with her friends. No one seemed interested in friendship with her, which she was mostly fine with. The longing of people was something humans could only push down and ignore for so long, though.

None of them acted in fear of their quick push to the western Azeran base. Like they might be walking to their potential deaths for the countries, they mainly seemed excited at the hope of action, and all their exhaustion from the day washed away.

Some sat around fires listening to stories from older soldiers or myths shared down the lines. The trip thus far was their first time in such a large group gathered at once; it was almost a party for them. Raye's mouth tasted bitter at what they did not seem to realize would be coming for them.

The sun no longer warmed their camp, and even after the hot day, the night grew slightly cooler. Raye tried to bundle herself up in her sleeping bag, but nothing felt warm enough in her loneliness. The breeze shook the branches from the trees; the shuffling was too loud to drown out. The moon was too bright even between the leaves, and her eyes would pop back open no matter how hard she tried to remain closed. She had traveled the entire country twice, alone: no family, friends, or even real acquaintances. Constantly alone and tired, she prayed to the gods that she might find peace and sleep, but her prayers remained unanswered.

Raye eventually accepted what the night was going to be. No more unanswered prayers or tossing and turning with the wind. So close to the capital she had never been to before. She felt it would be a shame to have never had the chance to see its beauty before being plummeted into a war they might not make it out of.

She hopped over sleeping bodies until she reached the edge of the camp in the direction of the city. She only made it a few steps before jumping, scared by a tap on her shoulder. Her head whipped around after her body's initial shock. When her eyes landed on Jin standing above her with a confused look, his strong hand still grabbed her shoulder.

"Where the fuck are you going?" an angry voice whispered at her. "You need to rest; we're not even halfway there yet. I can not have you getting tired before everyone else. Don't you dare embarrass my uncle." His deep, voided eyes had Raye memorized even in his anger. She managed to wrestle and weave her body out from under his grip, though.

"It will not be an issue. I can't sleep, anyway. I don't want to keep lying awake. It's boring," she protested. His eyes rolled while he let out a quiet scoff.

"Oh, I'm sorry, princess. I didn't realize you were bored," he mocked. "Go to fucking sleep." He pointed his finger back at the other sleeping soldiers.

Raye's eye started to twitch at his arrogance. *Dickhead.* She wanted to punch him across the face, for the love of all gods. *How dare he micromanage me?* She could not get onto his lousy side so quickly, though. She forced herself to relax.

She would not stand there and argue with him. Walking back toward the city, Jin stood speechless as he watched her walk away. He did a short jog to catch up to her.

"It's the middle of the night; what aren't you understanding? Or are you trying to run off after finally getting the soldiers you begged for? Tyrson—"

"Raye." she corrected. "Why aren't you sleeping then, Jin?" She turned to look at his face once again. He stared at her before answering.

"I don't always sleep well. But I also don't run off into the woods," he replied.

"I'm not running into the woods; I want to see the capital city. I've never seen it before." Raye started her walk again; she knew the city wasn't more than a ten-minute walk from where they stood. She had seen the city previously when they went around it to the wooded, less foot-trafficked path for a more leisurely trip. It was close.

That sparked Jin's attention, and without another word, he followed her to the capital. He seemed pouted over it, but Raye thought he was curious to see Azera's biggest city, too.

Even in the middle of the night, the city was still busier than she imagined. There were bars open all night long, addicts who roamed the nighttime streets, and prostitutes who stood in sections on the walkways calling out to any man who walked by. It was not the type of life Raye was expecting to find, but that was her fault for visiting in the late hours of the darkness when all the unwanted leaked out.

With every potentially dangerous person they passed, Jin would grab Raye and toss her to the opposite side of his body. A protective manner to some, but Raye found it obnoxious, and another way he enjoyed belittling her and not seeing her as any soldier of her own. Even passing by a drug addict lying on the ground in the dark corners of the shadows, Jin still felt it necessary to pull her closer. The last time he grabbed her, she pushed him off and told him to leave her be.

"These types of men are not kind to women, Raye," he said.

Like she did not know that. Jin did not realize that it was a lot more than those types of men who were unkind to women. It was those same types of men he had in his army who fought for their country and were unkind to women. His assumptions were naïve and irritating.

She wished he had not come with her at all if the only reason he did was as some 'protector.' He was far too self-righteous for her liking.

"Where are you taking us? I thought you'd never been here before."

The center of the city was easy enough to find. And what she saw there was exactly what she was looking for. "Right here," she told him. Raye pointed at the giant statue of a man in a stretched-out fighter pose with low bent knees.

His stance was broad and robust, and his arms bent into the readying pose, fists controlling the ground sculpted around him. One foot stomped into the ground, breaking the statue's earth under him in a dramatic half-thrown around him. Raye wanted to see the only proof of another well-known human like her.

"Who is that?" Jin asked, checking out the statue.

It stood two times the size of a regular person and remained on a pedestal above the roundabout walkway—the homage to the powerful Celestial. Raye was breath taken by the power the statue alone could convey, even from an inanimate object. She could only imagine the true power of his abilities; to control the earth around you, took a powerful being.

"A famously historical Azeran Celestial, Lucian," Raye explained.

CHAPTER SIXTEEN

May Death be kinder than man.

Fifty years prior; the city center:
The crash was so loud it shook the earth and buildings around them like they sat on top of the belly of a beast. Even Lucian, a master of his craft who could bend the earth to his will, had not felt an earthquake of this magnitude in Azera before. For that was no earthquake.

A second building collapsed hard onto the ground, the tall object crashing down with full force. Lucian caught a glance of the end as the top of the building hit the ground. The city was so noisy that he could barely hear his thoughts. Screaming and crying filled it all between the booming crashes into the ground and the high winds that whistled all around.

The streets turned to utter chaos like a flash of light. Lucian whipped his eyes around, examining the culprit. He planted his feet deep into the ground and let the earth sink them below, feeling through the earth for the cause.

There was no earthly cause, for it came from the sky. The debris and dust swept through the air, leaving a sandy mist throughout the city. Lucian coughed hard, then attempted to use his sleeve for further breath covering until the dirt would settle back down. His eyes forced to squint from the burning air quality.

Unknowing behind the reasoning, Lucian jumped into the rumble of the building to help get out any survivors. It was an expensive hostel for wealthy visitors from outside of the capital. Any whole bodies he grabbed. Most he found around the bottom of the structure were halves, mutilated and smashed open into a mush.

He threw entire bodies over his shoulder after ripping them from under the rocks, unknowing if they were living or not. Before Lucian had the chance to set the bodies down, another building started to fall, collapsing in on itself. He dropped the people into a nearby spot while others aided and ripped the fabric off a nearby deceased body to tie around his face as a mask.

Lucian ran as fast as his body would allow him toward the movement. Winds more vigorous than any tornado ripped buildings apart piece by piece. Stone bricks flung across the entire city one at a time until the wind would decide to rip the whole thing down. Precisely as he expected, it was no nature-related incident.

Up in the sky, floating above all else, the core of the element wrapped around him, the air only seen by the debris whipping around with it, the winds circling a man. A lifelong friend finally returned.

That was not the friend he once knew, though. Ripping senseless violence through the capital of a country they both spent years together in. Ruining the very world they both swore to protect with their entire beings.

This version of his friend loomed overhead mangled with blood and scars over his entire body through his tattered clothing. His dark hair, noticeably longer than prior, whipped across his face from his element around him. Lucian screamed his name as loud as he could as he ran closer and closer to the land closest to his friend, but he was no match for sound against the mighty wind.

"Silas! Silas! Silas!" He repeatedly begged for his friend; his voice was already hoarse from his roars. His throat was only getting scratchier, forcing him to cough from the mixture of air and screams. He went to the top of the building that stood nearest to Silas. Lucian jumped onto dirt platforms he raised in the air, floating with his ability.

Each step took him higher, then dropped, smacking back into the ground until he reached the top. Hoping his friend had not noticed him, Lucian ran full force across the roof of the building and then jumped off with all his might, slamming directly into a free-floating Silas.

Even his winds were not strong enough to whip away Lucian's massive build as he sliced through his air. With Lucian's arms wrapped around Silas' body, pinning his arms to his side to prevent him from further destruction, they headed toward the ground in a fast, free fall intertwined.

Silas twisted and turned in an attempt to remove himself from Lucian's hold, Lucian only squeezed his friend tighter. Silas' skinny body was eventually able to worm its way out of his grasp, and he pushed himself off Lucian, sending himself a short way away using his burst of wind.

Silas slammed hard into a wooden stand that was once a vendor's place of business, left only as a rumble of wood and broken, unintelligible items underneath Silas's body. He moaned and groaned at the pain from his impact. All the while, Lucian stuck his landing with his two feet planted into the ground, allowing the rock to absorb all of his impact, causing him no harm.

Silas forced himself up by his painful arms and legs with a sway as he re-grounded himself.

Lucian watched cautiously as Silas took slow steps closer to him.

"They are merciless humans, Luc." Silas's tears streamed down his face, and he spoke with a crazed look in his eyes. Without meaning to, Lucian took a step back, away from his friend. That was not the calm and intelligent Silas he knew so well.

"My brother," he called out to Silas. "Please be calm, and I will hear whatever you are trying to say. These people do not deserve—"

Silas knew he would not hear him out, or at least not believe him. Hatred grew inside his heart, and he felt his mind spiraling further with each look Lucian gave him. Like a monster to fear, he sent a massive gust of wind at Lucian, knocking his body to the ground.

While Lucian recovered from his hard blow, Silas used one hand to send his winds wrapping and twisting around another building next to them. The air squeezed the building, suffocating it and all inside, and easily crushed the brick inward in destruction.

Lucian was distraught. There would not be a single survivor inside the building. If they did not suffocate a terrible death, their bodies crushed within themselves painfully. The scene, horrendous.

Dusty airs hid the true horrors of the blood-filled stone and dirt clutter that lay. Lucian's chest felt like it had caved entirely inside of itself. His legs wanted to collapse under the weight of the destruction his friend had caused, but he had to stand as tall as ever.

"Silas!" he cried out in fury. How could he do that to innocent civilians? It was beyond out of character for him. Was that not the friend he grew up with? Or was Silas never the person he thought he was?

"All you ever do is their bidding, Luc. How can you not understand their pure selfishness?" Silas begged him to understand. Lucian had no intention of opening his mind to Silas anymore. All he had to do was stop, but he did not. The unnecessary violence he brought to the people of Nora had Lucian wanting to send himself into a rage.

"Vile evil flows through their veins, and the empire shall fall to my own hands if it must," Silas still screamed at him. Too wrapped inside of his mind, Lucian couldn't listen well.

Whatever had happened to Silas had changed him beyond repair. That was no longer his friend or ally. Lucian had no choice but to protect the capital from its impending doom from the violence of his new enemy. That was all he found himself willing to do—his duty.

Lucian shot his arms out to his sides, using his strength to rip up the surrounding ground, forming a giant rock mass. He flung it at Silas. However, Silas was always quicker than him; he moved with the winds.

His wind sliced his rock in half, allowing it to avoid Silas altogether. While distracted, Lucian stomped his foot onto the ground and flung his hands, ripping the ground apart again. The earth below them ripped a layer off the top and started to wave like the sea, flinging Silas off and falling to the ground.

Lucian ran over to where Silas fell, his body's imprint still left from his hard landing, but he was gone. *Fuck.* Lucian flipped his head and eyes around in panic, searching the area and the sky. A sharp pain in his side came out of nowhere—Silas' wind.

Crippled in pain from the impact, Silas had already lifted him up and into the air before he could even let out a sound of pain. Silas' air left Lucian unable to move an appendage. His entire body felt the pain and vital force of the air squeezing him tight. Silas could squash his body like he did the others if he wanted to.

Lucian felt the bruising inside his body on his torso and legs, and the dull pains only got worse. The exposed skin on his arms, neck, and face felt the wind the worst. It was like he was slicing his skin with a knife from the gusts that hit around him, still holding him in place. His face felt the burn first; he was sure his skin was turning red or blistering as he remained there. The wind was a burn of its own.

Trapped in the sky with no way down while Silas slowly suffocated him, his chest was panging with hurt. It felt like a heart attack coming from the inside. His eyesight was only becoming blurrier, so he attempted to use his connection to the earth to find a piece of it.

Lucian used the little movement his fingers had left to send a pebble from a nearby rooftop directly at Silas' eye in the hope he would falter.

The pebble did more than hit his eye. In a battle between their power, Lucian could send the rock faster than any of Silas's air around them. The sharp rock made contact with his eye and entered his head entirely. Upon impact, his eyeball split apart, shooting liquid and blood out of his socket. The entire side of his face was now covered in blood, still leaking from his gaping wound.

Lucian, freed from the wind, fell from his place in the sky directly toward the ground. His chest still caved in as he attempted to catch his breath, as his entire body felt unable to move, still trying to recover from the crushing. The fast fall toward the ground only made him panic more, making breathing even harder. He could only use his remaining strength to brace the earth to take his impact the best it could.

He landed hard on the ground; the earth created a crater around him. He lay in the crater, his body stunned in the shock from the landing. His insides were gnawing an unreachable pain. Vomit rose in his throat until he forced it back down with a tough swallow.

He sunk his hands into the ground to cling the rock around his fist. He brought his hands to his side once again; the rock formed to his hands now, one in the shape of a pointed spear to try to stab his enemy. He only had to find a wounded Silas now.

Hurt and rage coursed through his body. The pain and exhaustion of his impact and the anger he felt at his once best friend were too much for his body to handle. The only way he could get it out of him was through fury. Tears formed in his eyes. Trying to blink them away, they fell down his cheeks. His chest hurt even worse than before. Was it from his physical injuries? No, he did not think so. If it was from what he thought, he was about to do without choice.

He found Silas hidden by the side of a building, crouched on the ground with his hand covering his now missing eye. His blood soaked all around him. Before Lucian even had the chance to process what his friend looked like, Silas shot his hand out at him, knocking Lucian off his feet with a gust.

Lucian braced himself, and while his feet flung backward out from under him, he used his non-spear hand to bend the earth below him higher to catch himself. He quickly hopped back onto both feet. Silas was much weaker now, and he was losing blood too quickly from his head.

Silas had tried to make a run for the center of the city. He only got off on a jog, but Lucian allowed him. He followed Silas to the city center, marked by the biggest church in the city and its landscaped area around it. Beautifully decorated stones, plants, and colorful stained-glass windows surrounded the front of the building and walking area. Silas sat far back from the church on his knees, head looking up at the marvelous architecture. Lucian slowly approached him.

"Silas . . ." he attempted. "This was never our way. Why did you do this? We were always taught—" Silas cut him off.

"Every rich man in this city is responsible. There is no such thing as innocence in this world. To be human is to be vile, Luc. To be human is to wish wickedness upon one another. They will come for you next, all of you. Anything for another coin . . ." Silas trailed off, lost in his thoughts. His tears finally fell as he looked up at the church. His eyes closed.

Lucian did not understand Silas' claims. What were they responsible for? That was not what Lucian knew. He had only ever helped alongside those in the empire. Lucian didn't recognize Silas any longer—darkness consumed him and he lost all of himself and his core beliefs. He could not bear to see his friend in sucking deep agony.

What had happened in the time between their last visit? He could not roam the earth with that hatred in his heart. Wreaking havoc on the city's innocents could not be the goal. All the collapsed buildings and all the deaths he had caused in the last few hours, only to pay for another's sins. He wished he could read Silas' mind, for he seemed too lost inside it to give him the whole meaning of his words.

Lucian was used to playing by the rules given to him; he was not one to change that. They were above nothing, no government or law, just because they were something special. They were meant to protect, not harm. Who was he claiming to protect? And from what? *Gods on fucking earth*, he thought. Lucian wanted to scream out all his frustration. He did not.

Silas broke his silence, and Lucian suddenly found him standing in front of him a short distance away.

"You put far too much trust in the Azeran empire. Our home has been corrupted," Silas choked out. His voice was a dry, raspy struggle. He was going to die whether Lucian killed him now or not; he already injured him beyond repair. His hands laid at his side, his eye now a gushing bloody hole of flesh still bleeding down his face profusely. His body shook, and he could only stare his one good eye into Lucian's.

Lucian could not bear the guilt. To now face the destruction he caused upon his friend. To analyze the wound he caused his brother. He wanted to crumble within himself. Too pained by his grief from his friend's actions, he couldn't listen to what Silas was trying to tell him. Lucian was a man stuck in history, refusing to face the reality of the present situation and accept the world as it was. Changing, as it always did. Silas was still trying to warn him of what could happen, of what he saw and lived through, but Lucian could not hear him. It was far too easy to let things be.

He was no man of the future. Silas was wrong, Lucian knew. To blindly believe his friend or to follow the guide set for centuries by the gods of life to promote peace? It forced him to answer that question whether he knew it or not. Silas already knew the answer when it hit Lucian's face. Silas dropped his shoulders and closed his eyes before death took him over.

Lucian stomped his foot hard into the ground, causing the earth around Silas to crumble downward within itself, dragging him deep into the pit he had created. He refilled the hole and flattened the earth, suffocating Silas to death under the ground, burying his friend alive. That was the only thing Lucian would offer him. His last gift from the gods. Death from the world he found so wicked.

Dropped to his knees, Lucian allowed the silent tears to stream down his cheeks and laid his head upon the fresh dirt grave. Pushing down any regretful or doubtful thoughts in his mind, he felt there was no other option. Silas destroyed the capital of the country they had grown up in.

But had Lucian suddenly chosen a side he did not realize he was on? Of course, the empire would tell him exactly what they wanted him to hear and nothing more. Who was he to truly trust? Silas seemed to have some understanding of what they were after, but what would that be? The frustration overwhelmed his entire body. Had he just killed his friend for the wrong reasons? No, it was only the grief causing him to worry. It had to be.

What wickedness of humanity could drive his kindhearted friend to complete madness? Did it even matter at that point?

Lucian gave his brother a last prayer to the gods and another for himself.

He begged for their forgiveness.

The empire, so proud of the incredible Lucian's feat in saving the city from further disaster, they honored him. A statue of his likeness now stood in the city center outside of the church. Beautiful hand-crafted marble created by one of the country's greatest artists. Having such a powerful image given to Lucian sculpted into eternity should be an honor.

Portrayed as the strong elemental warrior, he was as his stone body stomped into the statue's ground, flinging it to his sides in an example of his Celestial powers. An honor it should have been. Instead, they placed it on top of his friend's grave.

Lucian would no longer visit the city center, as the sickness he felt from the view of it all was unbearable. His chest felt as tight as it did the day Silas had crushed him with the air. Silas now owned the own air in his lungs, it seemed.

The only cure he could find was to avoid any part of the inner city. To push the memories down further than he knew possible.

His chest, his heart, and his lungs were a gaping hole only filled with sorrow and deep pain. Pain that could knock the wind out of him.

Lucian spent his years completely outside the city limits—until no one had caught sightings of him again.

CHAPTER SEVENTEEN

Familiar faces are not always welcome.

He stood tall and more muscular than everyone else around him. If he could have grown in muscle in the time she had been gone, he did. Or she had forgotten what a strong man he had become. Raye could sense his charm and see his handsome face through the crowd. A familiar face after weeks of being trapped with strangers was precisely what she needed. An exhausting trip came to an end with exactly who she needed. Zeki.

He stood out, with his dark complexion against the mostly pale faces surrounding him. Even his proper commanding officer voice still found its recognition in Raye's ears.

Raye did not realize the smile that spread across her face as she approached him in the base courtyard. She pushed through the other soldiers surrounding him as he gave orders for whatever mission they were working on.

His voice boomed across the group of men. It was low and smooth as always, but had the new command of a leader behind it. Zeki's face was serious until he spotted Raye in the front row after shoving her way through. He spotted her bright, grinning face. How happy she was to see one of her best friends again.

Zeki's face lit up when he saw her. He finished what he was saying and sent everyone off. One of his big smiles that showed off his bright smile covered his face, and he made his way toward Raye. She was so exhausted and tormented from her journey that she threw her arms around his neck and embraced him fully.

She missed the only man who did not drive her mad or see her as an idiot woman. Her sudden physical affection surprised Zeki, but seemed to understand silently that she needed it. He wrapped his arms around her waist, returning the embrace.

"I'm so happy to see you, Ze," she whispered. She sighed into his shoulder. "This has been a long fucking month. They've had me traveling back and forth to the edge of the fucking country." Raye rolled her eyes, causing Zeki to chuckle.

"Yeah, but you've brought back the fucking Hiran army with you. Have the general eating out of your fucking hand yet?" Zeki whispered so only she could hear. She rolled her eyes once again at his stupid jokes.

"I haven't met anyone but the Azeran lieutenant general. I can't imagine anyone else will enjoy my company so much once they find out I'm not the powerful man they thought they promoted," she shrugged.

"You smell like shit, Raye. It would be best if you bathed," Zeki told her.

"I've been busting my ass bringing our aide back here, so I apologize for the stench, asshole." Raye shoved his arm off her, though he was much sturdier than her.

The courtyard was a busy mess of people wandering about. Carrying out preparations for the change of plans with the new aid brought. Zeki shoved through the waves of the sea with his singular left arm while his right hand gently rested on Raye's back, guiding her with him.

The man Zeki took her to appeared to have a few years on Raye and Zeki; the lines settled in his face more profound than any of the other fresh-faced soldiers. His light brown hair fluffed over his forehead, and his ears were casually unkempt. His skin wore a tan from the summer sun.

Despite being a strong man, standing next to Zeki cut his appearance in half—as it did most. Raye's only sense of comparison was his brooding strength and natural bulkiness. The man was even shorter than Zeki, but stood tall enough over Raye that her body felt much smaller than most.

"Ellerie, this is Raye. Raye, this is your captain, Ellerie. Me being the other one," he gave her a smile.

"Captain Zeki? How lucky of me to get stuck with you," Raye said sarcastically. Though she meant it, she was blessed by the gods to have one of her favorite people work directly for her.

Ellerie, suddenly stopping his conversation, snapped his head up to

Raye and gave her a proper salute with his straightened stature and perfectly placed hand. Raye's brow burrowed in a shock of confusion.

"That's not necessary, Ellerie." She reached out to shake his hand. His face loosened, and he shook her hand in return. "You've had plenty more years in the service than I; if anything, I should be giving you a proper salute," she flashed him a smile, which he returned.

"No, ma'am. You're my lieutenant colonel; I only owe you the greatest respect, not the other way around." He was genuine. The years of conditioning inside the military had worked wonders on a man who had given his life to the service.

"I never much appreciated the blind rules of a hierarchy. I ask for your respect, but anything more is a waste of time," she explained. Raye could tell he did not quite understand her method of thinking, but he would not further question his commanding officer.

Raye needed these people to see her as one of them, only so they may run into battles against an enemy they might not understand. They needed to stand by her, even with the knowledge of the monster she was.

Before their introduction could progress, the bell from the high tower rang with an intensity that the entire town could hear. The sudden noise made Raye jump out of her skin and find the culprit.

"Tyrson! Tyrson!" She heard repeatedly, almost drowned out by the ringing. She assumed it was her commanding officer running up to her and pushing through the crowds of people that swam around the courtyard.

When the officer found her, he grabbed her by the shoulders in relief and attempted to hold her still as the crowds of soldiers pushed her and the others around as they ran to their stations in anticipation of an attack.

The officer got close to her face so she could hear him over the bell, still rattling. His face spoke panic before any of his words did. Raye stared into his bulging, stressed eyes, waiting for him to speak.

"They've been spotted at the south shore. The lieutenant general has asked for you and your team to go. Take the Hirans and a troop and head down there immediately. We only just got word, so you should have time to reach the camp before they get to the shoreline for an invasion."

Everything was suddenly real. The Daos were about to invade their country after all these years. Not a second of rest for Raye before being forced to confront her enemy once again. Thank the gods for the Hiran army.

Though she was exhausted, she was glad it was her being sent down there. She would make sure to handle them. While they did not have the upper hand in entering Daoland like she would have wished, she could reach the south before their ship could even dock their soldiers.

"We will prepare here in case of an attack; go now."

"Don't underestimate them. This might be a ploy to send us down there, only to attack our biggest base here. Assume they know everything; they always seem to," Raye warned him. He seemed shocked by her response, but he took it well with a solemn shake of his head and left to prepare.

Raye turned to Zeki. "Prepare your soldiers to head south immediately."

He silently nodded once and went off, pushing his way through the panic of people disappearing into the sea.

They were too late. Somehow, they were too late. Raye could not understand.

As soon as they received word they left, how did they make it entirely into the camp? Even with an attempt to overestimate the Daos, she still underestimated them. She assumed there would be an attack up north, but there was no need to when they had already completely taken over their southern camp.

How had they not gotten word as soon as the ship was visible on the horizon?

Piles of dead soldiers already stacked in their neat little rows off to the side. The entire camp was knocked down and put back up again with their own better quality. They had already hung their flags in replacement.

Fucking, shit. She was so angry. Angry with herself, even though they had settled in, and she had no way of getting there early enough. She was mainly angry at them, though. They would pay. She would make them even if no one else could. Counterattack. That's what she needed to do. On her way back to where she left the army of soldiers, she devised a new plan.

Raye had them hold back a few miles while she scoped the camp out. She already had a bad feeling on the way down, and she was glad she listened to it as they had been walking into a trap.

Her nostrils flared with rage as frustration churned inside her head. They quickly slaughtered the entire camp then had probably sent word to

Duwan to allow them to walk directly into their plan. Her palms hurt from her unknowingly digging her nails into them. How easily the Daos always had the upper hand. Raye would not allow that to be their end. She would flip the game board.

"We go around and attack from the south," she told Zeki and Jin.

She ripped the map out of Zeki's hand and spread it across the ground as she explained her plan to them. While the numbers might be against the Daos, their soldiers were better trained and prepared. Azera managed to take any child, threw some leather armor on them, and told them to follow orders.

Strategy was the only way they could beat them and their barbaric soldiers. Raye hated the idea of losing time, but walking into the north was precisely what they expected of them. That would be the best chance they had of removing them from their country before they further sunk their teeth into their grasp.

The staggered breaths in her chest were from anticipating her first real battle. Despite being thrown into war, part of her felt like the little girl she once was when she first met her foe. Would she ever escape from that little girl, though? She wondered if she even could. Between most viewing her as a child and herself feeling like her still deep down, she doubted she could ever rid herself of her.

Raye could kill and bury every version of herself, but that young child would always remain. She would remain alongside the memories she wished so hard to get rid of. The first night, she met the Daos. The night she watched her mother's horrific end.

She assumed none of these soldiers were in the service when that happened, but seeing them entering another home stung—seeing the young men bearing the blue uniform of hatred. The indigo of violent ends. How dare they bask on the soil of a country that did not belong to them? The only way Raye would allow them on this earth would be if their blood covered it.

The soldiers raided the camp from the south as she planned. She watched as the dozens of soldiers ran around her into the camp. Their battle cries filled the air, and they quickly slaughtered through the first rows of unknowing soldiers. The green grass promptly became a mix of mud and blood, soaking the boots that stomped through it.

They were too quick with their turnaround. The shock had warned off, and they were now killing at double the speed any of Raye's own could. Their average fighter was much more skilled. Raye berated herself in her mind out of her frustration.

She ran out in the middle of the fighting with her sword raised, ready to show off her skill. Everything became a bloodbath so quickly. The poor farm boys had never had a proper chance, which would be their first and last wartime action.

Raye avoided oncoming swords and bodies flying around her. Her soldiers were falling with every slash of a sword. She killed any Daos she could manage to reach, but the battlefield had become a problematic terrain of random, cut off body parts and the deceased. Her boots squished with every step into something, blood flinging from the ground and the soldiers she mangled in front of her.

It felt like an eternity later by the time they finally got the catapults shooting in the north where she left them. With their full attention finally on the soldiers from the south, she threw another piece onto the board.

Fiery rocks shot their way into the camp, setting anything ablaze. The first thing to light up was their main tent. Flames took it over completely, setting off any artillery inside, creating a chain reaction of explosions that shook the ground, knocking many of their feet.

Raye's face burst into a wicked and quiet laugh. She could only feel the joy they must have felt when they lit her own home on fire. The explosion killed another few surrounding soldiers. Excitedly, she realized a sword was swinging right at her head. She turned to face it fully and ducked, avoiding the blade altogether, and stuck her sword into the back of the neck of the perpetrator.

The blade crunched through his neck and jaw. She could not see his face, but heard the painful choking coming out of his mouth. She ripped her sword out of him, and his body dropped to the ground as she turned her attention to others around her.

Euphoric massacre. A different version of her would have never thought those two words belonged together.

The catapults still swung burning rocks through the air, landing on any victim they sought, even those on their team caught in the crossfire. Raye used every sense she had, avoiding the bodies of people and the rocks and shrapnel flying through the air.

Dodging, parrying, and killing. She was utterly blood-soaked head to toe at that point, unrealized. The result was her being forced to fight more and faster than her entire army and the constant splatters of any pool soul she stuck her boots into.

Blood spewed across her face from her victim's neck. She shoulder-checked him to the ground while dragging her blade out. Out of the corner of her eye was the fiery ball she had been trying so hard to avoid. Raye dropped to the ground while grabbing her last victim's body and rolled under it—hardly a shield, but better than nothing.

She could not hear the blast. It was so close to her. The body protected her from burns, mostly. She threw the dead man off of her and forced herself back onto her feet. She only heard the ringing out of her left ear, closest to the blast.

Surveying the surrounding damage, she dared say she was winning. She tried to take a step forward when she felt a sharp pain in her left leg. When she looked down, she noticed a large piece of metal shrapnel embedded into her calf. Completely covered in blood, she could hardly tell how much was her own until it started gushing from the wound when she touched it.

She sucked air into her lungs quickly out of pain and groaned it back out. It would remain as such until she was able to receive medical help. She could force herself through the pain and walk around right, but it would slow her down significantly compared to her usual quick reflections.

Raye still managed to lunge forward to kill a soldier headed for her wounded self. She clenched her teeth, sucking the pain in as her jaw twitched.

A hand grabbed her shoulder, and she whipped around, expecting an enemy. She recognized Zeki before she attempted a blow at him. His lips were moving as he spoke, but she could still not hear properly and only shook her head and looked at him, confused. She could read his eyes as distressed, but her ears only remained a sharp ring with mumbled sounds as her hearing slowly returned.

Zeki grabbed her face with both hands and turned her head to the sea. He pointed at something in the distance, and when her eyes squinted to view it, her stomach dropped painfully fast.

Out in the ocean, where the sky touched the sea, a second Dao ship sailed its way there. She could not imagine how many more soldiers were on their way there when they struggled with as many as there already were. Raye's body could throw up if she let it. Her throat closed in on her. Instead of letting her tears flow, she swallowed her frustration and decided.

M. NEVILLS

CHAPTER EIGHTEEN

I own all the souls before me,
and all those after.

Retreating did not mean it was a loss. Raye knew that deep down. Sometimes, a good leader had to make the call when there was no point in wasting more lives. But the frustration was gnawing at Raye from the inside of her body. Her jaw clicked as she ground her teeth against each other.

"Fuck this," she whispered to herself. She wanted to scream out at the top of her lungs. A failure of a first attempt against Daos. It was a failure as her first attempt at leading. She could be the greatest fighter, but that meant nothing if alone. The Azeran soldiers were even worse fighters than she assumed.

"It's alright. It is better to save our lives than die fighting a losing battle. You know that, Raye," Zeki attempted to comfort her. He was the one who pulled her from the battlefield after she ordered a retreat, unwilling to go herself. She wanted to burn their boat down the second she could. If word made it out she was a Celestial, it would be out of her hands quickly.

Raye and Zeki leaned against trees as Raye caught her breath. Her wounded leg and smoke inhalation had her more exhausted than she would admit to him. Though Zeki said nothing, he allowed her a moment of rest.

"Let's go; I don't want to chance us lingering too long in their territory," he decided. Zeki went to grab Raye's arm to help take the weight off her injured leg when she pushed him off of her.

"How the fuck is it their territory now?" She was not particularly angry at Zeki, but he was always there to take the beating. A better friend he was than her.

"You know that's not what I meant," he claimed quietly. That fight trailed off as quickly as it had begun. Raye allowed Zeki to take most of her body weight. Her despair forced its way to the top of her body like bile. She swallowed hard and continued her limp walking. Her leg hurt much worse than it did a few minutes ago.

When Raye returned to the group, she was a paler and tired version of herself. She had lost plenty of blood, and it showed. Her soldiers offered her quiet grace while Zeki spoke up instead.

"This is no loss," he sternly spoke to all. "They already had the upper hand. We did more than we even expected of us. They must now rebuild and review entirely before they can make another move. You have all bought us time."

What a great leader she has been so far.

"Sit on the trailer on the way back," Jin told her. She wanted to argue something, but it got lost in the painful pressure she had in her leg, so she obliged.

She was sitting alongside supplies and injured, sulking. She should have been leading the victory home—warning the Daos not to underestimate them. But there was no victory. The harsh reality smacked her across the face blindly. From ruling over an entire school in abilities to being hit with such a sudden loss, it was hard for her to accept. She sat alongside the supplies on the bumpy ride back up north.

Raye could only assume the gods once again blessed her, as Anala was the one to help with her wound. She could sulk in her disappointment without judgment. It was more likely that Anala asked to aid her, though.

Her hair had grown since the last time she saw her. Her dark curls bounced around past her shoulders as she walked, though she did not tie it out of her face. Only Anala could manage wounds while making sure she looked her best. A sprinkle of joy in Raye's darkened corner of life.

Raye struggled in her sulking as multiple medics alongside Anala held her down and attempted to yank the metal that was burrowed deep into her skin. How badly she wanted to vomit everything inside her up.

After a while, the pain became so constant she did not notice it anymore. Suddenly, Anala was impaling her with a sharp needle to stitch her back up again. Before she could react, the others completely pinned her down. She could have thrown them off if she had not been so hurt.

Anala barked orders at the others that Raye was in too much pain to understand. She seemed to grow into quite the medic while apart. Though, maybe she always had been and Raye had just not noticed. She often tuned her retellings of class out during school together—Raye had her own things she was worried about then.

Anala sat next to Raye in silent comfort. Unsure of what would even help her. Raye could only find herself able to stare into her friend's eyes. For what words did she have to explain her emotions to her friend? Words could not express the years of buildup that only started with such failure.

Anala must have understood her pain enough, though, as it shone through the greys of Raye's eyes, the dark circles of restless days and nights, and the sliced and picked calloused hands she created. Had she always been such an open book? Anala knew her weaknesses—the exact places to look for when she became dim.

She rested a comforting hand on Raye's bicep with a gentle squeeze. Raye allowed herself to relax.

"Is there even life left to still save, An?" Raye was in a beaten daze. The question left Anala shocked.

"Of course there is. What about all of us in the country? What do you even mean?" Almost offended by her question.

"It just seems everyone might be dead already," her soft voice spoke. Raye's eyelids were feeling heavier and heavier with each breath she took, but she still shot herself awake. Unready to allow sleep to take her mind.

"But we're not," Anala replied.

Raye wished they were dead in her drowsiness. Then, it would be more justifiable to reign terror into the entirety of Daoland. Maybe then destruction could bring rebirth to a country. To allow Raye to destroy all, evil and innocent, with no remorse at all. To what evil deed was the final straw for her to impeach those who claimed unimpeachable? Too much of her wanted that without cause for justice. For plain revenge on her tiny home. *They deserved that*, she thought. But did the humans born to evil deserve that? Exhausted by a constant dilemma.

She was only an exhausted little girl, anyway. Destruction and all; how much harm could she indeed cause?

Azeran soldiers' lives fell to her shoulders. They were men and women. Human beings. Not just numbers to be played with—people with families and lives outside the military. Raye's own mistakes should not cost the lives of them.

She had to strategize carefully and not get caught up in the fight like the Daos. All those lives lost would be due to her. Their deaths could result in a life like her own. A lonely world forcefully endured. Human life was a sacred entity. She would lead the fight; it was the only way.

She was to stop the Daos from moving to the east town for a takeover. Her superiors ordered her to intervene, and while half her heart was mourning her last loss, they did not see it as such a significant loss.

She had managed more than they had in years and slaughtered more Daos than anyone else had. Raye enjoyed a quick fight, though. There was no reason to drag out a show if it was unnecessary. Her lack of fundamental wartime skills showed, and everyone else who thought otherwise was simply wrong.

They packed much lighter than before to reach the town before them. Anything she might have thought could prevent another mistake. Her captain, Ellerie, followed close behind her as she weaved through the empty towns.

The town maintained its eerily silent air. The town's stillness felt like death had already entered. Or was it only the feeling of what had yet to come? Raye could not let it be. She would win against the masses herself if she needed to. That was the decision she had made. If it came to it, she'd silence them all. She truly hoped it would not.

Dao soldiers would always be better in a hand-to-hand situation; that was what all three of them, Raye, Zeki, and Ellerie, agreed on quickly. Ellerie was well-versed enough in bomb-making compared to either of them, which was how they planned on winning the fight. As long as it did not cause many casualties of their own, it was their best option against the Daos. Raye and Zeki would be in the front, for their fighting was the greatest compared to all else.

Forced to be the waiting party, Raye hated the time she had to think of all the unknown. She assumed the Daos could easily guess they would have soldiers there waiting for them. She truly hoped their cockiness would blind them to a better choice and continue straight on.

Raye stood beside Jin, who also chose to stay at the front of their army, as they both stared into the abyss of the forest, waiting for their monsters to arrive. Her stomach churned at the thoughts. But with bombers and archers at the ready behind her, she had to put her faith in others for once.

The explosion lit the forest far enough to see barely. She could hear the booming, though. They were near.

Raye had men stationed, hidden among the trees, watching for the blues of their uniforms before setting off the first row of bombs. The pounding of the ground rumbled to Raye and her soldiers.

Daos soldiers took off toward them, trampling over their fallen comrades. The yelling of the men grew louder the closer they reached. Small towns hid no secrets. None of them, and none of the Daos. Raye and her team knew every placement of every building, unlike the Daos, so they might have a chance at hiding their more minor secrets long enough.

They remained still, even with the charging Dao nearing them. Ellerie and his team were watching and waiting, and Raye trusted them. So she stayed, even in her fears and worries; she stood tall with both Jin and Zeki.

Her fist clenched her sword tighter than she ever thought it could, waiting and itching for a scratch of blood.

The giant whoosh sliced through the air around them, and the archers shot into the groups of Daos, nailing all those in their way. Their deceased lay at their feet as they threw lit bombs into the remaining indigo-blue sea.

When any of the Daos realized they had been coming from the rooftops behind Raye and her army, it was too late to get out of the way. Body parts flew through the air, creating a rain of blood. Anyone left around the impact was an unrecognizable form.

There were fewer soldiers than Raye had even anticipated. Either they did not have the manpower on Azeran soil, or they did not see Azera as an opponent. Raye would bite her tongue in complaint either way.

There was a break in the bombings. Raye signaled to send her army forward. She charged at the enemy soldiers with a cry while her own followed behind her. The loud clanging of metal contact rang through her ears painfully loud. Her teeth ground through the annoyance, and she continued.

Ducking and weaving through the swinging blades, she rebutted by stabbing and slicing all nearby unsuspecting soldiers. Battling through the crowds, her legs were moving faster than her mind, and she tripped over a rolling head. Raye twisted her body, trying to fall onto her back instead, but only managed to shoulder-check the ground.

Her right shoulder and ribs pulsed with her heartbeat from her pain. She sucked the air in harshly through her nostrils and forced herself up before an enemy sword could impale her. She held her shoulder, squeezing it hard once before heading to her target. Her chest rose and fell dramatically with her intense breaths.

The officer stood at the end of his army, unwilling to put his life on the line. Raye was going to make her way to him to kill him herself. She ripped through every man in her way. Her blade easily sliced through the bodies of all in her path.

She violently tore the bodies apart with the firm and sharp force of her sword. She did not turn around to notice the trail of gory discordance she left behind her. The front of her body was covered in splotches of blood from her victims. Hardly noticeable on the black of her pants and boots.

The men left closest to the officer were better trained than the ones running on the front. Nothing stopped her, though. A brave man swung his sword right at her head, only for her to dodge it entirely and swing her sword at the side of his neck, slicing through it.

His head remained attached by the small side she did not cut through; the blood sputtered out all over his body as he fell to his knees, choking with what life he had left. When he landed on the ground, his head and neck sat at an angle, barely attached, profusely bleeding.

Raye turned her attention to the other men before even watching him fall; they stared at her with disgusted fear after seeing the horrific death of their comrade. Another died with her sword shoved through his forehead with a large crack of the skull.

There were no more men around to protect the officer. The fear conveyed in his eyes was more accurate than she had ever seen. Was it the vicious way she killed? A lady covered in the blood and body parts of her deceased, more than any other soldier there, uncaring for the monstrous way she looked? She did not even think it was enough to care. He was her prey.

His instincts finally kicked in, and his sword flung up at her with anger smeared across his face. Raye's blade went up without hesitation, and the metals clashed hard against each other as she blocked his attack. Raye was gaining exhaustion from fighting and was ready to end things quickly and burn off the anger that seared her skin and veins.

Blades pushing against each other in a fight of strength, Raye kicked the bottom of her boot into the officer's knee. Without breaking the eye contact she had against him, her boot landed harshly on his knee, forcing it backward in the wrong direction. The metal scraping together in front of them could not mask the distinct crack of his bone. The loud snap sounded just as painful as it looked. His face and body crumpled inside of itself, sinking him to the ground. One of his bones stuck out the back of his leg and pants; the white shone through slivers of the bloody scene and broken skin.

The town that once was now stood as a graveyard of their enemies. But it was also a sign of their success. The remains of human life spilled across a home for others.

Raye had spared the lives of two soldiers, only to drag their deceased officer back to camp. A message of her success personally delivered back to the Daos by their own. Azera was no longer a simple target, and she was there to rain torture upon anyone in her way.

With the day only getting warmer, they needed the town cleaned up as best as possible before it became a more significant problem. She had soldiers stack the bodies away from the buildings to burn them. With the heat rising, the putrid smell only got worse from the deceased.

They started using makeshift masks for their face out of clothes from any uniforms they could gather to cover their face. Raye was unsure if it helped or made the thick air harder to breathe. Even so, after she and the other soldiers carried the arms and legs of the last body into the pile, morale was higher than ever, and it felt good to be on the victorious side for once.

Raye knew they were in a temporary situation, but any failed attempt on the Daos' end brought joy to all. They were not all-powerful beings, like many had seemed to fear.

M. NEVILLS

CHAPTER NINETEEN

Will I ever atone for my sins?

The civilians could reoccupy their homes shortly after Raye and her team had deemed it safe. Raye assumed that with her soldiers maintaining occupancy, it could keep a safe home for them. Though only weeks after the Daos attempt, they proved Raye wrong.

All her soldiers gathered at the center of the town with plenty of space to listen and watch her announcement. Every soldier in the city stood anxiously waiting for her to arrive. Rumors had spread throughout that it was not a welcome gathering, and they shared their fears.

The ambiance surrounding the grown soldiers was one of thunderous fear. As graceful as Raye has always managed to be to them, rumors of her times in school and her attitude toward even her superiors had spread amongst them. Rumors claimed she was not the type of person to make angry.

While some cowered in fear of her, other men thought too highly of themselves for that. What could a woman possibly do to any of them? Some of the soldiers wrongly assumed that her captains would not allow her to become a wild woman.

Raye's captains not only followed any blind order she gave, but knew when to stand back away from her line of fire. Some of the soldiers even feared her much more than they would let on.

✦ ✦ ✦

Raye's fury reeked out of her body. Her calm demeanor was not one she purposefully released. It was all she could manage without exploding the entire city with her rage—an angry calm. Nothing could go right but everything could go wrong.

The group grew silent once she appeared in the center of town. Her teeth were grinding each other inside of her mouth. A young woman walked sheepishly behind her, refusing to make eye contact with any soldiers.

"Point," Raye whispered to the woman, only for her to hear. The eeriness of the situation hit them hard, though, so they made correct assumptions.

The woman pointed a measly finger at a man Raye had never thought of before. She hardly had the ability or care to memorize every plain face of every soldier that was hers.

Raye nudged her head toward the boy she referred to as an order for the two men near her to get a hold of him. She had learned to trust the two of them first in their abilities and respect and had begun to use them extensively to her advantage.

The two men grabbed him by his arms and threw him to the ground in front of Raye before he attempted further to weasel away from the crowd. They pinned him to the ground, waiting for Raye's next order. Raye could only look at him like the scum he was. How dare a vile soldier work under her reign? She had no room for those she could not trust on her team.

"Did you touch her?" she asked the boy forced into the dirt.

"What the fuck are you gonna do about it, bitch?"

Harsh words for the man with half his face in the filth. Raye crouched down to see his face better. She let out a tiny, dry laugh.

"You must not know who the fuck I am," she spoke softly.

She addressed the crowd instead. "How the fuck am I to trust any of you against the Dao when I can't even trust you with our civilians?" Her voice boomed against their eardrums with anger.

"I thought I made myself clear about our priorities previously, but I guess not. I thought I made myself clear I have no room in my troops for men who can't listen. But I fucking guess not." The anticipation thickened on their necks. She stood without a word, long enough to let her words settle.

"Right or left-handed?" she asked the boy loud enough for all to hear. She had her men bring him to his knees so he could face him fully.

He still did not answer.

"I asked you a fucking question," she boomed at him; her once calm anger had left as even more rage seeped through her cracks. He swallowed hard at her shouts but said nothing still. She decided to assume.

Raye stomped over to a corner of buildings where they stored extra weapons. She pushed her way through the crowd as they murmured their quiet questions. She eyed the variety of options in front of her before she decided on her best option.

She wrapped her hand tight around an ax, specifically built for battle, until her knuckles were white from her grip. She pushed her way back through the confused crowd, ax in hand, as the murmurs turned into wholly concerned voices speaking to each other. Her only focus was the man sitting in the middle of the huddle.

"Hold his hand down. The right one," she ordered one of the soldiers who held him. He pinned his arm down, dragging half of his body closer to the ground with his right hand.

Without hesitation, Raye raised her ax above her head and brought it down upon his forearm with one swift crack through the air.

The crowd erupted in shared gasps. The sharp blade sliced through his bones with a loud crack, and a spray of his blood through the air, covering the front of Raye's body and face. Though she did not flinch, her face was now splattered crimson red on top of her snow-like skin. Her jaw cracked moving side to side to contain her anger.

She stared at the mess she had made on the ground, his blood pouring out of his arm, creating a pool beneath it, his detached hand lying next to him. She stared her angry eyes of daggers at him, unrealized by the screams he let out from the pain, for she did not care.

Her chest raised and lowered slowly with each deep, controlled breath. *She was in control,* she reminded herself. While she could not be with every man every second, she would find out, and she would react.

"You're now medically discharged from the Azeran military. A one-time kindness from me to anyone," she claimed over his cries. Her cold voice left a chill through all the soldiers' spines. No one objected to her; no one appeared to disapprove of her.

"Let this be the rest of your only warning. While I do not wish to make another example of you, I gladly will." The rage in her voice had her practically yelling at them. She wanted to make sure everyone understood exactly who she was.

Darkness seeped through her teeth, out of the cracks in her mind. She was more terrifying than she meant to be. More cruel than she ever thought she would need to be. Her point seemed taken thoroughly, though.

"Am I understood?" she asked.

Yes, ma'am, they chanted in one response. She nodded once in acceptance. Raye tried to unclench her jaw as it started to hurt, but relaxation would not come.

She pushed her way out of the crowds of soldiers, deciding she was over it all. The soldiers dispersed slowly as she left. The town remained quiet since then.

Winter would come soon enough. If they could not maintain control of themselves, there was no hope of shared survival.

Raye knew her team, and others would be forced to the front lines out in the cold to maintain their positioning against the Daos. It was punishment from her superiors. If she would not learn the rules of their hierarchy, her team would receive constant punishment. She did not mind the front lines, though. They needed to stay under her control, though. It was the only way to get through the war.

If she could not trust her soldiers together, then they would not stay alive.

While Jin shared the same expression of disgust toward the soldier, to Raye's surprise, Zeki peered at her. She would not allow his opinions to have her falter. Her nostrils flared as she sucked the air in through her nose in heated breaths. How difficult he could be, agreeing with her one moment to viewing her with his own disgust the next. He should know better than anyone that this was the one punishment she could never go far enough.

Tears started to weld up in her eyes, which only created more anger inside herself. She rubbed her blood splattered face onto her sleeve in an attempt to wipe it off. It only smeared it in streaks across her face.

CHAPTER TWENTY

Why does their god save them but not me?

The first winter during the active invasion of the Dao in Azera had started. The days grew colder and never got warmer. In preparation, Raye and her team decided it would be best to keep Daoland soldiers trapped inside their area along the beach.

The ocean would only make the temperatures colder without proper shelter, and they would eventually run out of food unless they decided to bring another boat across the week trip in freezing weather. The Daos' lack of planning and assumption that Azera was weak led them here, unprepared for an actual battle lasting more than a year.

The winter had been more frigid than in previous years, forcing everyone to attempt to stay warm. Camps sprawled along the southern border, above where the Daos laid camp, to keep a close eye on them at all times. Winter or not, they were still enemies.

It only allowed them to hope the other was struggling just as badly and could leave them at bay.

The bitter cold kept everyone bundled up so tightly they could barely move. An icy frost covered the country like never before. An unforgiving death that swept across the nation, killing all that were not deemed strong enough. Forced to live out in the cold, Raye and her soldiers remained closer to each other than they ever thought they would.

They practically slept in piles on top of each other to keep any warmth at night within their shared tents. Raye had become closer to Zeki than she had anticipated, sleeping under any blankets they could find, squeezed together as close as possible.

They'd have large fires going at all times, heating rocks up on the bottom and then placing them under their blankets in more attempts to provide heat. The night grew so cold they could only hope everyone would wake up each morning.

Not everyone did, as the night would frost them to the bone and blue to the face. Raye did not want to face the heartbreaking reality of their deaths. To die during war, not even in battle, but freezing in your sleep. She hoped it was at least peaceful.

As much as Raye wished her team, or any team, could take the perfect opportunity to pick off the struggling Daos that winter, it was impossible. Her soldiers were in no physical shape in the bitter chill to take anyone on. It kept Raye's mind at ease that the Daos were in an even worse place than her, though.

As they took shifts taking watch of the Daos, every day seemed harder on them than the last. Azera made sure to always prepare for winter with food. But the Daos had not prepared for such an extended stay in the same place. With Azera forcing them into the same spot, they did not have an opportunity for food like Azera did. Soldiers would receive food from the northern base quickly, whereas the Daos did not have enough animals and fish within their base. They would become desperate. As long as their desperation did not involve Azerans, which Raye did not think they had the energy to, the Daos were of no issue.

When Raye had received word that their soldiers were either dying from starvation or the cold, she only thought how much easier it would make it on her once winter ended. The Daos would not die so quickly, though.

They made it through the rest of winter, eating off the meat of their dead soldiers. As much as it frustrated her about their survival, to think they had to resort to such barbarity brought a wicked joy in her heart. It was the least they deserved to feast on their deceased comrades.

Raye chopped wood with her ax for more firewood. Raised above her head, she slammed the ax down upon the wood until it split in half. Raye yanked the ax out of the tree stump she used to set the logs when it got stuck. She threw the pieces onto a blanket-sized cloth and grabbed the corners to haul the wood.

The snow crunched under the impact of Raye's feet. Each exhale steamed the frigid air around her mouth. The entire camp moved in slow motion from the cold. She tossed the pack of firewood alongside the others and entered her tent.

She crouched down on the ground and removed her gloves while attempting to blow hot breaths into them to try to warm her fingers up. She blew her breaths like a dragon while the crunch of snow came closer to the entrance of her tent. *Not even a moment of peace?* She whispered prayers beneath her breath that she was not needed by someone already. Zeki entered the tent.

"Hey, how are you doing?" he asked. She looked up at him.

"Fine," she answered. He looked at her like he knew that was not the entire truth. Zeki sat down across from her.

"Can I ask you something that's been on my mind?"

Raye looked at him in confusion and nodded. He fidgeted with his hands for a second before continuing.

"I guess I've just been wondering, like," he rubbed his hands together, "how do you do it so easily?"

"Do what?" Raye questioned.

Zeki sighed awkwardly, "How do you, like, kill them so easily?" Raye's brow went up in shock. "I just mean, it seems so simple for you. During school, I wondered if I would ever even be able to kill a man. I guess I thought it would have gotten easier after the first time, but I don't know."

Raye shook her head in understanding while she pressed her lips against each other, not wanting to share her answer. "I killed someone for the first time when I was . . . five, I think?" She nodded from her memory. "Yeah, that might be why it seems easy to me. These people ruined my life, Ze."

Zeki stared at her with his shocked face, a true sadness behind it.

"What?" An upset voice croaked out of him. Raye let out a dry laugh.

"Yeah."

"Do you want to talk about it?" he asked.

Raye contemplated whether or not she should share one of her worst memories with him. She had never even spoken its truth out loud. She feared that might make it much more real if she did. If anyone deserved to understand that part of her life, she thought Zeki ought to. He had a gentle kindness about him that remained, even after everything.

"The Gestige village, where I was born;. the Daos attacked at night," she started.

Young Raye sat on the ground of her home as the Dao soldier continued with her mother. Her mother, a long blonde mess of waves, similar to Raye's own, lay there unresponsive, lifeless, and pale. Raye did not know how long she had been dead, it seemed like she sat there for an eternity. Her eyes could not peel away from the atrocity.

The bright yellow fires burned the village down just outside her window. The screams of terror and murderous cries filled her ears. Raye clutched onto the knife she had hidden behind her. Her fear froze her in place instead of using it on the man.

The wickedly faced man crawled closer to her. His bright blue eyes haunted her with the daggers they pointed at her. He grabbed her by the left leg and dragged her closer to him. Tears flew out of her eyes as she shrieked out of fear. His hands climbed up her legs far too high as she screamed out. *There was no one left to save her,* she realized as she watched out the window. The flames engulfed the only place she knew to be home.

Her tears stopped as she watched the chaos outside unfold. Her own house had caught fire and would soon crumble on top of her and her deceased mother. Too young to contemplate her death, yet faced with a decision. Raye made the first decision not to die there.

She whipped the knife out from under her, stabbing his blue eyes, which bore daggers into her. In and out, she drove the knife into his face repeatedly until she knew he was dead. He cried out his treacherous pains, now blinded by the tiny girl slicing his eyes. His face bled tremendously over her, covering herself in his death.

She continued to shriek until she could not anymore. He fell on top of Raye, crushing her with his weight.

She shimmied and clawed her way out from under his giant stature. The smoke in the house grew as she tried to catch her breath. Her once pristine nightgown now soaked through entirely with blood.

The dripping red dress laid a path behind wherever she walked. She hid inside her parents' chest, where she was small enough to fit in while the house caved within itself. Alone in the dark, she stayed for days.

CHAPTER TWENTY-ONE

The in-between.

Once it had warmed up enough to allow for movement, the country was a muddy mess from the melted masses of snow. The beautiful greenery had become a brown-covered mess. The constant walking covered Raye's boots, forcing her to clean them off when she could.

Word had come that the Daos had received another ship of soldiers and planned to make their way to Azera's main compound. With no point in trying to wait in place while they made their way up. As strong a fortress as their stone boat was, there was no knowing just how many people and what type of armory they had until it would be too late for them to react at their base.

The hills roamed through there, and they would have the high ground at the north end if they got there first. Raye knew they would have no choice but to go in that direction, as avoiding it would send them into the Azeran's woods, which they would know well versus the Daos. They could be waiting for them in the trees, and such, the Daos would not make that same mistake of walking directly into a trap where Raye knew the land, and they did not.

A chill remained in the morning air, but the sun shone brightly without a cloud in the sky. The bright blue air kept Raye in a hopeful stance in their situation. She had made it to the valley before her enemy with the perfect view of all incoming.

The tall grass hid the mud well, but she knew once soldiers started to stomp, it would cling to the ground, creating a slippery mess for all. That was still their best opportunity to slow them down before reaching the fortress. If they planned to try to overtake their largest armory, Raye knew to assume they thought they had the manpower to do so.

On the horizon of where the sparse trees started and the tall grass met, the dark blue uniforms and pale faces began to pop out. They would be here soon; Raye's stomach started to drop at the thought. To each side of her were Jin and Zeki, as ready as she was.

The Daos had no archers or catapults. It appeared they only had the swords in their hands. Raye knew to be wary of them still. Once they had marched close enough, the first wave of soldiers proceeded into battle from the other lieutenant colonel's company.

Everything made sense to be on their side. The Daos soldiers had marched for hours, being forced into a battle and then exhausted. Raye could see all the Daos soldiers from where she stood; Azera had much more between the two of them.

The red and blue uniforms slowly mixed in a clash of swords. Raye remained on top of the hill to keep her view, knowing the Azeran soldiers were more than capable of their own in the battle.

The giant rumble beat the ground up to Raye's feet, with a massive explosion knocking her off her feet. Sharp ringing filled her ears, and she slowly blinked open her eyes, viewing the scene.

Dark smokey clouds covered the valley, the thick haze a result of the fires intermingling with the dense cloud coverage. A hand landed on her shoulder, and she turned to view them.

Jin's mouth was moving, his eyes in wide shock. Her head was pounding inside and out. She placed her hand on the back of her hand, where she fell, only to find blood on her fingers when she removed them.

Jin grabbed her arm and pulled her upward onto her feet quickly. His hands held her tightly, keeping her upright, as she looked closer into the scene in front of her. There were fires everywhere, but the ground was too wet to stoke the flames, meaning the only thing remaining to feed the fire was the clothes on the soldier's back.

The soldiers now lay dead on the ground: a blood field, no longer a muddy valley but a bloody, red-soaked graveyard. Dismembered body parts flung about; the scene was too hard to even understand at first. Both Dao and Azeran deceased soldiers lay sprawled across the land, their bodies ripped apart by the impact of the bombs the Daos deployed.

The air tasted of putrid death. If anyone was living in the mess, they were missing limbs or had skin burnt to the muscle.

The exact location she marveled at all those years ago on her way to her new beginning was no longer full of life but death. The sun could not even shine through the thick grey clouds; the grass was not green and fresh, but dark and chaotic.

Despair danced alongside the morning breeze. Nature's beauty taken by the death of man. Humans' anger rotted the soil, darkened the sky, and bittered the air.

The tug inside her chest could not be calmed. Even with everything on their side, how could they win a war history so clearly did not want them to? Where did mankind's slaughter end? Could it be here, in the valley of the once so living?

The valley had become a place no longer of life but not full of death. It was something else. The in-between: Life of the world and the Death of man. Would any god forgive them for their horrors? Repent if they must, Raye would not allow forgiveness.

Her body felt on fire, not from pain but from released anger. The lump in her throat left her unable to speak. Standing there, watching the bodies cling to any life left, every emotion she had seeped and poured from her skin. The breeze whipped the hairs left out in front of her face back and forth, hitting her face. She let it be.

The young men had no choice but to fight the rich man's war. She even felt sorrow for Dao soldiers. Raye had finally realized they all had a common enemy. There was no point in mindlessly killing the boys they forced onto the battlefield.

Evil or not, they were only pawns used by the men who sat on their comfortable chairs back in Daoland. They strapped bombs on boys whose only job was to kill as many people as possible, including themselves. Because they were right, why would Raye ever think they would do something like that? Who would kill their soldiers to kill more enemies? It was those who lost nothing in the process.

The wicked must die. And they shall.

❖ ❖ ❖

She walked down to the bloodbath. Death all around her. As she crunched through the bodies, the occasional face became familiar. Shock filled her when she recognized a lieutenant from another company. He lay there alongside his soldiers. *How admirable to enter the war zone first alongside his men.* If it were not for who he was, Raye might have thought that. She knelt to examine him further.

Yes, it's him. Sebastian. Her chest jumped when the bloodied face boy let his tiny breaths in and out. Barely alive, she still struck fear in his eyes as she stared into his eyes. The bright blue eyes that made him recognizable. Sebastian mustered out tiny cries of help. He would die there if Raye did not get him help immediately. Raye stood up and left him wide-eyed with voiceless screams he tried to get out as she walked away.

Her karma caught her quick. Before her mind knew what she saw, her body did, and her heart sank below the ground. Her body shook with uncontrollable fear.

"Finn," she whispered to herself.

His brown, wavy locks of hair flung over his head and around his young face. Her knees fell to the ground into a puddle of blood and mud. Jin stood behind her silently. Raye cupped the boy's face with her hand, still in shock. His pale face was so young still, even after all those years.

She held the little boy in her arms. The small boy slept against her chest as she pulled him in. He appeared the same as he did when she first met him. A young, quiet boy. He slept so peacefully, just like he did when they were little, so still. His breaths were almost silent. His body was so tiny she felt huge; when had she grown that much? Raye wished he would wake to see her. It had been so long. She never had the chance to reply to his letters.

The tears broke through her eyes and fell down her cheeks so fast she hardly noticed. She was content to see her little brother again, just as he had been when she first met him, the small boy barely older than a toddler.

Before, he had outgrown her in height like everyone else. Her tears started to fall off her face and land on his. His perfectly porcelain skin got hit with drops of wet tears, each one the color of blood red.

"My beautiful baby brother," she spoke quietly through her sadness. Jin grabbed her shoulder in anticipation.

Another bomb set off late, a few yards from them.

Raye awoke inside a medical tent alone. Whether it was the injuries or her mental state, she could not move her body. Her chest grew heavier and heavier with each breath she took. She felt no actual pain anywhere, though.

Jin entered through the tent flap. He was utterly unharmed, even though he was closer to the blast than her.

"You're awake," he attempted a fake smile. She could only stare blankly at him, confused and dazed in her emptiness. Too wrapped up in her well-being, she did not even attempt to question how fine he seemed. Her lips were unable to form words, only tears fell from her eyes.

"You feel alright?" he asked.

Her sadness sizzled out from her annoyance. She did not need Jin to feel any amount of pity for her. They were not friends.

"Obviously not," her hoarse voice choked out. His eyes spread wide with worry.

"I mean physical wounds, fuck. I'm sorry, Raye," he stated, the panic in his tone well deserved.

"Don't be fucking sorry to me," she snapped at him. "My body is fine, I think." She assessed herself better that time. She had no pain or injuries, no burns or stings. *What the fuck had he done to her?*

"I healed you," he stated, though she did not ask. "That's why you're fine. I have the Celestial ability to heal wounds. I figured it was time, you know."

She was going to choke him where he stood.

"You have godly abilities to heal people, and you left my brother laying in my lap dead?" Her voice cracked through her shouts. Jin stepped back out of fear and stuttered his following words.

"Raye, no. It doesn't work like that." He stared woefully into her pathetically saddened face. "He was already dead; there was no way for me to save him—you know shit doesn't work like that."

A silent moment passed.

"How did you know he was there?" Jin asked.

"He sent me a stupid letter. He went on and on about how brave he felt I was, fighting for a cause. When shit went bad with the Daos, he joined the front lines. *To truly help the fight,* he claimed . . ." she trailed off in her sadness.

She knew that, and she did not care. It felt much better to let herself be angry at the man who stood across from her, pitying her and seeing her in the worst possible state. Weak.

Her grief was so thick she thought it alone might drown her. It had its hands clawed into every part of her body, sinking her deeper.

However, there were no more boiling waters of rage there. The only thing left was a bottomless pit of endless darkness. She had her oldest friend, the one she had danced with so many times before. The loneliness she sank into, as she wanted to push everyone away for time alone with the old friend. All of her earliest memories seemed to be them. Grief.

Something was different at that time, though. She was unable to be alone.

Anala entered the tent. Her angel entered. The war did not affect Anala as it affected Raye. Anala's skin remained bright, while Raye lost sleep, and exhaustion only grew on her face.

Anala had a sad look on her face, though she always managed to make it look like genuine kindness.

She sat beside the cot Raye lay in and, without words, set her head next to hers. She wrapped her arms around her, and it was like she took away some of the pain for a moment. The darkness was not the only thing wrapped around her. Raye was not alone in her grief.

CHAPTER TWENTY-TWO

Greed be the hunger that is never satisfied.

Raye could no longer pretend to be some delusional optimist about the true nature of humans. Human nature is to be vile. She saw what they were capable of—the moves they made. Dead soldiers were a mere tally mark on a board for them. Raye knew she had to make the following tally marks matter to them more than any other. She knew what mattered most in the world to them. She needed to decide how to make it a tangible death. But plenty of people could still give her the answer she sought.

The Daos' base in Azera was easy to slip into in the dark.

Both Zeki and Anala were willing to join her on her mission. It seemed they would both follow her into the fire if she asked them to. Though Anala was not typically a fighter, she would be a good lookout, as she was quicker and quieter than a bulkier man.

While Jin attempted to convince her not to run off without permission from superiors, he knew he could not stop her. Unlike him, she did not care about proper rules and knew it was quicker and easier to do it herself right away. Asking permission to change plans took far too long, at least for something that minuscule.

A lone, sleepy soldier watching the southeast border of their camp seemed like the easiest option for them. He paced back and forth a few steps, maintaining his guard. They needed to be quick and silent. Raye grabbed a piece of cloth from her pocket and handed it to Zeki. He would be much more effective at manhandling another soldier than she would.

Zeki jumped up in one swift motion, wrapped an arm around the soldier's torso, locking his arms down, and covered his mouth. Raye hopped up, wrapped a rope around his flailing legs, and tied them together while Zeki shoved the cloth deeper into his mouth. The man attempted to worm his way out of his situation, but Zeki's grip was too firm. Raye helped him bind his hands before carrying him off into the woods. Anala followed from her position a few yards over, where she was maintaining a watch over the other soldiers.

They made camp a few miles north between the camp and the Azeran base. They were far enough away from any civilization; Raye made sure of it. Zeki removed the gag from the soldier's mouth, and he attempted to yell out for help.

"No one will hear you, besides maybe a coyote, I guess," Raye told him. "An, can you get a fire going?"

Anala nodded and got to work. She had an array of skills she was better at than Zeki and Raye. She built fires at half the speed either could and used to light them in the winter during school.

An up-close look at one of the men capable of such violence was strange for Raye. She assumed they would be more villainous. He was more of a fearful boy calling out cries for help. Leaving him alive and sitting in front of her made her queasy. Her body wanted to rip him open as she did any others. Compared to the boy sitting in front of her, she was more of a violent villain than he seemed.

"You're quite the baby for a trained Dao soldier," Zeki remarked. The soldier looked up at him in fear. He was childlike compared to Zeki. The fire Anala started lit his youthful face up in bright yellow. His pale face and light eyes shone from the golden rays.

"Your religion," Raye spoke. "Who are the highest respected people within it?" Her cold demeanor made the boy uneasy.

He glanced at her with fear and answered, obviously, "The emperor?"

Raye's nostrils flared out of irritation. She whipped a knife out and pointed it at him, only scaring him further.

"You gotta know that's not what I'm asking, dickhead."

In a classic Dao fashion, their captive assumed his usefulness far too much. His face grew too cocky for Raye's liking. Even in fear, those men believe they were much greater than they ever were.

"I don't feel like telling you demons," he whipped out. "I will not give you information to hurt my country's victory," he claimed triumphantly.

"I'll kill you if you're useless," she claimed plainly.

"Then you won't get your information," he replied.

Zeki laughed at the boy. "Then we'd grab another one of you, fucking idiot." The soldier gulped down his embarrassment and weighed his options. Raye had grown too impatient. She stabbed the boy in the shoulder with her knife. He let out a scream of pain. Zeki and Anala both had looks of shock planted on their faces.

Raye was not done yet; her time had been wasted far too much, and her respect would be gained back. She grabbed his bounded hands and shoved them onto the ground laid out flat, looking into his tear-filled eyes before moving again. She raised her eyebrows, allowing him a chance to answer her question. He only stared at her in pain.

She blindly chopped her knife down without breaking eye contact, as if cutting vegetables for a stew. When she felt the resistance of the bones in his fingers, she pushed down harder. The crunch and cracks of the snapping bones filled the air before he could even let out a scream of pain.

"You can die slowly or answer my questions," she explained.

Sobs fell down his face as he stared daggers of disbelief at her. She raised her eyebrows again, waiting for his answer, and lifted her knife, ready to slice her vegetables again.

"P-Priests! I think that's what you're looking for. We have them at every military camp," he choked out. A big, beautiful smile spread across her face.

"Good. Where do we find them?"

Before the sun could come up over the horizon, they dumped his body near the border of their base, where she knew the dogs would pick him off. She doubted they would waste any manpower hunting down who might have killed a lone soldier.

Raye had not had the opportunity to previously meet the Azeran military general, but now she needed to properly pitch her plan. All the upper officers in Azeran gathered around, Raye now included. General Norverro had yet to speak up and let them argue it out amongst each other. Raye grew hot with exasperation.

"We do not have the manpower to look at this like it's a numbers game," she felt like she was practically yelling over them to be heard. "We will continue to lose this war unless we hit them where it hurts. Our country is bleeding dry; they are occupying more southern land as we speak; without those crops, we lose food."

"Well, sounds like you have it all figured out. If we lose no matter what, we might as well wait it out anyway," one argued with her. No one would listen to the little girl.

"How the fuck would you know where to hit them? You can not sail over to Daoland and braid the emperor's hair—" more shouts erupted.

If that was how they solved problems, no wonder decades have passed without anything being done. Most of them wanted to maintain their home soil and simply prevent the Daos from killing too many people, but assumed their takeover was inevitable. It was not inevitable if they would listen.

Raye could only scream into the void so much. Their own opinions grew inside them like tangled roots.

The general's fingers stopped bouncing up and down, causing the group to turn to him, expecting him to speak. Raye did not give him the option and took the sudden silence as an opportunity.

"I am taking a team over to Daoland and executing my plan. With or without permission from my superiors, I do not care." She left the table in a silent shock for her disrespectfulness. The general did not seem bothered.

"You should have warned me better about her, Lieutenant Zion," he said jokingly. Zion bashfully smiled in embarrassment at her outburst. Speaking out of turn was no outburst for Raye.

"However, we may feel Miss Rayana is not our greatest concern. We must admit that she was able to move us along quicker than any of you in this war."

The table remained silent. Raye maintained her composure and ignored the cockiness she wanted to shove at them.

"Rayana may execute her plan; if she fails, we remain as we always do. If they die, they die. If they somehow win us the fucking war," he paused, "well then I guess we shall see."

The greatest of words she could hear in that moment. The consensus that the Daos may kill off Raye in her stupid plan kept morale high at the table. Raye paid them no mind, anyway.

Raye needed to let her team know she was a Celestial. Before she took them across the ocean, her trusted few had to know everything. She could not risk scaring them while she threatened the Dao emperor. They were her allies, and she needed to trust them. She needed to tell Zeki first, though.

Zeki looked at Jin in shock at the entire conversation they were having. Jin's unbothered attitude confused him further.

"I already knew," Jin spoke. Zeki let his words settle in his mind before his jaw shifted in anger.

"What do you mean you already knew?" he questioned.

"How else do you think she convinced Hira to aid your government?" Jin said with a chuckle. Zeki did not laugh back.

"So, Jin knew this entire time, but you did not tell me until now?" Zeki turned to Raye. Raye's eyes zoned in on him, scanning him to reassure his genuine anger.

"For years, you didn't tell me, you didn't trust me, but Jin knew?" Zeki's anger grew with each further realization. Raye could not understand his frustration.

"Of course, there was no one I could trust about this," she explained plainly.

"But Jin, right?" he scoffed.

"I had no other option. We would have died without their help. Hira is different from the Azeran people—who have made Celestials out as monsters. My life is not a game to take a chance on here."

Zeki's eyes widened from shock before he spoke.

"But it is. Everything is a fucking game to you. Everything is a strategic game for you. You didn't tell me because you needed to make sure I would follow you anywhere, even defying our own country. And now, who would deny a god?"

"I am not a god," Raye reflected.

"I do not believe that you truly think that." Zeki's nostrils flared with anger from the words he kept in. He left Raye and Jin alone in silence.

M. NEVILLS

CHAPTER TWENTY-THREE

If someone were to ask for a display of god amongst men, I would so kindly answer.

Raye took it upon herself to answer whether someone asked or not.

For the first time in two decades, Raye stepped onto the soil of what she used to consider her homeland. Indescribable feelings of guilt and sorrow slithered up her body and around her bones. No matter the time that had passed, it seemed her body

The loss of life gnawed at her soul, a painful twisting of hurt caused by the ancestors and neighbors she would never know. How could she step back on their land, alive and well, while she allowed their murders to reign tyranny on the same earth they have now become?

She had no choice but to push her bile down with a hard swallow and keep moving. They docked their boat on a shore with no civilization.

No one had ever invaded the Daos before, a single small boat being successful was unlikely. They had no reason to be seen or found in the middle of nowhere, as their land was far too vast to keep eyes on all that well.

Zeki's hand found the spot on her back in between her shoulder blades, causing her to jump out of her mind a little.

"Are you alright?" He ducked down a little to ask her quietly. He could always read any change of vibe she gave off, no matter how tiny. As much as she hated it, she could appreciate him. Raye shook her head, yes, but he did not seem all too convinced. He always saw right through her.

The only option Raye would consider was the churches inside of their military camps. Dao civilians were not something she was trying to entertain in war. With only a handful of soldiers with her, she hoped they could get in and out quickly without harming or notifying anyone. Assuming for the worst, though, she doubted it would be so easy.

They wore all black and silently invaded at night, the dark lessening the probability of being spotted. If they found out they were on their soil, there was no telling what might happen. Using knives and rags, Raye and Jin took any pairs of soldiers watching the guard, while the other three took out their own across the way.

They shoved their gags into their mouths while shoving their blades deep into their necks, right under their chins and up toward their head. It killed them quickly as they choked on their blood.

When their limp bodies fell entirely into their arms, they laid them on the ground. That proved a quick, but messy, method as each person became soaked in their victims' blood. Their missions proved successful in multiple other camps.

That night, a single soldier got up to take a piss.

Noticing the six dead guards in his half-awakened state, he yelled out. They had grown too confident in their final attempt.

Fuck, fuck, fuck, of fucking course. All that seemed to come to Raye's mind at the moment.

They only had to get out of there with the priest. Raye whipped out her sword and started slashing. She killed more than her fair share of men quickly.

One foot in front of the other, stepping, twisting, turning her entire body, dodging each swing the tired men threw at her. One-handed swings of her sword sliced through any flesh it found. Her left hand grabbed any body part she could find, discreetly killing them with a bolt to the heart.

She did not care as she watched herself kill the boys, who let out vicious cries of pain they could not contain. The way their pain forced tears out of their eyes, just like the other soldiers before, almost humanized them. Almost.

Boys or not, they would die that night. They would not humanize her if given the chance. No one ever had—why should she? She did not dwell on her thoughts for longer than a moment.

Amidst it all, with plenty of chances to run away with the others, she remained. Anywhere she saw the blue uniforms, she rained red upon them. She had slaughtered the entire camp. It then smelled of rancid burned skin from the victims.

    She lit up in rage. So many young faces lie around her, lifeless, forced into a war with no gain for them. She headed toward the camp to find her comrades. Her boots crunched under the bones beneath her feet. So much closer to her goal, she felt ecstatic.

    If she had better morals still, she might have cared more about the child-like soldiers who could no longer return to their mothers. But that meant nothing compared to the close reality of victory.

    And victory she will have.

    Fifteen men of the Daos' god laid her as their captor. Suppose it were only so easy to feel a lack of guilt. Even under the eyes of a god she did not believe in, she still felt the heaviness of her sins on full display. She did not even know their official titles within the church for sure. She had no care to educate herself on their religion built on destruction.

    The more sinister part of her wanted things far worse than death brought upon these men, even if they did not personally deserve it. It seemed like most people were paying for another's sins.

    These men preached for a god, an emperor, who wanted to claim all by any means necessary. They pray for the soldiers who murder and rape innocents. Worship a deity who gives no rights to those besides man. They stood before a church to tell all who would listen that their king was a descendant of their lord himself; for he should then claim all he wished.

    The people of Daoland worship no god but a single man who claimed their throne while giving them structure and rules to follow mindlessly. He can claim their lack of sinning gets them into eternal Heaven, but anything done in the name of god was then no sin to them.

    The uncivilized Gestige and Azerans who lost lives uselessly to them were simply an act of their god. Not to even think of those elsewhere in the world Raye did not know about.

    Sickening rage. That was all Raye could feel within herself. The longer she allowed herself to get sucked into their world, the less and less guilt she felt for each of them. Eternal damnation she would face if their god revealed itself as true.

    The emotional turmoil made her want to vomit. Her head could explode from the pounding coming from inside of her. She could not tell if the intense pain she felt was real or the anger trying to escape her body by clawing its way out.

Her teeth remained clenched and ground on each other. Her heartbeat outside her chest, in her fingers and her toes; she felt unreal. They would die for their country's sins. Raye was now the lone decider of their mortality; no god could stop her, for she was Death. No longer may they glory in their pride. Her scythe would come upon them.

Each one she executed quickly and efficiently. Kinder than any Dao deserved. She held herself to a slightly higher standard of respect for their religion than they had hers—even after all these years.

She shoved her sword into the heart of each tied-up man and watched until their life leaped away. Fourteen holy men died in minutes at her hand. When she headed closer to the last man alive, she heard him whispering a quiet prayer to himself.

"Are you so certain you will go to Heaven?" Raye interrupted his prayer. His eyes fluttered up to look up at his end. His breath was shaky; she knew he feared her. The only way she would have it. His last prayer was one last great reach out to his god in hopes of being saved. He remained silent in response to her question.

Dirt and dried blood covered his nightgown as a result of them extracting him. His light grey hair indicated he had probably spent a long life assuming he was serving his religion. Only for him to end up tied to a tree in the middle of Daoland woods by their barbaric enemies. Raye grew impatient with him and shuffled to end it already.

He choked out his final words, at least. "You have the devil in you, don't you, girl," he said in an eerie whisper. As he shoved the words out of his mouth, tears spilled out of his eyes. Raye squatted to his level to view his face closer in the dark. She leaned her arms onto her squatted legs and stared into his eyes momentarily.

She allowed herself to remain calm and collected by presence, but inside of herself, she was boiling with anger at him. She would not allow him to think anything he could ever say would affect her. She had to choose her following words carefully and not out of rage. Raising the end of her blade to her heart, still low to the ground in front of him, she stared a deep look of putrid anger into his soul in his final moments.

He let out a scared gasp of air as she put slight pressure on the tip of the sword on his chest. She was burning with fiery anger; he could probably see the flames behind her eyes.

"I am the fucking devil," she spoke slowly with a low chill of hatred infused in her voice. Once she was sure he understood every single word she said, she grasped the hilt of her sword even tighter before smashing it deep into his chest cavity.

It sliced through his flesh and bones easily with her push forward. Through his buttery muscle and into his heart, her sword slid effortlessly. A sick, tearing sound from his skin ripping apart filled her ears as her blade dove through his body. Her last lamb of the night slaughtered, at last.

Fifteen pale, lifeless bodies sat still tied to their trees, now incompletely blood-soaked clothes. Raye removed a small knife from her belt to make her final political statement.

Raye was Death, and Death was her; the two entangled so close together, like vines covering a tree intertwined within itself.

She had become a slayer of divine creation.

Raye killed any Dao soldier who stood in their way—violently electrocuted to their death with the people of the capital watching. She and the small army of soldiers she brought were untouchable. No range was too far for her to shoot them down if they dared.

The gong echoed through the silent air and bounced off the pillars before the palace. Raye led their march through the Daoland capital, followed by her parade of soldiers carrying the fifteen men nailed by their hands and feet to the wooden boards.

Their blood dried where it had poured from their chest wounds from their assaults the night before. Blood covered their faces and nightgowns. Raye had marked their foreheads with the same cross they wore around their necks.

The crowds had gathered nearby as they watched and sobbed silently at their acts of horror. The uncivilized people of Azera they always assumed them to be. The air was thick with fear of anyone who would lay hands on their holy men. The march of her soldiers drowned out any cries.

The Dao emperor stood before his palace door, waiting for them to approach him. His son stood behind him. She stood silently before him, staring intimidation and fear into him before she spoke. She wanted her actions to be settled into his view and understanding before she continued.

"Fifteen men, for the fifteen years of war I've feared while living in Azera, which is not including those I haven't feared since joining the military. I thought it was awfully kind of me," she stated factually.

He stared back blankly at her.

"I expect you count us equal after the countless you have killed. That is my compromise. If you step foot into Azera again, I will destroy your country to rubble."

The emperor started a chuckle, but she would not allow him to finish. The threats she made were not to be laughed at.

Sparks flung off and around her in large magnitude. The crowds burst into screams and chaos from their fear. Her lightning traveled up the pillars and buildings, cracking and burning them thoroughly scarred. She stopped just long enough for him to let out yells.

"You blame me for your suffering while your own emperor is the one who captured and sent me all those other Celestials in your nation to be killed. All the others like you, who claim godly power, struck down by their own emperor. What naïve imbeciles," the emperor shouted alongside a wicked laugh. How could he act in such a way when presented with her power. She must show him the true power of a Celestial—one who knew the truth of mankind.

Raye knew the Azeran emperor was no saint, but these accusations changed everything she thought she knew about him. They seemed to align with the type of emperor he was. The twinges of electricity through her body snapped and popped on her skin as her anger rose and rose.

She sent bolts that struck the emperor's body, forcing him to collapse onto the ground in shame. The plan was only to scare him. It seized his entire body and left parts of him scarred from her forever. But that was not enough.

In front of her laid the man behind all of her misery. An emperor who gets to live a lavish life, hiding behind the piles of bodies he left. A man who knows no suffering. He did not deserve it; the lack of suffering, the lavish life. He did not deserve life.

His body thumped to the ground face first. His thud echoed through the city. The Daoland emperor lay dead on the ground in a crimson pool of his own blood. That was not her plan. It was only to be a warning.

She blinked away the fear she caused herself from her lack of control.

She only needed to make them even. But that would never have been even. Death was the only thing that would make them equal in her heart, even if her mind thought it knew better.

Agony and fear rushed through the bystanders, while the emperor's son bent down to his father's body. His son, probably Raye's age, looked up at her from across the way—pale in the face.

Still covered in her light, she took a small step closer to him.

Pivoting, Raye spoke, "I shall spare you and your lineage your lives if you heed my warning, boy." She narrowed her eyes into his like he was the only one there.

"If I hear even a whisper of Azera or Hira from Daoland, I will be back before you even realize what has happened. You will sign a peace treaty and no longer occupy the land. Am I understood?" Her voice projected across the scene so everyone may witness.

His eyes wanted to falter from her, though he did not. He straightened his back and shook his head firmly in agreement.

"I understand," he stated, pain in his voice and a look of terror across his face.

A once untouched family had now been struck. Let them not make the same mistakes against Raye twice.

Raye watched as those gathered sobbed over the loss of their men. They did not even know the actual loss. Fifteen was not enough for what they had done.

She was vile; she knew. She did not care. When she turned around to exit, Jin stood there staring at her with a face she did not recognize. Did he hate her and her actions? Did he decide she had gone too far? He was a leader; he should understand when things must be done in war.

Raye did not stop to wonder and kept walking without looking back. She heard the pounding of his footsteps behind her as he followed.

She felt neither guilt nor joy.

While everyone else felt victory for her feat, she felt nothing. They did not have the knife to kill the priests; they had not witnessed their final breath. Azera had won; what else did they have to worry about?

The only person who seemed bothered was Jin. She thought the two of them quite the same; it was why he irritated her regularly. It was why they butted heads so quickly. It was why she hated him. He was exactly like her. But suddenly, he decided he was morally above her. How dare he. Jin will not complain once she brings justice to the Azeran people and removes the emperor from his throne.

Her army adored her. The people loved her. She was the savior, *their* savior. Hira was on her side. She was a god. And only a god could rid the power of the emperor.

CHAPTER TWENTY-FOUR

We are born in blood; we will die in blood.

It was written poorly across the wall in the red ink of the victim who sat below, hunched over, lifeless—some wealthy man known for his gracious contributions to his community. The community was already filled with wealthy individuals flourishing on their own. In the impoverished parts of the country, the people knew of him because of the large farm he bought in recent years. He would claim it was to help the owners who were struggling. The reality was he sat back and made a profit off their land while the workers did the laborious tasks, paying them enough to survive but not adequately compensated.

The country was too busy celebrating its newfound victorious defeat against the strongest nation in the world to notice the rebels had been gaining more and more power within the people.

Raye noticed the perfect opportunity as if it had willingly handed itself over to her. She had waited the one year of war against Daoland, and time had come for justice against their own Azeran emperor. For she had known what he had done.

She practically jumped to volunteer her team to stay down south and closely watch the rebels. The empire did not see the rebels as an actual threat. Once Raye could get her hands on them, they most certainly would.

On the side of the building, in the alleyway off the main street, the dead man remained. It appeared like the civilians turned an eye to the scene, uncaring. They sent Raye down there to eliminate any rebel outbreak in the area. Unfortunately for General Norverro, Raye had no reason to follow that order. Raye stood silently within the alleyway as she watched Finian, their leader, and his three lackeys finish their masterpiece.

They did not notice her until they had finished, as she stood in the way of their getaway plan with the soldiers now policing the streets. Panicked eyes set on the four of them as their eyes searched her entirely, surveying the situation. Dressed as a military officer, Finian's eyes went straight to the sword attached to her hip. Raye broke into a cocky smirk and a dry laugh. Lately, she had found the fear of her often humorous and enjoyable. Her laugh only confused them.

"I enjoy the slogan. Did you think of that yourself?" She gestured to the writing on the wall with her chin. *Born in blood; die in blood.*

Finian shook his head in a nod firmly at her. He was a tall, skinny man, someone she assumed grew up in starving poverty his whole life, not the definition of a fighter. She appreciated a man who found his strengths, even if they were not physical, and managed to use them to cause the havoc he wanted. His men beside him looked to him for an answer in their fear.

"Fin . . ." one of them started in a whispered cry for help. Raye's angered eyes shot to him in the ring of that name in her ears.

"If you're going to fucking arrest or kill us, just do it," Finian gritted through his teeth.

She laughed briefly. "I know you don't think that's why I'm here." She gestured her head deeper down the alley to follow her.

She made her way with slow steps further into the between. Finian watched with quiet distrust while he decided. His decision was short-lived when he saw the movement of other Azeran soldiers out of the corner of his eye who trapped them inside the alley without a way out. She only gave him the illusion of an option, and without choice, he dove deeper into the sides of the buildings, his men followed close behind.

Raye took her spot amongst her highest-ranking men, Zeki, Jin, and Ellerie. All willing to stand by her against their own country. They stood at the dead end of the alleyway, far enough off the main street and wholly blocked from regular view. Finian's calm demeanor had become scattered again at the sight of them all.

"In the simplest terms, I'd like to help you with your end goals, Finian," she claimed plainly. Raye thought over what she said, tapping her fingers on her crossed arms. "Well, actually, that's not entirely true," she started with a coy smile. "You will help *me*."

She could see the confusion across Finian's face; he did not know whether to be threatened by her, which made her giggle. As bright as she knew him to be, he had not yet caught up to the conversation.

"I'm not sure I understand," he trailed off. "Doesn't seem like you're truly asking me. It seems you already have the answer you want." He nodded at the men standing behind him. Raye narrowed her vision to only him.

"The choice is still yours, though yes, I assume the answer already. I needed to make sure you would meet with me," referring to her soldiers. "You can help me fix the brokenness of our country. You may find this a much larger task than you fathomed. I could use you greater than you can use yourself."

Finian still gave her an uneasy eye, but she already knew his answer.

Finian took Raye and her accomplices to an older abandoned part of town, where he and his group converted it into their base of operations. It was an old factory building that had started falling apart, deemed no longer safe for workers then. They left the outside decaying and covered in vines and overgrown greenery while transforming the inside into a livable environment.

"When we set up base here, we realized the two upper floors had collapsed with no easy fix, so we simply stay down here," he explained.

Finian took them through the lowest ground level. There was a mess of people and smelled like sweaty men and mold. Even so, it looked much better than the outside of the building and seemed like organized chaos. Whatever they had been doing was working well enough for them.

"And you're sure the building is safe?" Zeki asked.

"We added some extra support beams throughout each of the other floors, and it's been alright for some years now. I'm not too worried about it," Finian explained with a smile.

Raye examined the boards full of written information in the middle of the wall for all to view. It was a map of the country with pins locating each spot where they had placed a victim. One of Finian's boys stuck a new one right off the alleyway where they had just been. He wrapped a string around the pin and brought it to the information set that matched the victim.

They had managed dozens throughout the years, a slow and steady way to play the long game and remain unnoticed in their shadow work. It had worked in properly dehumanizing the elite to the regular civilians of Azera.

While Zeki and Jin stayed examining their collected information and artillery, Finian took Raye to the old manager's office on the second story. The dingy old stairs creaked with each step she took. He took her to a small room with only a desk and chairs and a map of the country displayed across it. It had no markings like the other as if he was only studying it.

"I can point out every single military camp we still have operating," Raye told him. He opened the desk drawer to pull out more pins and had her place them.

"Sit. I'm going to tell you exactly what I need you and your men to do once we make it to the capital." Raye sat in the chair across from him.

CHAPTER TWENTY-FIVE

Corruption runs through the veins of mankind.

Anala lived in a large manor full of staff to support them. The staff led Raye up the stairs and down the hall to Anala's bedroom. It had been months since the end of the Daoland war and even longer since Raye had seen her friend.

"Why did you come to my home?" Anala asked her, still shocked she was standing in front of her.

"I wanted to see you. I wanted to tell you of my plans," Raye told her, confused by her friend's hostility.

"You can't just come into my home, Raye," she whispered her anger at her.

"You're my friend, I'm sorry. I didn't think it would be such an issue. We write to each other all the time, I assumed—"

"We stopped writing as much, though. I was not expecting you to come to me unannounced," Anala scraped for an excuse.

"I don't know if I understand. We stopped talking as much because I had to go off to Daoland and win the war, An. Or did you mean afterwards when I was sent to the south to manage the towns? I did not think our friendship could dissipate so easily. I've come to you to ask you to help me save our country alongside my own army." She did not mean to be angry at her, but she was.

"I know, I'm sorry. I didn't mean that. I mean really we were friends in school, it was so long ago. I have just had other things preoccupying my time," she was trailing off, unwilling to say what she needed to.

"What? School was only three years ago, and we've spoken since then. How do you justify only being friends in school?" Raye tried to speak softer this time.

"I did not say *only* friends in school, I don't know, Raye. I've just done my time. I want to stay with my family; I can't go join you and your . . ." she paused, "My father would greatly disapprove, and I do not wish to disappoint him any further, Raye. I've found a husband, I can have everything I have wanted. I do not wish to ruin this. And I miss my sisters so much. We have a bond you could not understand."

Raye let out a sigh of air, frustrated by the words that stung, but in no mood to fight with her. She could have mentioned the brother she truly cared for, how she had found him dead in the mud, how much that had hurt her., how she could never understand that. But what was the point of an argument with a person who did not even want to fight for their friendship?

Raye would move on to bigger things, to change the country in ways that would even help Anala, while Anala remained without her. Raye's chest felt hollow, but not empty of her emotions. A strange sorrow for the person who had abandoned her.

"I understand, I'm sorry. I wouldn't want you to ruin your life for this; I'd never make you do that. You're my best friend." Raye's words came truefully.

She had a man to marry, she could finally be a wife. She finished her father's obligation and got exactly what she wanted. She no longer needed Raye for any intimate relationship. Even though it was a tactic of Raye's own, she was blind to her friend's ability to do the same—Raye was a mere stepping stone onto the thing Anala truly wanted.

Anala flashed her big, gorgeous smile at her, the one that melted Raye's heart like nothing else. Her face relaxed.

"I love you, Raye. Thank you for understanding." She folded her fingers together as though a prayer had been answered. While she did not know Anala to lie, her words felt fake. *She was so quick to write Raye off, how could she claim love?*

Raye wanted to run away and sob to herself, but she also wanted to stay and interrogate her with questions she was not sure she could handle the answers for.

"Will you continue medicine?" A question left her lips faster than her mind thought of it.

"Well, no I don't think so. Unless I have to, I guess," Anala said. Raye did not bother with more.

She wanted to grind her teeth against each other in frustration. Time ago, she could never have imagined Anala would bring her any amount of genuine anger.

Things had changed. *Had I done something wrong?* Time apart did not seem like something that would pull them apart that greatly. She had lost so many people, and if Anala no longer wanted to be the close friends they once were, she would force herself to accept it.

Raye knew that all Anala wanted was to find a husband and start a life with him; she did not understand why she would not be willing to keep her friendship where it was while she did that.

Why was a man more deserving of her than Raye was? After everything she had been through with her, the emotional labor she brought, how dare someone who would hardly know her deserve more of her simply because they were a man.

She blinked away any trace of her tears and left. If Anala no longer wanted to fight alongside her for a better country, she would not force her. Raye could not linger on relationships if they were useless to her. Anala was different, though. She loved her so deeply that it brought her physical pain at the thought of losing her.

Raye had never felt such distress over someone who had not died.

The city of Nora was lit up with excitement. Winning in an impossible war created joy throughout the city and within the palace walls. The emperor had thrown a banquet in honor of the country with all the wealthiest and most critical attendees. It had taken almost a full year to plan since Raye had actually been on the Daoland soil. The new Dao emperor had visited and made official peace with Azera and Hira. A part of Raye never thought it could truly happen.

Three years since she first entered the university, to now being the winner of a war at only twenty-four years old. She prayed that her ancestors rested peacefully from then on. Only the lost Celestials were left to avenge.

High-ranking military officials, lords, and ladies throughout the country gathered around the palace entrance, shuffling through the grand door to make their way inside. Arrays of colorful formal outfits filled the emperor's largest hall.

Within the palace walls was like its own perfect land. It did not seem as though the largest city in the country surrounded it. Within the tremendous walls were the greenest grass and trees, ideally taken care of by personal grounds staff.

Brightly colored gardens full of beautiful flowers maintained to perfection. Gorgeous trees with branches and leaves that hung low from its great height, casting shadows onto the ground. It reminded Raye of the Kryf's home, which she once called her own.

Being away, and placed into the hard realities of not only poverty but war, had her forgetting the lavish life she lived for many years. She did not find comfort in the similarities.

The palace grounds being highly guarded did not stop Raye from walking through the front door in her formal officer uniform. All high-ranking individuals had an invitation, so technically, Raye had every right. She walked through the large arched doorway, met by the palace staff attending to the visitors.

"May I take your coat, Miss?" Raye turned to the staff to her right, an older bald man with his arm stuck out.

"No, thank you. I'm not staying long," she responded. He bowed his head and stepped back from her without another word.

Raye entered the hall; the two large doors opened for her by the palace staff with a creak. Most of the room's eyes turned to her as she entered; her loose waves fell over her back and shoulders, a bright contrast against the darkness of her cape and uniform underneath.

Unbothered by the attention, her stride remained a steady pace forward. Across the room sat the Azeran Emperor Oswin on his dramatically decorated throne. Raye's teeth clenched harder at the sight of him. A vile man, casting poverty and class war, sat pretty and comfortable in his beautifully embroidered robes, practically one with his body.

Hair groomed to the perfect standard that Raye had known no man to care that deeply about. She knew his truths and secrets and would no longer allow him to sit so comfortably on his cushioned throne sitting high above all else. She would no longer allow his spectators to smile and laugh as joy surrounded him while they were by his side.

By the time she had gathered her thoughts, Raye had found herself directly in front of the emperor, with only a few soldiers next to him in between them. How easily it would have been to kill him then, Raye reminded herself kindly. However, it would be useless for all.

Raye felt the stagnant air in the room as they all glanced at her and her subsequent move to the emperor. What type of unknown soldier girl would walk toward the emperor himself? Probably one who wanted trouble. Raye could gather the room's consensus from the airy whispers that flung to her ears.

"What do you want?" One of the guards scolded her. Though the emperor only watched her as entertainment. She was sure he was somewhat aware of who she was; it would be harder for the military to keep her from him than not.

"Leave her be," Emperor Oswin spoke, the booming voice of an emperor one would imagine. Raye assumed it was a part of the royal blood they passed down. The guard straightened himself back into his position as the fear of the emperor's voice struck the back of his neck.

"Of course, one of my greatest officers should introduce herself to me," he continued. He did not seem intimidated by Raye's chilly personality. She did not expect him to.

"Rayana Tyrson." She remained upright and unbothered while quiet dramatics went through the crowds due to her lack of respect. The emperor did not even seem to notice; instead, he gave her a smile with an underlying wickedness she felt only she could see. He raised his brows, telling her to continue with whatever she had approached him for.

His casual pompousness irritated her. Every little nonchalant movement he made seemed like an intentional move of power to show the room that was in charge. He leaned his head on his hand, propped up by the arm of his throne. A slight tilt in his head to show her his interest. She was unamused.

"I am allowing you to remove yourself from the throne immediately." Raye's voice was calm and boomed across the room for all to hear easily. Over the months, her voice had transformed into the voice of someone who controlled the nation. Someone who was the strongest in the room. She was no longer someone who kept the strongest parts of her hidden in the corners of the room and the darkest shadows of the night, out of view of all. They would all soon come to light.

Emperor Oswin spread a more prominent smile as the crowd sought justice for Raye's words. The only thing protecting her in their eyes was that the emperor waved them to hold back so he could continue speaking to her. She waited for his response, which she knew was coming, but she had to wait for his deep laughter to stop pouring out of his mouth.

"And why is that Miss Rayana?" he asked, humor in his tone.

Raye maintained an unthreatening demeanor, remaining unbothered by the emperor's attitude; her arms lay at her sides underneath her cloak. She had not allowed her anger to be released yet.

"You have driven the country not only to a magnitude of poverty and class divide unlike anything ever seen in history, but you have somehow managed to make rules and laws inclining towards sexism more so than ever in the last few decades. The only few who benefit from it are," she paused and let out a dry laugh, "sitting in the room with you. The elite few you allow to do as they please—same as you. If you wanted, I could list the actual crimes you and your friends have committed against the nation of your people." Raye lifted her eyebrows as if asking, though she knew he would disagree.

He was no longer humorous with himself, but visibly angry with her through the irritated movements of his mouth.

"Who the fuck do you even think you are here?" the emperor asked her.

"I suppose now—I am your enemy."

He released a dry laugh at her egregiousness, thinking she had no real fight against him, even if her statements brought out his anger. The same guard as before spoke up again, angered by Raye's accusations.

"How dare you pledge some sort of war against the emperor himself?" he shouted. "Your little quarter of the military has nothing against the remaining empire army and our Hiran allies, you fool."

The emperor let out a genuine laugh at his guard's statement, rubbing his chin with his fingers.

"But she has the Hiran army, not I." The guard's face turned to confusion from his statement. "She is the one who retrieved the Hirans; they follow her, not me. It seems you brought them here on your terms. It seems you have had your hand in every plan for quite some time. Sat waiting, playing the long silent game." He was not worried, by the looks of him. "I suppose I have nothing else to do besides kill you in here then." He shrugged his shoulders as his men poured forward at her and out from every door in the room, as he had gathered them all in the hall while they spoke. She could see now they were playing the same game, finally.

Her arms flung out to the side, her cloak still hanging over them until she lit up the room brighter than ever with the light of her god. Unlike the rest of the room, the emperor appeared unimpressed by her sudden abilities, shouting in fear of the Celestial monster in front of them.

Her cloak hovered over her arms, and her hair floated around her due to the electric energy she was giving off. Immediately, she attacked the guards nearest to her with ease. She sent the shock directly into their hearts, stopping them instantly. Bodies dropped to the ground with hard thuds all around her, while the static noise she gave off drowned the screams of the guests.

She had gained such control of her element since she was young that it moved around the room like liquid. It differed from the lightning bolts in the sky on a stormy day. Her own was a part of her body entirely, an extension she controlled to an exact amount, flowing through and around her like her own blood.

It only took little hand and arm movements to kill dozens of guards within the room, but she needed to work slowly. It was not about killing them all; she needed to leave the palace. They had her trapped in from all exits, which only meant their deaths. While the brave guards attempted to get anywhere near her with the tips of their swords, the elongated metal only allowed her to be more creative with her slaughter.

Raye's fingers spread wide with her arms out, allowing the flow of her lightning to travel up the swords around her, wrapping and twirling around the blades in a beautiful display of vicious light. Once it reached the hands of the soldiers, they all instinctively dropped their swords out of pain as she burnt the beauty of each swirling light into their skin until it made it throughout their bodies and killed them.

The room quickly stank of burnt flesh. That, and watching their first violent death in front of them, caused the remaining bystanders to vomit up the food from their stomachs, only adding smells to the room.

It seemed the military officers knew better than to jump into the battle against Raye, or the shock of the young girl they served alongside revealing her godly power to them stunned them in their places. It was easier for her if they stayed back. She did not need to see Zion's face after all he had done and given her during her time there. He should have known nothing was ever so simple with her Master Sai.

Raye decided she had done enough against them and was ready to leave. She ran toward the exit shoulder, checking and dodging any incoming attacks or anyone in her way, not even bothering to kill them as no one was quick enough to lay a slice on her. The guards attempted to follow her as she ran out of the exit.

She was a much faster runner than any of them with their heavy weapons. She made her way to the wall of the palace grounds, grabbed hold of the vines and greenery that covered it, and hoisted herself up by her upper body strength. Flinging her right leg over the wall, she straddled it while looking down at all the soldiers that ran with all their might to her. After catching her breath, she swung her other leg over and dropped herself onto the ground.

The lake was just south of the palace grounds, where one of Finian's men sat in a boat waiting to take her home. She jumped into the boat, causing it to rock a little as the man started paddling as quickly as possible across the lake until they got sucked away downstream by the connecting river that would take them back south quicker than any chance the empire would have to follow.

Raye did not look back once; she knew no one was following.

Without a second thought, a new war had begun.

CHAPTER TWENTY-SIX

The shadows of war.

Finian let the others in through a second-story window on the back part of the palace. Zeki weaved his hands to create a platform for Jin and one of Finian's boys, Arlo, to climb up through the window. They each stepped into Zeki's hand and pulled themselves through to the second story.

Zeki held onto the stones that stuck out with his hands, positioned his feet against the wall, and climbed up the wall. He grabbed onto the windowsill and pulled himself up and through the window with a grunt.

He found the others standing in an empty spare bedroom. Finian wore the palace guard's uniform that he removed from a man. Finian opened the door a crack to view the scene outside. The hall was empty, and the four of them made their way out. Finian led them down the hall when they heard the commotion begin.

Raye's distraction had begun. They could hear the feet stomping as they ran towards the main banquet hall where the emperor sat. The four set off quickly toward the emperor's daughter's room before their distraction ended.

Finian motioned with his hands that the door at the end of the hall was their target. Zeki opened the door slowly so as not to make a sound. When his eyes peered through the crack, he saw the back of a woman's head. She sat in the corner, her face facing a window away from them, her long brown hair fell down her back completely loose. The room smelled of rich perfumes that hit Zeki's nose the further he opened the door.

With the other two watching silently while Finian watched the hall, he entered the room quietly. He moves one small, gentle step at a time. He could see the beginning of her pale face as she read the book in her hands.

If she had not been focused on it, she could have spotted him in her peripheral vision. He continued each step until his right foot hit the wrong floor panel. The ground made the slightest squeak possible, which brought the princess out of her concentration, and she turned around.

Zeki's hands shook. Before she had the chance to take another breath, Zeki dashed at her in a quick move. His hand covered her mouth instantly, while his other arm wrapped around her as she panicked.

Her body attempted to flail out of his grasp, and her fingers clawed at his hand that covered her mouth. Her big brown doe eyes bulged in a massive panic that sank Zeki's heart.

Jin ran over, gagging her properly the second Zeki released his hand and bound her wrists together. Zeki threw her body over his shoulder while her screams muffled through the gag. He ground his teeth and swallowed his shame.

They needed to leave before Raye did.

Thumping down the stairs to make it to the first level, they find themselves caught between their exit by a single guard. The young palace guard only had a mere look of confusion on his face, unaware of anything happening.

Without a thought, Jin sliced his throat in a bloody and quick death before they exited through a side door on the main level. The boy's instinct led his hands to wrap around the painful wound, instantly soaking his arms as the blood pumped quickly out of his body. His face turned a quick pale as he choked on the ground in a bloody pile.

Finian and Arlo stopped in their tracks momentarily by the shock of how effortlessly Jin had executed someone. No hesitation in his mind made him second guess, killing the man.

Zeki saw their anxiety, but they had no time to worry about moral decisions in war. Something that made it very clear they had never been soldiers.

"Let's fucking go," Zeki barked at them, waving them to get through the door. They snapped out of their shock and followed them to the outer wall of the palace grounds.

Jin sat on top of the wall, straddling it, while Zeki passed the princess to him. He grabbed her and hopped onto the ground on the other side. Once over, they ran back to their boats. Zeki sat in the boat with Jin, Finian, and the princess and started rowing them across Lake Eery. Arlo stayed low inside the other boat as he waited for Raye.

Each leg bound to a leg of the chair and her hands tied behind her back, she looked up at Raye with fury in the forefront of her glare. Raye knew she was attempting to hide her fear of what they might do to her.

Her dark, frizzy hair hung over her lean limbs. Her face was pale, not necessarily by nature, but due to the lack of harsh sun upon her skin. Not a blemish on her smoothness. Raye almost felt jealous.

"Hello, Princess," Raye said. "I'm not here to hurt you. We need your help."

She scoffed at her dramatically as her whole body flinched in annoyance.

"Then why the fuck was I stolen from the palace, tied up, and tossed around like a piece of shit?" she exclaimed. Raye maintained her normal plainness, which only seemed to make her angrier.

"All things considered, they were quite gentle," Raye responded coldly, with a raised brow.

"How so?" she questioned.

"You sit perfectly fine within the beautiful corridor of your home, a literal fucking palace. Your country is suffering beyond what you could ever comprehend."

"It's not my country," she trailed off. Raye squatted down in front of her so she could look up at her.

"It can be if you want it, Princess," she said. The princess looked down into Raye's light eyes. The darkness under her eyes was one of someone who did not sleep well. "It is your birthright, no matter what your father decides. I will bring you the throne if you are willing."

Raye spoke gentler to her. "I'm sure being the eldest daughter of the throne and being trapped inside your room with nothing of your own is not how you'd like to live your life."

"What would I need to do?" she asked quietly.

"Change your father's darkness, Princess."

They remained in silence while confusion and pain washed over the girl's face. Raye only remained how she was, comfortable in the quiet.

"Calista. That's my name."

Calista cautiously walked around the upper floor of the old factory base. She touched nothing as Raye took her to a room she could have.
"It's quite dirty in here," she told Raye. Raye rolled her eyes and scoffed automatically at her.
"Feel free to clean up, then." Raye's eyes shot at her like daggers. Calista swallowed down her fear with a large gulp.
"Sorry," she looked away awkwardly. "I've only been inside the palace gates." Her voice was like warm honey. Of course, it matched the poise and beauty of the rest of her. Raye wanted to grind her teeth at the sound of her.
Raye pushed the squeaky door open to reveal the tiny dust-covered room. The room was empty except for a single chair. Calista winced at the sight.
"I'll get you stuff to sleep with. I know it's not great, but the door locks from inside," Raye explained.
Calista entered the room. "Why does that matter?" She examined the room closer.
"For your safety," Raye said, obviously. "This place is full of men we don't know too well." Calista shook her head slightly. Raye was not sure if she even understood.
"I'll clean it up a little, and it should be fine. Thank you," she said.
Calista caught Zeki by the corner of her eye. She darted out of her room past Raye to grab him. Her fingers wrapped around his arm in an urge to stop him in his tracks. His head whipped around to find her.
"Zeki! Could you get me some stuff to sleep in my room?" Calista asked, dolled-eyed. Raye's face twisted into disgust. Zeki's eyes darted back to Raye's irritated face.
"Uh, yeah, of course."
Calista twisted into a big, sweet smile. "Thank you so much," she exclaimed. She ran off in search of rags for cleaning.
Raye stepped closer to Zeki, arms crossed. He grinned at her in anticipation.
"I fucking told her I'd get her shit already," Raye snapped. Zeki raised his shoulders in innocence with a laugh.
"Why'd she ask me then? Didn't think you'd deliver, I guess," he said through his grin.
"You know why she did it."

Zeki raised a brow. "Because she has a thing for me?" He leaned against the wall and flashed his stupid smile at her. Raye recoiled from his words.

"What? I assumed because you're a man and she didn't respect me," Raye snapped. "You think she has a fucking crush on you? You're so full of yourself anymore."

His smile dropped when he shook his head. "You're so oblivious." Zeki rested his head on the wall his body leaned on. Raye snarled at his rudeness.

M. NEVILLS

CHAPTER TWENTY-SEVEN

*They claim that grief is love,
but I think mine is guilt.*

Raye sat on the cold ground, staring into the brightness of the fire before her. With each day growing colder at their base, they found themselves gathered by warm fires every night.

Her mind was zoned out of her body, and she could only put her energy into making sure she was breathing. Zeki's hand pressed firmly against her back in a comforting way she did not mind.

His touch brought her comfort. Raye's eyes felt like tears could fall out unwillingly at any moment with him. Zeki's head ducked, so his lips almost touched her ear while she watched the fire flicker.

She could see his dark figure out of the corner of her eye. His big brown eyes looked at her as gently as they always did. His low, soft voice started to whisper words into her ear, but she did not understand what he said in her daze.

She blinked herself back into her mind and turned to face him and ask him what he said. Within a blink, Zeki went from the soft skin of his face touching against her cheek to sitting, leaning forward, spooning his soup into his mouth.

Before she realized he was missing right before her, she asked aloud, "What?" her voice coated in a raspy tiredness. He was not there; he was never right there whispering in her ear as she had known him just to be. She would only blame her lack of sleep and exhaustion.

"Me?" Zeki's eyes perked up at her from his hunched-over stature. Raye was snapped back into reality.

She only misheard. She decided she should try to eat the food she held in her lap.

"Never mind, sorry." She pressed her lips together and chewed them with her teeth.

It was obnoxious and confusing to be too tired to function properly. She reminded herself that it could be the stress getting to her, pushing any anxiety she had about it to relieve herself of some stress. She scooped a spoonful of the watered-down soup they had for dinner as the sky set for another cold night.

The breeze ruffled the branches above them, no longer full of bright leaves. Each day, they woke with less warmth than before. Winter would be a rough battle, but stopping their success now would only allow the empire to regain what they had lost. Raye could not let that happen. She would instead force her army through winter and hope the weakest could survive.

As quickly as she used to stand up for the littlest, weakest soldier, the darkness she allowed in had eroded her own heart. The numbers grew higher while her care fell lower. People died in the war; she had always known that. They would die for their country's turnaround into greatness and equality they had never known before.

She planned to make it through the south's most challenging parts of winter and continue north after.

Raye bound Zeki's hand in makeshift insulation for gloves with a poor attempt. She had not learned the proper way to bandage a person, which might have helped her through it. Her only goal was to make sure Zeki did not get frostbite. She covered her work in a mitten to keep the heat in.

"It almost makes me wish An was here," Zeki paused. "Though you'd hardly pay me any mind if she were." He looked up from where he sat at Raye with his dark eyes. His exhales puffed into the cold air around them.

"I don't, fuck her," Raye spoke quietly.

"Didn't realize you were that angry with her about not coming with us."

Raye scoffed at his accusation. "I'm not upset about that. She's been quiet since before the war ended, all because she's with some man now. I just saw our friendship as more than that, I guess." Raye focused on wrapping Zeki's second hand, ignoring his big eyes staring at her.

"Maybe she just has different goals than you," Zeki offered.

"Quit trying to play mediator. She has become a complete ghost toward me. After everything, that's it?" she spoke quietly, her voice covered in sadness.

Zeki shrugged. "Your grudges . . ." he shook his head as he spoke.

With each town they made it through, they climbed further north. The empire did not care about the smaller towns and villages in the middle west of the country, so they did not have many of their soldiers occupying them already.

Raye quickly gained access, slaughtering all of their men and allowing the townspeople to join her cause if they wished. It only grew her army. In her Celestial display of light, the people saw her as a god of hope for their rights.

Without the emperor able to take the southern farm's food supplies, everyone gained access to food under her control. To see the surplus for herself that he would sell off, leaving his people starving and at high prices, she could see his true greed for money.

She knew the emperor would save most of his army for their main base in Norsan, though. It held the stockpiles of all their military equipment and the country's most extensive and substantial base.

He would care more about ammunition than feeding his soldiers. The easy defeats meant nothing until they got a hold of Norsan.

The journey up north would prove the easiest part of their future. With winter on its ascend, there was no more time to waste on towns and villages the emperor had no care for.

M. NEVILLS

CHAPTER TWENTY-EIGHT

Those who persist in sin shall face my wrath.

Norsan held the same power as it did when Raye first entered the city. The entire city built up upon the first disaster the Daos had caused them. A stone palace of military grade.

The entire town was empty. A silence Raye had not seen ever before. They knew she was coming for it; of course they did. She did not expect otherwise. They were no match for her abilities and her army, though. No one in the world was a proper match for her abilities, the Daos ensured that.

To an outsider, it all seemed like it would be over quickly and easily for them. Raye knew better than to judge a situation based on appearances, though. The emperor had done his job longer than she had been alive.

She was sure he had tricks that no one knew about. He could have been hiding a new weapon from her or even created one in the months she gained control over the rest of the country.

Most of her army remained at the camp they set up along the border. Raye and a small group entered the quiet city of Norsan with caution. She was sure any weapon he might have would mainly be against her. She could handle whatever it was. There was no reason to drag her army through when they would only be a hazard.

Raye entered through the main gate of the stone fortress to find it empty of an army. Almost empty.

Raye's body swayed back and forth as she stood still in disbelief. This could not be real life. She prayed it was not, but it was. And this was the war she chose.

Her stomach churned. Something was not right, and she beckoned her soldiers to leave. Zeki wanted to argue, but she ordered him away from the fortress. The emperor had gained a weapon more significant than anything she could have thought possible.

✦ ✦ ✦

Anala stood tall and unaltered across the way from her. Alone, she stood with no army to back her. That could only mean the situation was worse than Raye could have imagined. Anala was not there to simply speak to her. To convince her to stop her motive. No. It would never be that simple in Raye's life.

She could feel the tears forming in her eyes. *Don't fucking cry, you bitch, not now.* Anala had stabbed a knife through Raye's heart and killed her. Why would she do that to her? Why would she leave her only to fight for the other side? As far as Raye knew, she was only ever a medic and not a great fighter. Why was she sent there?

"What do you want?" Raye shouted to her, a voice of anger she never thought Anala would have directed at her.

"You need to stop, Raye." Anala's voice stood firm and projected confidently across the way. Raye scoffed at her.

"And what the fuck are you gonna do about it?" Raye screamed at her. Raye's arms shot out widely at her sides, practically begging her to hit her. A part of her wanted Anala to love her still and be willing not to hurt her, but the more significant part knew her being there already told her all she needed to know.

Was it always easy for people to betray someone they cared deeply about? Or was the love for her not as deep as Raye's was for Anala? Had I been so blind this entire time?

Anala's face read that she genuinely wanted to do what she was about to, but to Raye, everything she did seemed like a cheap facade she would not fall for. Anala would not have come there unless she was willing to do whatever the emperor told her.

Anala's entire body lit up in flames. How interesting this had become.

Raye remained unbothered and only allowed her eyebrows to fly up, intrigued. She was dying inside, but if she could manage one thing, it would be an emotionless lie. Hiding things was all she was used to.

Anala stood covered in her flames, expecting Raye's scared or shocked emotion, but she received none of that. Raye flashed a cocky grin as she stuck out an arm and covered it in the powerful electrical fire of the sky.

Her lightning had become more powerful than ever imagined, and her control had significantly grown. The sound was much louder than her crackles of fire, and the snaps and pops filled up the entire courtyard of the military base. Raye was unbothered by her threat, but Anala's flames lessened when she saw the power Raye displayed. Raye could see the shock in Anala's eyes, she was expecting this level of power from Raye.

I guess we both had some secrets.

Even Anala could tell that Raye had mastered her element with the control and power she showed without even a flinch of her trying with her one arm. Raye controlled enough lightning around her arm at once that the bright white light completely lit up the entire shadowy courtyard.

Anala thought she could have an advantage over Raye, as she was practically a non-fighter compared to her. Instead, Raye planned to make a fool of her.

Raye took off running toward Anala as she still stood in shock. She would get no special treatment from her if Anala wished to be her enemy; she would be her enemy.

Raye sent a powerful punch right at her head, still surrounded by her lightning. Anala got herself together and quickly threw herself to the side, dodging her attack. Raye's fist slammed into the stone brick wall, leaving a dent and burn from her punch. Her knuckles bled, but she felt nothing. She was a god.

There were significant differences between Anala and Raye. Raye would always confidently attack first. Anala could not keep up. She feared Raye, and Raye could see that, which would only make Raye fight better.

Anala was only running away from Raye the best she could, shooting her balls of fire at her whenever she had the chance. Anala thought keeping her away would help her fight against her. If only she knew Raye could have killed her from any distance with her bolts . . . though she was secretly afraid to.

Anala had made her way up the stairs, now the two of them at the top of the outer wall. Anala ran towards the giant tower in front of the base that stood over the water. Raye wanted to hurt her, but she did not know if she could kill her. Maybe she could injure her and take her back to speak with her.

No, she wouldn't. Her entire being wanted to kill her, except for her fucking aching heart. If only she could rip it out.

The two got to the top of the tower, now standing above all else in the town, high in the air. Raye assumed she had a plan of some sort but did not know what it was. They stood on top of the tower together—trapped.

"This will be the last chance I give you—stop. Whatever Emperor Oswin has done to scare you, I can protect you from him," Raye claimed. Anala's face read disbelief with her furrowed brow.

"I have a family, Raye!" Anala cried out. "He'll hurt them; this isn't just about me. You can't—you haven't—protected everyone. I have people I actually care about."

Raye watched her silently for a moment while she drank in Anala's desperation. Anala's big dark eyes begged into Raye's soul while her mouth twisted from the pain of her own words. Raye had people she cared about. Anala no longer understood her; everything she had done was for others. Every choice she made was about saving the greater good and preventing hundreds from suffering.

But, how quickly one's love can turn to hate.

Raye shot her with a single bolt of lightning. Anala yelped out in pain as the bolt electrocuted her, forcing her onto her knees.

Her body collapsed onto itself as her muscles fought against each other. It was less than anything Raye had ever done to herself accidentally; she knew she would be fine. Raye expected she would have longer before she broke out of it and brought herself back together until she jumped up and ran full force into her out of nowhere. Her plan seemed to be to kill them both.

Anala tackled Raye with her entire body, sending them off of the highest point of the military base. How beautiful it had once been when Raye stepped foot through the gate. A powerful aura was conveyed from the building.

They did not deserve such a fortress. When Raye fell off the tower, Anala clung to her body still, and she could see the entire base from a completely different view. It honestly looked like a castle. A castle that she no longer belonged in.

The two fell through the sky until Raye grabbed the wall's top ledge with her entire upper body. She tried to pull herself back up and over the wall until the sharp pains whipped up her leg. She dropped down to only her hands, holding herself up.

When she looked down at her bleeding leg, she found Anala clinging to her leg with one hand as the two hung off the edge over the harshest part of the ocean's waves, crashing into the bottom side of the base. Raye could not swim; if she could, it would not be well enough to get herself out of the intensity below her.

The pain swirled up her leg further. Anala was burning her leg with the hand holding tightly onto her. If Anala were to be sent to the harsh ocean, she would take Raye with her. Anala sent a flame up and around Raye's leg, causing an even bloodier scene. She looked up at her with a face Raye had not known before.

Anala's job was to kill Raye, and she was determined to do that—even at the risk of losing her own life. Anala planned to serve her country well. She would not let her claws out of Raye's leg and only sent more searing pain up Raye's ankle and calf, burning her flesh.

Raye could only smell the putridness of her flesh being cooked. The pain settled in so badly, Raye could not help but let out a cry of pain. Her hands attempted to maintain hold of the wall, but between the two bodies she held up and the agony of her leg, she only wanted to grab it out of comfort and release the wall.

They both knew there was no other option in their situation. Anala was only trying to get her last jabs in, probably hoping to make sure she would drown in the ocean, unable to swim away.

Raye's fingers slowly slipped off, raw from the painful stone wall, until she could no longer hold them. The two fell into the crashing waves, dipping below the surface quicker than they fell through the sky. The sea sucked Raye and Anala up into its undertow. She did not even get the chance to take a deep breath before being quickly plunged into the water.

It took her down quickly. Further and further, the light of the surface faded away, heading down into the ocean's darkness. Anala was nowhere in her surrounding area. Raye did not care about her anymore. How fast pure love can turn to pure hatred when that person chooses something else over you, especially after only choosing them yourself.

Raye belonged at the bottom of the ocean, she thought. Deprived of all light, only surrounded with shadows. While her mind was still awake, she enjoyed her sink to the bottom; she deserved it.

The shackles around her ankles drug her down with the despair they carried, deeper and deeper to the place she belonged. The blurry vision of the remaining light faded; the darkness could eat her whole with a single gulp.

The loneliness she consumed and almost enjoyed surrounded her there. Her chest ached with the pain of betrayal, the darkness shining a light on her reality. Drowning would be a painful death, she knew, but maybe she deserved it. The pain stopped bothering her altogether there. She could barely feel the sting of salt water on her burned leg.

Anala was always the only person in the world who could make a terrible mistake and leave Raye feeling guilty. Guilt in her gut that could last an eternity.

CHAPTER TWENTY-NINE

I cling with my claws.

The feeling returned to her body; eyes still dark. A hard pressure built up inside her chest. The drowning water she could imagine in her lungs as the pain returned to her. Her chest felt like it was being crushed.

Ever so conscious, her eyes flung open from the shock of pain. They opened to Zeki's lips pressed firmly against hers while he shut her nose and blew a deep breath into her. When his eyes reopened to see her awake, he stopped.

The salty burn inched up her throat quickly enough that she could not react, and she started to choke on everything attempting to come up. Her hands wanted to cling to her throat as if it might help the pain of her breathlessness. Her body arched in pain as she tried to get it up and out of her mouth. She felt like that moment lasted forever.

As quickly as it started, Zeki grabbed her body and rolled her onto her side. He pushed back the wet hairs that clung to her face as she vomited the seawater into the sand right beside him. His hand lingered on her cheek in an attempt to comfort her. Raye found comfort in nothing at that moment.

Once her body had forced out everything but air from her lungs, her eyes fell as heavy as ever. The last thing she saw was Zeki hovering above her in worry. His wet clothes clung to various parts of his torso as water beads dripped off his nose onto Raye's body. Zeki had successfully saved her; all she could do was drift and flutter in and out of a conscious state and watch.

Her heavy eyes fought with her mind. She only wanted to stay awake and accept the comfort Zeki was so willing to offer. To lie on the uncomfortable beach while sand stuck to the entire side of her face. Raye went dark again.

Her head now laid against a warm body covered in damp clothing. Her body bounced up and down as he walked with her in his arms. Raye could feel Zeki's heartbeat. It seemed to beat quickly, probably out of worry for her life. She hated that she had him worrying about her. Though she always seemed to escape death, he need not worry.

Zeki carried her back with his arms wrapped around her legs and ribs as if he were holding a child. His arms felt so warm to her as she shivered from the cold water. His body warmed up quickly—she was quite jealous as her cold skin clung to him. She felt his fingers grip her body tightly as if she was going to be snatched away. She did not deserve him.

The next time she awoke was to Jin's hands brushing against her skin. A faint blue light lit up the dark tent she lay in. The light surrounded his fingers as he healed the inside of her body. She could see Zeki's watchful eye on Jin through her blurry vision as he touched her.

Raye stared into the void of her nothingness in silence. She sat on the outskirts of the camp, facing the dark wooded area. She knew her team worried about her, mainly Zeki, as he always did. The days blended in meaningless agony. She had a wound even Jin or any Hiran could not heal. She replayed every second she and Anala spent together, attempting to find an answer for her betrayal.

Zeki sat beside her as she stared further into the woods in Norsan's general direction. She felt his presence next to him, though she did not look.

"I don't know if I can do it, Ze," she spoke softly. He had not heard the softness in her voice before. The softness was a sense of defeat. It shocked him for his friend to sound in such a way.

"I think you can probably do anything," he told her.

"I don't know about this." He put a hand on her shoulder to turn her body towards him.

"Fuck Anala. She didn't just abandon us, Raye. She's fighting for the other side. She's fighting for people who don't even respect her as a human," he said.

"Most of me hates her so much right now," Raye spoke slowly; her mind found the words. "But right now, I'd be less sad if she died. How could she do it? I thought we were everything to each other." She stared with large, upset eyes at Zeki. He did not have any words to take away her pain. He pulled her into his chest and wrapped his arms around her. The only thing he had to offer her.

Her face turned to the side, facing the dark woods again. She swore she saw the dark shadows move quickly in the corners of her eyes. It was like her mind was leaking out of her body. Zeki's heartbeat thumped in her ear as a constant sound.

"Calista said her father doesn't typically spend time in his bedroom but in his observatory. So that's probably where you'll find—" Zeki explained before being cut off.

"I didn't realize you were all that close with Calista now," Raye scoffed at him, jerking her head off of him. Zeki rolled his eyes.

"I'm not, but she's not our fucking prisoner; I talk to her sometimes." Raye crossed her arms with a shrug. "I guess."

"What?" Zeki sighed at her.

"You're supposed to be my friend. Mine," she hissed.

"What the fuck are you talking about?" he mumbled. "Look at you all jealous. I can't have other friends now?"

"So, you are friends then?"

"Dear gods, Raye." His hand rubbed against his face.

"What?" She bit the insides of her cheek while her nostrils flared uncontrollably waiting for his answer. Zeki sighed loudly once again.

"Never thought you'd have so much insecurity." His light laughter filled the room.

"It's not fucking funny," she whined. He flashed a grin toward her shown in the moonlight.

"I think it is." He raised his brow. Raye hated even showing him the slight jealousy she craved over him. After years of knowing each other, she would let it slip out every once in a while. He seemed to enjoy it more than he would admit to her.

"Don't worry about it, alright? I'm all yours, no matter who I talk to." He extended an arm around her shoulders to embrace her again. Raye pushed him off.

✦ ✦ ✦

The soldiers grew thicker the further east they went. The emperor would put most of his protection on himself.

The swords swung high and low, clashing against each other. Raye's team had become a mix of trained soldiers and civilians willing to fight for her. She attempted to keep the untrained back further in hopes of less loss. The military wanted them slaughtered, though. The empire's soldiers ripped apart the volunteers. Raye could not save everyone.

The civilians of the town were still in their homes while the two sides fought against each other. Houses could be lit on fire from the bombs or Raye's ability. It was not the place for her to use it; there was too much to catch the flames.

A battle ax her team had found inside the Norsan fortress had become her new weapon. She had missed the physical act of violence. Hands-on the hilt, the sizeable, sharp blade felt like it sliced through anything, anyone. It only took her two swings to cut her enemy's torso in half.

The same way she chopped wood in the wintertime for constant fires. She swung the ax upon the soldiers' heads like a log in one strike. They were so close to the capital.

She did not waste time cleaning up the town of their massacre, for it was not her problem now. They continued forward to allow time to set up a camp on the city's outskirts.

So close to the final enemy. So close to victory. Raye could taste it on her tongue. She felt it in her bones. That would be their final battle. It was their final battle until they had it all. The country was theirs to place Calista on the throne. Raye wanted to do something she had not done in a long time.

Raye stepped away from the camp to head toward Lake Eery. She slipped her shoes off and rolled her good pant leg up before stepping into the entrance of the lake. The breeze brushed her hair across her face. She released the two ties that held her hair pulled back and braided to let her hair flow entirely into the wind. She stared into the beauty of nature in front of her. Her eyes closed, and she heard rustling from the wind. The fishy lake water smell filled her nostrils.

Her chin tipped up to allow her face to soak up the sun. She prayed to her gods. She prayed her graciousness to them.

CHAPTER THIRTY

Every choice I make is me; maybe I'm not as good as I think.

Zeki lay on the ground across from her inside their small tent. He was in deep thought and unaware.

"Something wrong?" Raye asked him. He turned to his side gently to face her.

"Do you think we will die tomorrow?" he asked.

"I think I'll die every day," she replied. She rolled over to lie on her side and fully faced him. "I no longer let it linger."

"I wish I wrote to my family more," regret written on his face. Raye paused before deciding if she should speak her mind.

"I don't regret anything, I think," she stated. Zeki raised a brow at her. "I can't change anything I did in the past, so there's no reason to let it muddle my mind with regret. Any hauntings I've had grow to be my friends are no longer an enemy I battle with."

Zeki let out a dry chuckle at her. "I wish I had none."

"What are your regrets? Anything we can fix tonight?" she whispered to him. Zeki smiled at her, a sad smile compared to the old charming ones he used to give out so quickly. Raye feared she had broken all her friends.

Zeki's hand brushed the side of her head and tucked her wild hair behind her ear. His hand lingered on her. His deep eyes stared into hers while his fingers twirled in her hair casually.

How could he look into her eyes, so full of hatred and violence, and still give her the softness of himself? Could she continue to drag her friend through her darkness? How far was she willing to rip him toward herself?

✦ ✦ ✦

"Maybe you don't have to kill her, Raye," Jin attempted to suggest. He had known the secret weight Anala held in Raye's heart. A deep and heavy burden. He had not known the hatred it had turned into.

"I will do what I must, Jin. That's the end of it," she scolded him. It felt unlike him to wish well on an enemy—even one that was once a friend of hers. Jin did not take her attitude well when he only meant kindness. He stormed off from her to check the area before they were all sent into battle. Raye knew the Azeran army would be waiting for her own on the main road from where they stood. Raye also knew Anala would be waiting for her inside the city.

Once the hours had passed and Jin had not returned, Raye's chest tightened with anxiety. She knew in her mind the truth before she genuinely accepted it. As much anger as she held for him, Jin had changed the course of history alongside her in exchange for nothing. He was the selfless human she once was so long ago. Seeing him so much like her and having turned out to be that person put pain in her chest, she admitted to no one.

That was why it pained her so deeply when she saw him.

His decapitated head stood stuck on top of a pole in the middle of the street before the city. His pale face had lost even more color, and his hair fell messily around his face loosely, not pulled back in his usual late style.

Old memories she was not aware of had flooded her mind. The old and the new flashed between each other, and it was hard to know what she was living at that moment. The victims' heads stuck about the streets of her home. She suddenly remembered crawling out of the rubble to find the village once filled with living, breathing, Gestige left only with death. They displayed the bodies as prizes they had won or a threat to anyone who entered the old haven. She recognized the predicament Jin was in, as she had once seen the men of her hometown in the same, violated even after death. Anala and the empire were no different from the Daos.

Raye thought she might cry at the disgusting sight of her ally, but she did not. Instead, it felt as though something sucked the air out of her body entirely. As if made of stone, she lost all control of her body's movement.

"What the fuck..." Raye whispered aloud. Before her legs attempted to give out on her, Zeki grabbed her from behind and gently lowered her to the ground in her collapse. Her body started to shake.

"How the fuck could she do this?" Raye cried.

"You don't know it was An," Zeki held Raye in his chest as she panicked.

"Oh, it was her." Raye's eyes bulged, her jaw clenched, while her nostrils flared. A scoff was forced out of her throat.

"I can't believe I ever believed her to be soft and kind. She is none of that. She's exactly like me. She is still on their side, Ze. She doesn't care about any of us," she raged. Zeki tried to calm her with gentle hands, but she would not allow it. Her rage consumed her.

The breeze brushed Jin's hair to the side. Raye stood up, and as her fury burst out, a dark lightning storm rolled into the sky above them. The grey clouds took over the sky quickly, swirling around her as their source. Zeki and her army stepped away as sparks of light began to fly off her uncontrollably.

The thumping began as they marched to their location. They marched forward on the main street for their battle against them while Raye would kill any of the fearful soldiers without guilt. She unleashed her abilities with a strength she had not before. The light blinded all around. She shot the trees, the buildings, and any soldier who fell too close.

Raye screamed out as she let out her rageful power onto the unsuspecting enemies. Crackling filled the ears of everyone, unable to hear the shouts and screams. Scorched and stabbed by the flames of the sky, the bodies fell quickly. Raye's forward stride did not stop. Lightning flung off of her, striking down anyone in her vicinity.

The two enemies clashed against each other, their swords striking metal with loud clangs. Raye's soldiers held back, continuing their battle, while Raye sought out her true enemy. The position of Raye's soldiers caused the empire's own to step over the bodies of their comrades.

M. NEVILLS

CHAPTER THIRTY-ONE

To be woman is to be god.

The wind picked up, rushing against anything in its path. Signs on the buildings flipped back and forth with a sway, and the air became chilly, even in the height of summer. Those in the street got an instant shudder from the cold. Above, the dark grey clouds started coming over the town quickly with the wind. The sky swirled in various shades of grey above the city.

The thunder followed shortly, rumbling the streets and buildings from the impact. Something was coming, not just a storm. The people could feel the energy shift in the air. Some shared looks of worry, and others watched the sky as the sun sucked behind clouds of darkness. The air was tense and uneasy, and civilians slowly entered buildings as the darkness approached them.

The silent mass understanding—Death was coming.

The dark clouds loomed high in the air directly above Raye, swirling with each step she took. Like the start of a tornado that would never form, she was in the end. Within the clouds, sparks of light flew about. A bright mix of blue and white light flung about in the sky, none yet reaching the grounds of the city. As Raye made her way into the inner city, she became more visible to those around her. Her eyes had darkened with sparks of blue lightning-like marks inside.

Tiny sparks and lightning pops snapped in the air around her body. They flung off of her, lighting up the space with each spark. Her clothes had practically become rags, sleeves, and lower pant legs ripped off in shreds. The burns at the bottom of her leg were sketched in detail, and the deep scars given to her by herself were both visible. The lightning pulsed around like veins within her iridescent skin. Her usually maintained hair now fell in a loose, free golden wave so full of electrical energy that it lay inches from her body, floating about in the air. Strands of hair flew mindlessly in the air like it was swaying in the bathtub full of water. Her fingers twitched with every closer step in search of her victim, itching to end things quickly. Each little twitch caused a small pop of light to fly off and in between her fingers.

Her eyes shifted through the town in search of her prey.

Anala stood near the city center. Her maroon dress hung off her skinny body in a childlike way. Her stance read as a powerful being, but her aura tasted like fear. Raye could lick it off the air.

Raye's eyes twitched uncontrollably with each step closer she came. Her soft footsteps exposed the aggressive storm raging around her. The wind whipped the two's hair around their heads. Raye was close enough to see the teary-eyed girl standing in front of her, hidden behind a facade of power. *Pathetic.*

Anala's fire lit the air suddenly. A large explosion of flames burst out of her body toward her opponent. Raye ran full force into the flames with eyes on her target. Fire brushed against her skin through the tunnel of flame. Anala attempted to strike her again before she got too close, but Raye dodged her heat.

An array of electric lights followed Raye's body. Raye struck a bolt at an unforgiving full force in her direction and instead hit Lucian's statue from her evade. The great Celestial Lucian crumbled like the rock of his element. His body parts lie in pieces on the grounds of the capital, above his dear friend's grave.

Anala dashed away in another direction, knowing she could not win in a battle against arms. Raye did not run after her; she kept her eyes focused on her movement, like a tiger hunting its meal.

"You can't win by running away," Raye's voice boomed, whipping against the wind. Anala stopped in her tracks to look at her. Her big brown eyes stared into her soul even from meters away. It made her sick to her stomach. Anala entered the building next to her, and Raye followed suit cautiously.

The wooden floors creaked with every step Raye took. She tried to listen to Anala's location but made no noise. The smell of smoke hit her nose by the time it was too late, making it difficult to breathe as the smoke thickened. Tall flames now blocked the entrance. By the time Raye realized what was happening, the roof collapsed on top of her, crushing her to the ground. The ceiling was still on fire as it lay on top of her; the heat it gave off roasted her to her core. She would be cooked alive if she did not get out of there.

She squirmed to remove herself from under the weight while pushing up on the roasting fire. Her skin was being scorched with each touch, but she had no choice. She escaped the rubble, only to find her shirt on fire. Patting it out aggressively to stop the flame, she hacked and coughed the smoke out of her lungs. Each breath felt like thick sludge in her lungs. Raye had no choice but to run full force into the collapsing wall with her shoulder in an attempt to knock it down. Shoving her side into the wall, she heard the creaks and breaks of the wood, but it still stood tall.

The air felt impossible to breathe, and she shoulder-checked the wall again. It crumbled under the weight of her body, landing her outside on the ground. She rose to her hands and knees, trying to let her fury-filled gaze find Anala. She was nowhere to be seen. Raye realized she had no use hunting down someone who did not want to be found. She needed Anala to come to her. She regained her footing and set towards the city's southern edge, where it met the lake.

Shooting down everything she could see; she sent lightning bolts into the stone buildings with such power that it sent pieces flying off in chunks. Her sparks destroyed entire stalls and buildings with one strike; it caught fire to anything flammable. Panicked screams and terror erupted within the buildings, forcing people to run outside, away from the cause. The crash and booms of each strike shook the earth's core. When Raye turned to view the skyline of her destruction, the dark smoke and crumbled city filled her vision. The capital was in distress, and tragedies struck the earth like lightning.

"What the fuck is your problem?" Anala cried out to her. She came running behind her, blasting her with her strikes and knocking Raye off her feet.

"What the fuck is *your* problem?" she shouted back at her. Raye shot bolts at Anala, slicing up her skin as she tried to avoid them. Anala retaliated with a two-handed blast of fire directed at Raye, but Raye refused to stand down.

The bright white light mashed against Anala's red and orange fiery blast, divided in the middle, neither meshing with the other. Raye's nostrils flared while she thrust her right hand forward, forcing her power to push against Anala's. She finally stood up off the ground and gathered more power against her. Anala's feet slipped backward as she used her hands and body at full force against her. The pain started creeping up throughout Anala's body, and she got shot backward onto the ground.

Raye walked over to her as she lay on her back, looking up at her. Raye grabbed hold of her dress and yanked her up while Anala attempted any ability she had left to strike her with fire. The small flames did not harm Raye; they only toasted her skin and singed the ends of her hair. She grabbed Anala's dress, balled it up in her fists tightly, and drug her body, throwing her near the lake's shore. Anala groaned and cried with each movement as she tried to get onto her elbows. As Raye walked toward her, she crawled backward, creeping into the water. The ends of Anala's hair and her dress quickly became soaked.

Raye stepped into the start of the lake, where only her feet got damp. She squatted down to be closer to eye level with her.

"Do you think water is the best idea, An?" Raye asked. She stuck her fingers into the pool of water and let the light dance off her fingertips, shocking all around her gently. Anala shrieked from the sudden electrifying pain, and her body quickly seized. "Come on, it wasn't even that painful. Just a tiny shock," Raye claimed.

Anala started to sob, her entire face contorted in her despair. Raye stared at her silently.

"I don't have the same choices as you, Raye," she muttered between sobs. "It's not too late. I'll protect you." Her words struggle out with her tears. "I'll protect you from fucking anything, you know that." There was a deep desperation in her voice.

"I don't need protection from shit." Anger coated her throat with each word. "We will never be enough. It will never be enough for them."

It was no longer a battle between gods but between girls. And oh, how they were girls together.

"I wrote to you after I left your home," Raye told her. Anala's cries slowed as she appeared shocked by the statement.

"I couldn't bring myself to read it." Her sobs became quiet tears, and Raye's anger turned to fury.

Raye got closer to Anala and into the water, where it hit her shins. She gritted her teeth painfully from her hatred as she grabbed the neck of her friend with both hands and shoved her underneath the water. Pure shock popped into Anala's eyes as her muffled screams drowned underneath the water. Raye watched as she writhed under her grip. She could see her face entirely through the clear waters. The genuine fear in her face as she fought for her life was all under Raye's power.

Under the water, Anala thrashed about screaming and begging for air. Raye's hands maintained her below the surface. The water's temperature grew warmer from Anala, a last resort to save her life with the little energy she had left. She tried everything to rip Raye's hands from her throat to pull herself out from drowning, an impossible task. She stayed under the water, thrashing about, and Raye just watched, emotionless.

Raye watched as the bubbles stopped, and Anala's body stilled. She released her hands, and her body floated, her face being framed by the water. Her wet, round curls clung to her skin. Her eyes remained open; the sun brought out the gold in the center. Raye pushed Anala's wet curls out of her face. Her once beautiful face. Her best friend's face.

Raye's hands cupped Anala's face like it were her child's. She pulled her body closer to her own. Embraced in her chest, Raye kissed Anala's cheek, still as warm as she had always been. But Anala's fire was gone.

Would either of them make different choices if they had known where they ended up?

M. NEVILLS

CHAPTER THIRTY-TWO

For I am divine Death.

Raye drug Anala's soaked, limp body out of the lake. Her arms flung over Raye's shoulders while her legs dragged behind in a damp trail before Raye reached the city's pavement. Anala's head rested entirely on Raye's shoulder, her wet curls draped over the front of Raye's chest.

How different they both looked now. Her once flawlessly bronzed skin now filled with slices and burns, much too similar to Raye's. She never thought Anala's skin would reflect herself so greatly.

Raye continued to drag her body through the silent city toward the capital's staple—the palace gates.

The old man sat in his chair, a smile on his face as Raye entered his chambers. Her hand laid on her knife, strapped to her leg, at the ready.

"Took you longer than I expected to revisit me, Rayana. Though, how impressive you've proved yourself to be," Emperor Oswin spoke low and calm. Raye's jaw clenched at the sound of his voice hitting her ears.

"Do you not care that your empire is falling? That I will not leave before you die?" Hatred coated her voice, her voice hoarse from her emotions.

"The older you get, things tend to bother you less and less . . ." he trailed. Raye snarled at the emperor unamused by his response and snarled her face at him. The emperor let out a laugh.

"I've had a long lifetime of rule over my country; I will die soon, nonetheless. At the end of the day, I've been here for decades with wealth and power. What has your life brought you, little girl?" Raye's eyes bulged out with anger, but she bit her tongue. She reeled herself back in; her emotions already spiraling.

"Not even saddened at your bloodline's loss?" she asked, appalled.

"Why should I care about a thing after I die? Fuck all of them for all I care." He shook his head from side to side.

She stared into his cruel eyes. Soft, elderly eyes hid decades of deep, vile thoughts without care for anyone but himself.

"You always have to go and make it more complicated than it ever needed to be," he started. "I always watched you closely, but now it should have been even closer." He sighed at his thoughts.

"I remember seeing those soldiers you killed. Their bodies violently mutilated before death. To then sneak a peek at the little girl in the medical tent who caused such destruction." He made a clicking noise with his tongue a few times, annoyed at his past self. "I knew then I had a rare catch on my hands, and I couldn't let that go. No."

Raye felt he was mumbling more to himself than trying to explain a thing to her. She supposed he was attempting to play the poor old man.

"If that's a game you're trying to play, I already know. I already know you placed me with the Kryfs," Raye told him.

He laughed. "As much as I wish that it wasn't true, you've proved me wrong repeatedly. You somehow always seem to know everything around you at all times. If I think I'm one step ahead, you're already there with advancements. Even when I thought there was no way this time and that you had grown too cocky in your abilities, you do always prove me wrong. Might drive a lesser man mad, I'd say." He paused, leaving them in silence. "How I've always enjoyed such a fun game, though."

"You playing with victim's lives is no fucking game. You're the same as the Daoland emperor. You're both sick," Raye said.

"Then what have you been doing?" He scoffed at her. "I even thought throwing your friend at you would shake you, stop you maybe. But it didn't; it seems you already knew my plan to use her."

"I had no idea about Anala. Fuck you for using her against me and forcing me to kill her," she yelled at him, her anger seeping through.

His brow shot up in shock, and he settled comfortably in his chair.

"Could have fooled me with how easily you killed her. I forced you to do nothing, Rayana. Do you even have any idea of the great abilities you've been granted? Do you even understand after all this time? No one could stop you, not even your best friend." He licked his teeth like he enjoyed the taste of her death.

"Shut the fuck up." She stepped toward him, whipped her knife out of its slot, and pointed it at him.

"You don't mind hearing me speak; if you wanted me dead, I'd have been dead. It's very unlike you, Miss Tyrson, to leave your pests alive for so long. You want to make sure you have all the information, I assume. Make sure every calculation you made was correct. Trust me, you already know everything you wanted to know."

Raye lowered her weapon. She remained silent. Was that why she wanted to hear him speak? She came here to kill him, yet he's still alive with a palace full of guards. He could be buying time to kill her. She wasn't sure if she cared. She needed to confirm the truth.

"Where is Sai, the master from the school?"

"Must have known we were coming—he was dead before we found him," he stated. Raye's heart sank to her stomach. How had she caused so much harm?

"You could've had it all. My plans were so excellent for you. The Kryfs could not live up to the task of you, though. I thought giving you a life of luxuries would be enough. That was the first time I underestimated you. But you loved to wander to places you were never invited to."

"What exactly was your plan? Have me killed? Send me to Daoland in exchange for your continued safety, just like you did all the others?" Raye asked.

The emperor laughed at her ignorance.

"Suppose you don't know everything after all. You would have married my son. You would've been an empress. You could've been the fucking empress."

Raye stared at him with a sickly confused face, which only brought him further joy. How disgusting for a man to view her as a personal weapon. He would have forced her to marry his son. She did not realize the whispered *no* that left her lips.

"No one on earth would have touched the Azeran Empire. Not with a god like you helping rule over it. Even if the Daos did take land, they would never touch my family or me. Not after all I handed right to them." A craving for power brushed off every word he claimed.

"They would've killed me. Or you would've just handed me to them like the others," she denied.

"You're not like the others. You're much greater and stronger than any of those other Celestial fools. You could wipe out all of humanity if you wanted to. Did you not see how you fought against Anala? You've proved time and time again the amount of power you possess with such ease," his voice and face screamed with the greed he wanted.

The power he saw directly as his own. His voice grew with each sentence as his stomach grew hungrier for what could be. "You just had to think what you were doing was right," he snarled, practicing yelling at her.

Raye had not feared in so long; she had forgotten what it had felt like. She understood how the emperor maintained his position for so long, unbothered. He was twisted and addicted to anything he could get his hands on. He wanted his hands on her, and it made her stomach churn.

"You're a foolish child to think anything you have done will change anything in the future. The Daoland emperor might never step foot on Azera, but he will continue to conquer the rest of the world. You've only saved us."

The emperor's temper had risen, and like the grown man, he stood up and gripped his hands around Raye's throat. To her surprise, she dropped her knife out of her hand and clanged onto the ground while she did nothing. He grabbed her so tight she could not breathe, and in her shock, her hands flung up to attempt to fight him off. Like the little girl she was, she dangled in the air as he lifted her by the neck, forcing the air out of her while she remained in shock.

His thumbs gently rubbed the bottom of her face while his other fingers kept their grip. He caressed and manhandled her in a way she had not been in so long. That struck a sense of fear into her. No matter how powerful she grew, how godlike she became, the man who grabbed her without shame still scared her.

Sparks flew and wrapped themselves around his arms, reaching the emperor's body. He instinctively let her go, and she dropped to the floor on her knees. His body soon followed as the bolts surrounded him and seized his body.

He laughed maniacally as his body dropped to his knees and his back arched backward. His laugh overpowered the sound of Raye's lightning sparks. She forced herself off the ground, knife gripped tight in her hand once again, and shoved the knife through his throat.

She dove her short blade through the soft flesh of his skin until it hit the edge of her grip where her hand held the hilt. As blood pooled out of him and her sparks traveled through and around his body, his laugh continued, gurgling as the blood pooled in his mouth. He laughed through the pain she caused him. His eyes welled up with forced tears, and he laughed at her.

Her own eyes poured tears out of frustration and anger. *How dare he, how dare he, how dare he.* He treated her like a fool, like a child. She was not a child anymore; she had not been for so long. Why was that so difficult for everyone to see?

When she removed the knife from his throat, his limp body fell hard onto the ground. A thud loud enough that he had guards banging on his door attempting to enter. Raye knew she only had a little time to leave unless she wished to slaughter the palace. She was too tired to want to do that. She should have left then; she knew it.

She dropped onto the ground next to the emperor's side. His wrinkled, evil face pissed her off—dead or alive. She stabbed her knife through his face, not once or twice, but over and over again. She could not stop; her anger would not let her. Her sadness would not let her.

Every insert and exit into his skull flung blood into her face and body. Raye did not care, though. Each time, she let out a cry or grunt of her frustration. When the guards became too worried and attempted to bust the door down, she stopped and looked at the newly mutilated face of the once emperor. She left his face like a smashed pomegranate.

Seconds before they managed to break the door down and find their emperor violently murdered, Raye squeezed through his window and climbed down to the ground.

Red streaks of blood covered her fair skin, and her sandy hair blew and frizzed in the wind. Dirt and blood stained her clothes—she was a feral sight to be seen. She dashed to find her friend where she left her.

CHAPTER THIRTY-THREE

I am my own undoing.

Raye bore the weight of her own exhausted body alongside Anala's. The chill wind hit the trees as she entered the wooded area surrounding the city. She needed to be alone and was not ready to return to her troops' camp.

Raye sat Anala upright against a tree while she started a fire.

"You were always the best at starting fires," Raye said. "Guess we know why now." She let out a short, dry laugh. Raye lit some dry tinder on fire with her sparks. She turned to look at her friend while it caught.

Anala was much paler than ever, still possessing the usual beauty she tended to have as if she were only sleeping. Her long dark curls fell loosely around the frame of her face. As the sun set behind the trees and the darkness crept in, the fire lit their faces in orange. Raye watched as the light flickered off the tree trunks around them. Her eyes lost focus within her empty mind until Anala's voice rang in her ears like a bell that brought her back into her present body.

"Will it all end up alright, Raye?" Anala asked her, her smooth, soft voice that always hung heavy in Raye's chest.

Raye did not have an answer. Even after every decision she made, she did not know if anything would be all right for their country. Fog filled her mind. Heavy, tired eyes made their way over to Anala. Only she met her big black eyes with her own. Bright eyes, glowing skin, and complete, rosy lips that hardly moved when she spoke softly. Her hope-filled eyes met with Raye's tired, exhausted eyes.

"War is boring and slow, I've learned," Raye finally told her.

"How so?" Anala asked.

"It's long and lonely," she paused. "It's not what you'd think it to be. It's starving in the frozen winter or isolation from your friends and family. It's hiding in the shadows, hoping no one finds you. It's no great battle; it's merely hopelessness."

Anala did not have a response to her, which left them both staring into each other's eyes, silently yearning for the other to say something.

"I missed you," Raye spoke again. "I miss being happy with you. I haven't been happy like that with anyone else."

"I don't think that's true," Anala replied. "Zeki makes you happy, too; it's just different," she spoke quietly. Raye did not know what to say to that.

"If the Devil only punishes the vile, are they truly evil?" Raye whispered aloud.

Anala's head perked up. "What?"

The question had been plaguing her mind for a while. There was almost a comfort in it, one she did not realize. The Daos may think of her as a devil woman, but she had started to believe they were most misunderstood. The Devil could be a god alongside all other divine.

Both were far more similar than anyone was willing to admit, she had been discovering. How good could a god indeed be? Power corrupts, after all.

Raye pulled her hood over her head to keep her warm as she lay on the chilled ground. It seemed there was no absolute comfort left.

"I dreamed of you at night in ways you'll never understand. All that time apart, all I did was think of you. I have never been close to another human like I was with you. I thought you saw me for what I was and loved me. I thought I saw and loved you, too," Raye spoke aloud, unsure if Anala was listening. She faced her in the early morning while the sun rose and the embers of their fire were all left. She looked attentive to Raye, taking her every word in.

She's dead, she knew. But when things felt so real, who was Raye to question the universe?

"How we changed as we grew. If only it was together and not apart." Raye looked into Anala's teary eyes. She always felt her emotions strongly, like Raye, but how drastically different they were. Anala could cry over anything, whether it be anger or happiness. Raye only wanted to destroy the things that upset her or love those that didn't.

"I think your ghost will haunt me until death," Raye told her.

"Then may you find eternal rest, my friend," Anala told her through tears.

Was my short-term happiness worth the pain you left me with? Raye could ask that question to almost anyone in her life, past or present. But with Anala sitting before her, she had no answer. It became so hard to remember her happiness alongside her. She had no one but herself to blame, though. She had her hand in every plan. Her sticky fingers maintained the suffering, heartlessness caused the chaos, while her loneliness brought the terror.

The undoing of others was nothing compared to the undoing she caused upon herself. Anala might beg to differ, though.

"I haven't been feeling myself lately. And I feel like only you would understand how. I don't know how you always did, but you got me like no one else," Raye told her friend.

"Because I was your best friend, silly. I understand you because I just got you," Anala said with a smile. A smile she had not seen in so long. Her bright teeth were between her plump lips, raised rosy cheeks, and squinted honey eyes. Strange how one does not know what they miss until they see it again. How deeply they crave something until it is thrust upon them once again. A tear fell out of Raye's left eye. She did not know why, for she seemed happy at that moment. However, it was complicated to understand what emotions she was feeling. Everything was numb.

Raye did not know how many days had passed before she returned to her comrades. She entered the camp a different person than she left.

All eyes were on her as she walked through the camp to find Zeki. Too afraid to look directly into her eyes, the soldiers' eyes would quickly shutter to the ground away from her gaze. Everyone seemed to be aware of the general atmosphere beside her. She dragged her feet to the large general tent where she knew Zeki would be.

She pushed the flap and ducked her way inside. Shocked eyes stared upon her grotesque appearance. Ellerie and Finian stood to either side of Zeki, hovering over the splayed-out map plans. Raye's pathetically exhausted eyes met his unemotional ones. His jaw shifted side-to-side, dead-eyed.

"Leave us," he demanded. Raye's head turned to watch the two exit, leaving her alone with Zeki standing across from her.

"Where the fuck were you?" The hostility surprised Raye. Zeki had never been angry with her. Her palms sweat at the thought.

"Coping," she claimed. He shook his head back and forth.

"We all assumed you were dead. Then we get news about the emperor," he spoke with his hands aggressively. "Where the fuck did you go?" A mix of genuine worry and frustration shook in his voice.

"I killed her, Ze. I wanted to be alone." He huffed and puffed at her.

"You could have come back. I could have been there with you. I could have helped you—" Raye rolled her eyes.

"No, I wanted to be alone. I didn't want to be with you; I wanted to go off alone," she fought back. "You couldn't have helped me."

He looked like she punched him in the gut.

"What about me then?" he asked, defeated. Her brow rose. "She was my friend too, Raye, for the gods' sake."

The darkness under his eyes looked prominent then. The anxiety about him. He was mourning the loss of his friend and the potential of Raye. Raye's eyes zoned in on him, in no mood to bicker.

"I needed to be by myself. I'm not the great character you've made me out to be inside your mind, Zeki." She scoffed at him. "I wanted to be alone without you."

He clenched his teeth tightly. "My life doesn't revolve around you, but it fucking sucks I don't even have a friend to comfort me back. After everything I've done for you—"

"I didn't force you to do shit," she said. "You don't need to worry about me like I'm some lost child. I wanted to be alone for a few days, my gods!"

He stared at her with confusion written. Her arrogance grew tiresome.

"You were gone for over a week, Raye," he snapped.

It had only felt like a couple of days had passed. How much time could have gone by without her noticing? Her mind swayed with the confusion laid out in front of her. When she looked up at Zeki's eyes again, he shook his head and turned to leave. She locked eyes as he grew closer, looming above her.

"Did you know, back in school, they wanted us to spar? They begged me so often, seeing us as good competitors to each other. I told them no, so many times," he started.

"You said no?" she asked.

"I told them I'd never fight a friend," Zeki said. She could see his nostrils flare from his frustration.

"I suppose that's where we differ," she stated harshly.

"I suppose." He looked at her with disgust. "I need you to know you're not the only victim. You care more about killing the oppressors than saving the oppressed."

His shoulder hit hers where she stood while he exited. She remained in the tent alone as her eyelids twitched.

M. NEVILLS

CHAPTER THIRTY-FOUR

Cremate me in what I wear,
for even after death, I do not wish to be seen bare.

Filip,
I've never asked a thing of you. I will ask for this one thing and nothing else. The empire will fall. How far you all fall is up to you. I must have his son while his daughter is to replace the throne. Her birthright is to right the wrongs. Neither of us wants a child boy to replace the throne.

Raye's pen inked the paper in her sloppy handwriting from when she wrote far quicker than she should. But her mind was going faster than the words on the page were being filled out.

I shall atone for my sins . . .

She wrote her request in her letter before signing.

In one life or another,
  Your Sister, Rayana

Placed inside an envelope and sealed it with wax, she sent it off.

"You're not as good as you think you are." Sebastian sat in the chair in the corner of her room. She had not thought about him in so long. His matted hair and face dyed red from his own blood. His burnt uniform showed the gaping wounds through. Exactly how he looked on the brink of death.

"I never really thought I was all that good, though," she replied. She did not know why she would give him the time of her thought. Even if her mind attempted to convince herself to feel guilt over anything she had ever done to Sebastian, she did not. He and every other miserable man deserved the fate she gave them. Every Dao soldier she killed, young or old, every man who stood alongside the emperor and his selfishness. They all deserved it.

"Maybe that is the guilt you feel," Sebastian spoke again. "You feel guilty because you don't feel guilt over the murderous things you have done."

Her jaw shifted, grinding her teeth hard. *He's not real, just make him go away. You're in charge of your mind.* Though, was she?

"Yeah, I might be a dick, but I was fighting alongside you. Same as everyone else. You could have saved me and you didn't. You ignored my cries and let me die a slow painful death. What a great leader you are."

Raye attempted to blink away the visions of him. He only grew blurry from the tears stuck in her eyes.

"What do you know about saving Azera, huh?"

She jumped off of her blankets to exit her room. If she could maintain control then she would run away.

Raye was still determining how her eldest brother would take her letter or if he would even open it. She was sure he hated her even more due to Finn's death. She knew her own choices led Finn to want to join the military without officer training. He tried to help people and fight for people on the front lines. He knew they did the bulk of the work. She wished she had warned him not to. She should have written to him even once.

Her chest grew heavy with each passing second; she held the letter in her hand. She had waited a week for his response.

It only read:

You have my word, Raye

The city center.

Filip Kryf

They would go to the city center.

◆ ◆ ◆

The factory still smelled of mold and sweat. It grew accustomed to her daily activity. It was her palace, where everyone inside followed her every order. She might even miss the lingering stench and dirty rooms.

"I've handled things," Raye said. Zeki's eyes peeled up off his reading to look at her. He sat hunched over on the desk in the dingy room. The window behind him brought sunlight in, lighting him up from behind.

"How so?" he asked.

"I've made a compromise; we shall meet them tomorrow." Raye sent a tall bottle onto the desk in front of him. *Honey Wine,* it read.

"I owed you a bottle," she paused. "Congratulations on your promotion." He did not ask questions that floated around in his mind. He already knew the answers. "A bad apology for everything I've ever done to you."

"Raye . . ." He searched his mind for the right thing to say. However, there was no right thing. They were merely two humans, too tired to say precisely what they were thinking. They were dragged through far too much shit to be standing where they were. Far too young to feel so old.

"Everything you've done hasn't been bad."

"Debatable," she faked a chuckle. She felt terrible for all the poor souls who had met her, for she seemed to ruin everyone around her.

Zeki picked up the bottle of wine to examine it and rolled it around in his hands. Raye left a small note tied around the bottle for him. She watched as his eyes zoned out while his fingers messed with the bottle. There was nothing left to say.

Raye had killed both her friends.

◆ ◆ ◆

Raye's body shook, from her hands to her breath. She could barely breathe. The sweat dripped off her palms, and her stomach churned in anticipation of what would come. She held back the tears in her eyes. They would not see her shed a tear; they had already thought her mad enough.

Her army stood behind her. They were ordered not to move, that they were there for peace and resolution. Zeki remained behind to guard Calista while they were gone; an excuse Raye would not argue. The emperor's son was their only target—a token from the empire to make certain Calista would become empress.

It was her first time seeing her elder brother in so many years. He must have looked a decade older than the last time she saw him. She hoped she caused him stress. Raye's body swayed in the wind during the silence. The view of the palace from the streets of the capital was quite breathtaking once she looked at it plainly, without malice.

The emperor's son stood in the middle of the street bound by ropes, turned against by his army. They knew they would not win against Raye with him as emperor. She would never stop until she won. *Crazy woman*, they would call her. She was a victor.

The single archer to the right of Raye drew his bow back to his face. It only took a second of concentration before his fingers released the string and let his air zip through the air, landing penetrating the prince's skull. Gasps and noise popped up through both sides, but neither moved. They were almost equal, ready for a restart of their country.

Her brother stood tall across the way. Raye often wondered how he felt about the loss of Finn. Did he even hold a place for him in his heart? Or had Filip outgrown him? She often felt confused about the place his family held inside his mind. Strange how long it had been since she thought about any of them besides Finn. Now, at the front of her mind, she wondered if they would ever recover from the war. Hopefully not.

Filip drew his bow back, aimed, and released quickly. His archer skills were far more advanced than that of the sword. Raye wondered why he did not take up archery sooner. He was too stubborn to be a traditional swordsman soldier. His arrow sliced smoothly through the air. Cutting the wind like a sharp knife.

Raye found the accusation of not knowing the future was fear-inducing wrong. Knowing what was coming was worse. It could be quite overwhelming, as someone who always seemed to know exactly what would happen. To understand those things without the option to force a change. She found herself not afraid of much as of late. There was nothing on the earth that could beat her. So, why was she unable to win a war against herself? Her mind was poisoning her, and to have such power with poison was not a mistake she would continue to make. She feared what came next.

The sharp tip of the arrow broke through the skin on her forehead, ideally in the center. It broke through the bone and into her brain until it finally slowed down, attempting to exit the other side. Her head jerked backward by the neck. The rest of her body eventually followed suit and fell completely backward onto the ground, where her blood flowed right out of her head wound. She lay there. Her blonde waves sprawled about in the pool of crimson red around her, while her skin maintained a white hue, and her light eyes stared into the bright blue sky. Her muscles twitched, a last jolt of energy as her body lay deceased.

Her army remained at a loss for words, which quickly turned to anger until Ellerie ordered them to be silent. The two sides had paid for their sins and could start new beginnings in Azura.

CHAPTER THIRTY-FIVE

I thought I was being good.
I thought I was being good.
I thought I was being good.
I thought I was good.

Death is peaceful.
Was I ever as victorious as I once thought? I die a lonely life—same as all I killed. For all I did, did I save anyone? I stopped nothing, for it was always set in stone. To look around and know no matter how much time has passed—nothing has changed all that much. Dare I say, I am happiest now.
 I melt into everything. Not my body, but my being. I melt into the rivers and the ocean and grow intertwined in the trees. I shine light with the sun and sing with the breeze.
 I am everything; I am nothing.

✦ ✦ ✦

Rayana (Raye) Tyrson: (ray-AH-na [ray] tier-son)
    Young woman trying to save her new home from the Daos.
Kryf: (kr-IF)
    The last name of the family who adopted Raye.
Anala: (AHn-a-la)
    Raye's best friend she meets at school.
Zeki: (Ze-key)
    Another of Raye's friends she meets at school.
Celestials: (Suh-lest-EE-uhls)
    Humans blessed by the gods with elemental power.
Azera: (AZ-er- a)
    The country Raye currently lives in.
Hira: (He-RA)
    Land bordering country to Azera and longtime ally.
Daoland: (D-OW-land)
    Country trying to colonize other nearby countries.
Gestige: (G ae-ste-eg)
    Group of people who lived in small villages and worshiped the earth and gods. Were wiped out from their home by Daoland.

ACKNOWLEDGEMENTS

Over a year ago, when I started working on this book, I never would have believed that I finished it. I gained inspiration one day to simply start putting together a story and spent every day off I had inside coffee shops researching and typing away. I had no true end goal in the beginning, but I always hear people saying how the time will pass anyway—which was originally said by Earl Nightingale, motivational speaker and worked in the radio industry, I believe. He truly must have been a good motivator because I see this quote often, and every time I feel quite inspired. The year and a half did pass, only now, I have my first finished book. As a young woman with absolutely no direction in her life, I'm so happy I have found a passion.

Thank you to Dr. Nicole Morin at The Assist LLC for her copyedits and helping me bring my debut book further to life. I assume half of what I write is incoherent. Thank you to my mom, for being the first eyes on my story and not telling me it was awful. Thanks to my entire family for always being encouraging in whatever hobby I pick up. Thanks to my friends who support me and the vague things I shared about my story.

Thanks to anyone and everyone who advocates for reading and a big thank you to anyone who read this book.